Mandy Magro lives in Cairns, Far North Queensland, with her fiancé, Des, their daughter, Chloe Rose, two adorable pooches, Sophie and Sherlock, and the largest personality of the household, Charlie the cockatiel. With pristine aqua-blue coastline in one direction and sweeping rural landscapes in the other, she describes her home as heaven on earth. A passionate woman and a romantic at heart, Mandy loves writing about soul-deep love, the Australian way of life, and the wonderful characters that call the country home.

Also by Mandy Magro

Rosalee Station
Jacaranda
Flame Tree Hill
Driftwood
Country at Heart
The Wildwood Sisters
Bluegrass Bend
Walking the Line
Along Country Roads
Moment of Truth
A Country Mile
Return to Rosalee Station
Secrets of Silvergum
Riverstone Ridge
The Stockman's Secret
Home Sweet Home
Savannah's Secret
Road to Rosalee
Back to the Country
Jillaroo from Jacaranda
Gum Tree Gully

One More Time

Secrets of Riverside

MANDY
MAGRO

FICTION
HQ

Secrets of Riverside
© 2024 by Mandy Magro
ISBN 9781867264637

First published on Gadigal Country in Australia in 2024
by HQ Fiction
an imprint of HQBooks (ABN 47 001 180 918), a subsidiary of HarperCollins Publishers Australia Pty Limited (ABN 36 009 913 517)

HarperCollins acknowledges the Traditional Custodians of the lands upon which we live and work, and pays respect to Elders past and present.

A catalogue record for this book is available from the National Library of Australia
www.librariesaustralia.nla.gov.au

Printed and bound in Australia by McPherson's Printing Group

MIX
Paper | Supporting responsible forestry
FSC www.fsc.org FSC® C001695

For Des and Chloe, my family, my world … 143,
to the moon and back, I love you both with all my heart,
always and forevermore. xx

There is the kind of fire, lit by man's hand, that can warm or consume us, mesmerise or terrorise us. Then there is the kind of fire that smoulders inside all of us, one that craves to be ignited by another's sparks … both are forces to be reckoned with.

PROLOGUE

Blue Mountains, Christmas Day

This can't be real, this isn't happening. Wake up, Amelia, please, wake up!

Try as she might to claw her way out of what seemed like a terrifying nightmare, fifteen-year-old Amelia Price was already wide awake. Now seated out of harm's way, with the kitten her mum and dad had gifted her only hours earlier cradled tightly in her arms, she felt paralysing fear hanging heavy in the air as the emergency crews hurried around her. Amid the mayhem, a familiar voice wavered into her hazy awareness, the woman trying to soothe her as a blanket was placed over her shoulders. Her kitten was gently lifted from her lap and into Mrs Strathmore's arms as her neighbour and best friend, Ebony Strathmore, wriggled even closer to her.

With her vision blurring, she tried to blink the horrific images of smouldering rubble and coiling hoses. But she couldn't. She rubbed at her stinging eyes with her fists. It was meant to be the happiest day of the year. She should be sitting at the dining table now, with her family, eating the roast turkey her mum had been slaving over since they'd finished opening their Christmas presents bright and early that morning.

But her family was gone forever.

And now she was forever alone.

This despairing thought pounded over and over in her dizzy head as she winced at the recollection of her little brother Zack's desperate cries for help and her mother's tortured shrieks. Just like theirs had been, her own heart-wrenching screams were now silenced, and although the flames had licked at the suffocating air like some ravenous fire-breathing demon as she'd frantically tried to reach her family, she couldn't feel the pain of it any longer. She also couldn't tell the police who the person was that had carried her to safety. Other than that it was a youngish guy, with strong arms and a calming voice.

What she was acutely aware of right now was Ebony's supportive presence at her side, her own ragged breath, her swirling nauseated stomach, and the tears streaming down her cheeks, and yet, at the very same time, she felt oddly numb. It had been so suffocatingly dark within the fire's wrath, and she'd truly believed she was going to die, but then someone had scooped her up and carried her to safety. Who would risk their life to save hers, only to disappear into thin air? The whole scene before her was whizzing by, but at the same time moving in such painfully slow motion. She wanted to look away, to squeeze her eyes shut.

But she couldn't.

'Why don't you come inside, Millie?' Ebony's voice was soft, kind. 'So my mum can take care of you.'

Biting her bottom lip, Amelia shook her head.

'Okay then, I'll stay here with you for as long as you need me to.'

Blinking back heavy tears, Amelia nodded, grateful for her one and only true friend.

As Ebony's fingers interlaced with hers, she drew in a long, deep breath and watched the black smoke twisting and twirling upwards from what had once been her home, and into the dead of night. The sirens had long been silenced, but the blue and red spinning lights still flashed over the smouldering debris.

Only hours ago, her mother had hugged her close and kissed her cheek. Only hours ago, her father had lifted her from the floor and spun her in giggling circles. Only hours ago, she'd been playing with Zack, their laughter and Christmas music reverberating through the house. She wanted to believe her family had been as lucky as she had, that they'd been rescued too, and taken to someplace safe that she was yet to discover. But that wasn't going to be the case. She knew that in her heart of hearts. She was alive. They were dead. Other than Ebony, she had nobody now. She was very alone. She was very scared. And she was terrified of what was going to happen to her. And with that very thought, she was pulled down in engulfing darkness, to a place that was filled with nothing but resonating emptiness.

CHAPTER 1

Sydney, fifteen years later

An electrical storm had cut all electricity to the Sydney suburb of Parramatta, leaving Amelia's tiny bedroom hot and humid. It had been hard enough falling asleep at midnight, but now she couldn't rouse herself from her torturous slumber. Her exhaustion from the aftermath of her persistent nightmares had become a burden too heavy to carry any longer. With her sweaty limbs thrashing beneath the sheets, she felt the constricting grip of the ghosts of her past closing in on her. Reaching for her, their clawed fingers pressed through her flesh and clenched her insides, squeezing her racing heart so tightly she could barely take a breath.

Wake up Millie, please, wake up!

With every bit of might she tried to heave herself from the horrors of her dream. But just like every other time, the looming shadows had her at their mercy, the faceless beings skilfully pulling her under. Terrified, she scratched and clawed at her unconsciousness, desperately trying to climb to the surface. She didn't want to go through this anymore. But just like when her worst nightmare had become her reality all those years ago, she was stuck in a kind of hell, and it was dark, so damn dark, and scorching hot.

Helplessness consumed her and she slipped further into darkness. A strangled sound escaped her as everything spun in crazy circles. Then the fiery floor she was scrambling upon gave way, and she was tumbling defencelessly into an even blacker abyss. Thick grey smoke furled around her like a giant snake, asphyxiating her. Over her wheezing breaths, she could hear her father's frantic roars, her mother's bloodcurdling screams and somewhere in the fire-engulfed house her little brother, Zack, was crying out for help. Begging for her to save him. She tried to suck in a breath, and then another, so she could call out to him, so she could somehow soothe him, but there was no oxygen left. Her lungs burnt with the lack of it. She had to get to him. Or die trying.

On her hands and knees, she endeavoured to crawl beneath the flames devouring the walls, so she could get him, but there was nowhere left to go. There was no escape. She was trapped. Powerless. Dying. Backed into a corner where the red-hot flames stretched and reached from the walls, licking at her skin, scorching her, melting her flesh right through to the bone. The pain was excruciating. She wanted to die, so the hurt would stop. There was a loud boom, and the flames got closer, bigger, ravenously engulfing her world. Crying out, she tried to shield herself with her arms, hoping it would somehow help her survive the roaring fire that was swallowing her home, her family, and her breath.

'Millie!' Her name carried, ec consumed ceiling. 'Millie, wake u

Over her laboured breath, Millie hea then an overhead light burned to blinding li her fastened eyelids and drawing her towards iridescent surface. She instinctively knew there was pea found there. But would she make it? Could she? Then ha were upon her, shaking her. Begging her.

'Millie, you're having another nightmare, please wake up.'

Ebony's shrill voice grabbed her and quickly lifted her to the surface of reality.

Whimpering, she finally woke, and before she could form words in her dry mouth, Ebony's arms were around her. 'Shhh, Millie, I got you, hon,' she cooed, rubbing her back. 'It's okay, you're safe now.'

Her hands coming to rest on her flat, empty belly, Millie's attention snapped to what had become her heartbreaking reality. A renewed rush of profound sorrow overcame her. Somehow, she'd rather be back in her nightmare than having to face the raw emotions over her miscarriage.

As she pulled back a little to look her in the eyes, Ebony's expression was one of complete sadness. 'I'm so sorry you're going through this, Millie, I just wish there was more I could do to help you come out the other side of this incredibly hard time.'

'You're doing everything you can, Ebs.' Beyond grateful for her one and only true friend in what had proven to be a big bad world, Millie fell against Ebony's shoulder as her hands came to grip the back of her friend's nightshirt. 'Thank you for letting me stay here while I figure things out.' Her words were muffled. 'I honestly don't know what I'd do without you.'

[illegible]ey stayed like that for a few moments more, two broken, [illegible]ply connected souls holding one another tight, until Millie's [illegible]ars slowed and she untangled her arms from Ebony. 'I'm so sorry for waking you up again, Ebs.' Sniffling, she wiped at her tear-stained cheeks. 'I swear these bloody nightmares are going to be the death of me one day.'

'It's all good. I get it, and I got you, always and forever, my darling friend.' Ebony smiled sadly. 'After what you've been through lately,' she rested a hand on Millie's bouncing leg, instantly steadying her, 'and with what happened to you as a child, well, they are things most people could never dream of going through.' A frown creased her forehead. 'Add in the living hell your bastard of an ex has put you through the past few years, and then losing your baby because of what he did, well … let's just say you know how much I wish I could make him pay for treating you so horribly, and I don't mean in a legal sense either.'

'I know you want to hit him where it hurts, Ebs, but violence doesn't solve anything.' God only knew just how much she was aware of this after being Jason's punching bag for way too long.

'Yes, I know, but it doesn't stop me dreaming of doing to him what he's done to you.' Ebony tucked wisps of copper hair behind her pixie-shaped ears that were dotted with a myriad of piercings. 'And just for the record, you don't have to keep thanking me for helping you. You've done your fair share of being there for me when my world fell apart too, don't forget.'

Looking into her friend's desolate gaze, Millie briefly recalled the night they'd gotten the call four years ago, telling them that Ebony's parents had died in a light plane crash, but she quickly swallowed down the heart-wrenching emotions that came with the recollection. 'Yeah, I know we've both been each other's rocks, and partners in crime sometimes too, over the years.' She nodded, trying to smile while sniffling. 'But with the shifts you're pulling at the hospital and then over at the youth centre, you need your beauty sleep when you can get it, instead of being up at all hours consoling me.' Ebony had been saving money for her dream trip to Africa, and Millie was excited for her.

'Meh, I'll sleep when I'm dead.' Ebony grinned then nudged Millie's arm. 'And for your information, Miss Price, I don't need beauty sleep, I mean, just look at me.' She pulled the most grotesque face possible. 'I'm gorgeous just as I am, don't you reckon?'

'Oh my gosh, you loon.' Chuckling, Millie kissed her friend's cheek, and then gave her a playful shove, unwittingly propelling Ebony from the edge of her bed and to the floor. 'Oh crap ...' Flopping to her side, she hung her head over the edge of the bed and matched Ebony's sassy grin. 'Sorry, I honestly didn't mean to do that.'

'Yeah, right, just come right out and admit it, you're jealous of my insane beauty.' Ebony pulled the same humorous facial expression again, sending both of them into uncontrollable laughter.

Gathering what she could of herself, Millie wiped tears of both misery and mirth from her cheeks as she rose from the bed and offered Ebony a hand up from the floor.

Accepting the offer, Ebony jumped to her feet and then plucked her knickers from where they'd crept up her bum. 'Right, I'm going to go back to bed, to try and get a few more hours sleep before I have to get back to the grindstone of back-to-back shifts again.'

Millie nodded affirmatively. 'Yes, good idea, you do that and I'll make sure to stay super quiet while I get ready for another day spent job hunting.'

'I'm sorry that arsehole fired you from the service station for not being able to work the days following your miscarriage.' She huffed and shook her head. 'I really hope you find something you'd love to do this time, like cooking or working in a quaint café, and not take any old job just to make ends meet.'

Millie crossed her fingers. 'Let's hope, hey.'

Ebony grabbed both of her hands and gave them a squeeze. 'Are you sure you're okay with money, on top of everything else? Because I don't mind lending you some cash if you're struggling.'

'I'm okay, Ebs.' She had a little bit tucked away, but a job would have to come sooner rather than later if she didn't want to land in hot water, and she also wanted to contribute to staying with Ebony too, as soon as possible. 'You've kindly given me a place to stay until I'm back on my feet again, and that's priceless.'

'Don't speak of it, I love having you stay here with me, so stay as long as you want to.' Ebony gave her a quick hug. 'I love you so much, hon.'

'I love you too, Ebs, to the moon and back.' Millie smiled through her melancholy as a crazy thought came to her. 'Hey, seeing as we don't get to hang out much lately, how about I come with you on your jog Monday morning, so we can spend a bit of precious time together before we sail like ships in the night for the entire week again?'

'Really?' Ebony pulled an are-you-sure face. 'Because you're not really an exercise kind of gal.'

'Yes, really.' Millie's trim body owed more to her having a fantastic metabolism and good genes, rather than her hitting the gym or treadmill.

'Righto.' Ebony smirked, and her green eyes twinkled with mischief. 'Whatever happened to your motto of "why run when nothing is chasing you"?'

'Ha, yeah, there is that, but I miss you, so I'll brave breaking a sweat to hang out with you for a little bit.'

'Alrighty then, it's a date, my friend.' Ebony grinned and waggled a finger at her. 'And I'm holding you to it, so no excuses at six o'clock Monday morning, *capisce*?'

'Yes, ma'am,' Millie replied spiritedly and gave a salute.

'Good.' Ebony nodded. 'Night then.' She paused and offered a kind smile before she disappeared through the doorway.

'Sleep tight,' Millie called back as a drawn-out meow brought her gaze to the huge tabby cat now pressing his face up against her bedroom window. 'Oh hey, Felix, oh my gosh, I've been worried about you, buddy.'

Padding over to the slightly ajar window, she pulled it up and reached out to pluck her feral, and very heavy, moggy visitor from the fire-escape ledge – the safety feature that had been one of the main reasons Ebony had snapped up the pokey rundown apartment a year earlier. Millie understood Ebony had done it for her, for the occasional nights that she slept over, so she'd feel safe if there was ever a fire. Now that she'd finally plucked up the courage to escape from her violent boyfriend's clutches – with her Suzuki Jimny that was almost as old as she was, a backpack of clothes and personal items, and nine hundred and seventy-two dollars in her pocket, along with an empty thousand-dollar credit card – this room was her haven. And she had Ebony to thank for her new path, which would hopefully lead to new opportunities and a bright future. Her forever friend had been her driving force, and her saviour, as she'd helped her to flee like a thief in the night three weeks earlier, leaving the man who'd ruled her with an iron fist and tight money strings passed out on the lounge room floor as drunk as a skunk once again. Thank goodness those days were behind her now, gone, part of her past. But leaving the skeletons in the closet was easier said than done. To this day, she longed to know who the guy was who had saved her from the fire.

Cuddling the cat, who had been visiting the apartment ever since Ebony had moved in, she placed herself back in the present moment as she relished Felix's purrs that were so loud he sounded like a mini generator. 'I was starting to think you'd skipped town, buddy, or one of those horrid alley cats had finally gotten one over you. Thank goodness you're okay.' She gently ruffled his head. 'So what have you been up to the past four days, you scallywag? Huh?'

Felix responded with a string of meows, as if understanding her concerns and filling her in on his adventures on the streets of Parramatta, as she carried him into the kitchen of the small two-bedder apartment and plonked him down on the floor. Purring louder still, he furled himself around her legs, lovingly rubbing her ankles with the grace of a ballerina as she poured him a bowl of milk, placed it onto the floor to his delight, then grabbed a can of house-brand tuna from the back of the cupboard. After peeling back the lid, she tipped it onto a saucer and plonked it next to his now empty bowl. Folding her arms, she rested against the bench and watched him eat like he was starving. With his ginger coat and playful, loving nature, Felix reminded her so much of the cat her parents had gifted her on their last Christmas morning together. She'd even named him after her feline friend who was now in kitty heaven after succumbing to cancer. Felix the first had gotten her through countless nights of sobbing herself to sleep as a fifteen-year-old girl, and now Felix the second was doing the same when he dropped in for a visit.

'I really have missed you lots, buddy.' She smiled as he glanced up at her through wide eyes and then got back to his food. 'Don't be leaving so many days between visits next time, my friend.'

Turning to the early-morning light now spilling through the kitchen window, she was momentarily caught up in the splendour of the kaleidoscope of colours bouncing off the pretty suncatcher she'd made at one of Ebony's Art for Healing classes down at the youth club. Along the windowsill sat her recent addition to the apartment, three pots of herbs: the parsley, basil and mint were flourishing in the warmest spot. Growing edibles brought her happiness. As did music – country, seventies rock, old crooners, none of this modern-day stuff the radio stations quite often played. It was little things, the simple things, things with heart and soul, people with old-fashioned values, that filled her with joy, along with wide open fields, being around horses, sunshine on her face, the smell of freshly cut grass, the scent of leather in a tack room, the stillness of a star-studded country night sky, a campfire – all the pleasures that came with country life.

Apart from the sunshine on her face, she lacked for all the rest. As an orphaned fifteen-year-old who'd known nothing else but country values, life in the big smoke had been like a slap to the face, over and over again. The hectic heartbeat of Sydney didn't provide such simplicities. The skyline of the city she'd called home for fifteen years now was a far cry from the untainted

Blue Mountain landscape of her youth. Ebony and her parents had moved to Sydney not long after the fire, to start afresh, and Millie had come with them. Shirley and Greg Strathmore had taken her in as their own, loving her and caring for her, and Felix the first, unconditionally. And for that, she would be eternally grateful. It made Ebony the sister she'd never had, and Ebony's wonderful parents the only family she'd ever been graced with after losing her own.

Plucking a leaf from the mint, she popped it into her mouth, savouring the refreshing flavour as it took her back to happier days, when she would spend time with her mum out in the garden, playing beneath the sprinkler with her brother, or in the heart of the house cooking up a storm with the fresh produce they'd just picked from the lush vegetable patch and laden fruit trees, not to mention the deep orange-hued eggs from their healthy, happy, free-to-roam chickens. Her proud-as-punch father would always arrive home from policing their little township to a feast fit for a king. And as for her little sweet-toothed brother, he'd always had his hand in the biscuit tin her mum kept filled with homemade delicacies like crispy Anzacs or gooey jam drops. And Lilly Price's lamingtons had been to die for. The Country Women's Association ladies had always tried to lure the recipe from her, but her mum had remained tight-lipped, vowing it was a secret family technique, passed down through generations. If only Millie could get her hands on the recipe, but just like everything else, the fire had taken it.

Life back then had been filled with so much love, so much security. Just. So. Much. The fire, deliberately lit by a group of hoodlums, had changed all of that. Thankfully, some justice had been served, and the ringleaders, both sons of the well-known mobster Carlo Martino, had been caught. As for the others, being involved with the key players of the Kings Cross underground must have had its perks, because they received only a slap on the wrist – just another example of life being extremely unfair. Joey, the younger brother, got away with it. He'd been let off scot-free, in her opinion. The older brother, Luca, had served almost eight years in prison. He should have been given life, after taking three. It frustrated her that she knew so little about this man, or why he had done what he did. She didn't even know what he looked like, aside from the court sketches she'd seen in the newspaper reports; he'd kept a jacket draped over his bowed head as he was hustled in and out of the courthouse. Why they had targeted her father, a dedicated police officer who lived hours away from their cartel, she hadn't a damn clue, and neither did the investigating officers. They'd been unable to provide the answers she so desperately needed. To kill a man and his family over nothing; she'd never be able to let the anger of the injustice go. Not ever. She would be taking it to her grave.

Sucking in a breath, she shook off the distressing thoughts. She didn't want to focus on the hurts and injustices of her past. Instead, she wanted to hold dear the memories of her family. That's what brought her some kind of peace – the fragments of each of them that she held locked away in her jaded, shielded heart. Most fond memories were of billowing barbecues, and stirring bubbling pots, of chopping vegetables while sitting on a stool and licking delicious mixtures from beaters with her little brother. Her mother had lived in her apron, and food had been at the centre of their lives – it had been what had brought them together every day, laughing and chatting and sharing stories while they ate.

Her stomach growled. Thinking about all the yummy food they'd shared around the dining table made her think about the fact that she should really eat something now, before heading off to look for a job. Glancing at the clock above the stove, she swore beneath her breath. Time was ticking. She needed to get a move on so she could put her best foot forwards, and hopefully return with a job at the end of the day, one that she might actually want to get out of bed for.

A glance in Felix's direction made her smile from within. Curled up on one of the dining chairs, he was fast asleep. She took comfort in knowing she and Ebony made him feel welcome and at peace. Flicking the kettle on, she then grabbed her favourite mug from the draining rack to make her first strong cuppa for the day. Coffee was the only saving grace from her sleepless nights – the caffeine helped get her from one minute to the next, to the next, day after day, week after week. As she popped a heaped teaspoon of the instant dark-roasted grains into her cup while longing for a freshly brewed latte, it made her ponder running her own café or a quaint teashop where she could embrace the love of cooking her mother had instilled in her. It would be like a dream come true. But it was a pipe dream. Never could she afford such an endeavour. If life had taught her one thing, she rarely got what she longed for and she certainly wasn't one of the lucky ones.

As she busied herself making a couple of pieces of toast with a thick slathering of Vegemite, and with the remnants of her nightmare still at the corners of her mind, her thoughts wandered to the places she'd travelled to many times before. Yes, her nightmare was a terrifying reminder of how close she'd come to dying that day, and it should make her grateful for every breath she got to take when her family's lives had been so brutally stolen, but then the reality was that her real life was frequently a living nightmare too. After years of living in an abusive relationship – because, like Ebony had lovingly explained to her, she'd believed she deserved the mental, emotional and physical hurt just for being alive when her family was dead – it was hard to find daily gratitude in the mess of her existence. Even so, with Ebony's help, step by step, she was doing everything within her power to make things right, so she could finally be at a stage in her life when she could honestly say she'd placed all the broken bits of herself somewhat back together. Then, maybe, possibly, by some miracle, she could find the elusive eternal happiness she longed to feel.

Ha, and pigs might fly too!

She had to learn to at least be fair on herself.

And brutally honest.

After going through such a traumatic event as a young girl, would she ever get her life back on track? Could anyone ever get back on track after what happened that night? She was starting to believe the answer was unequivocally no. Because no matter how hard she tried, she just couldn't seem to shake the shadow of it. Bad things followed her. Shit happened. She fell over, time and time again. Dusting herself off was becoming exhausting. Fifteen years on, and she still couldn't move past it. She couldn't stop picturing her family being burnt alive, then what was left of them being buried beneath ten feet of earth while she sobbed at their graves.

She'd survived what the newspapers had stated was 'un-survivable', because of her brave, quick-thinking, nameless rescuer. But as grateful as she would forever be to whoever her saviour was, the guilt of surviving still sat like lead in her stomach, and all that talk about time healing wounds was absolute bullcrap. The grief never got easier, nor did the cavernous sensation in her heart. She'd just learnt to somehow, some way, live with it. Most of the time. Other times, she crumbled into a heap. And all the while, time marched on, and she just had to march along with it if she was going to survive living. No amount of counselling, or meditation, or praying to a god she wasn't sure she believed in – what kind of god would take people in the cruel way he'd taken her family? – had ever freed her of it, nor would it ever. She couldn't even set foot in a church now because the last time she had done so was to bid her family one final goodbye.

Anyway, enough overthinking everything, she thought with an almighty huff.

It was time for her to spend her day pounding the pavements with resume in hand, and from what she'd experienced the past week, also deal with getting knock-back after knock-back, only to arrive home to an empty apartment, too exhausted to eat anything with substance, before hitting the sack. On the plus side it was Friday night, which meant she could enjoy a drink or two, but no more. She knew all too well where hitting the bottle to numb herself got her. Waking up with a hangover from hell.

And that was no fun, no fun at all.

* * *

Twenty-three hours later, and still jobless, Millie was slapping off her offensive alarm. In her drunken state, when she'd basically faceplanted on her bed, she'd forgotten to turn the damn thing off. Glaring at the empty hipflask of vodka and packet of cigarettes on her bedside table, she rolled over and heaved her begrudging body out of bed. She needed caffeine. And lots of it. Tugging on her robe, she skated her feet into her well-worn slippers. Then, plucking a menthol cigarette from the almost empty packet she'd only bought yesterday, she thrust it between her trembling lips. Thinking she'd be able to savour just one, after quitting smoking almost three years ago, had clearly been a massive mistake.

Hindsight was a big ugly B.

Shoving open her bedroom window, she leant on the sill. There was no sign of Felix. Which sucked, because she could really do with a cuddle and idle chitchat with her feline friend. He must be off on his adventures again, somewhere out in the yonder of Sydney. Illogically, she found herself jealous of his freedom and his escapades. If only she could enjoy the same liberties, and hit the road, destination unknown, on some wild quest, without a care in the world, knowing there was a safe place to call home when she felt like a meal, some tender loving care, and then curling up for the night.

The weather had gone from hot to cold overnight, and a chilly draft whisked up from the backstreet below, snapping her from her thoughts and tempting her to retreat inside. But she stubbornly dug her slippers into the rug-covered floor. For once, she wasn't going anywhere until she was good and ready. Cupping her hand, it took three attempts to light the cigarette clenched between her teeth. Her first deep inhale was pure heaven, so she quickly had another. She knew the right thing to do was to put it out, and throw the last few remaining cigarettes into the bin. But, rebelliously, she took another satisfying drag. To hell with caution. Life was short. She wanted to live it while she could.

Her exhaled rings of smoke spiralled upwards and then dissipated into thin air. As hungover as she felt, she really did love this time of the day, when most of humanity was still sleeping, and she could find a moment of peace. With her chin resting on her hand, she watched the early morning unfolding as if on time elapse. Dawn was busy painting its sky-face with strokes of rosy blush upon its cheeks – it wouldn't be long before the sun rose high in the bold blue sky to brazenly claim ownership of the day. A few floors below, a baby's sharp cry broke the rare moment of silence, followed by a hacking cough from someone above, and then a vicious-sounding catfight erupted from the back of the apartment block, near the abandoned train tracks. Her heart thudded as she honed her hearing and held her breath. Hisses and strident meows ensued. Metal clattered and clinked. More catcalls echoed. This was one all-out cat brawl if ever she'd heard one.

Oh no, please don't let it be Felix.

She couldn't bear to think of losing another she loved.

Thirty breath-held seconds later, Felix the second appeared, strutting his stuff down the passageway below, and she breathed a huge sigh of relief. She quickly stubbed out her cigarette. 'Hey, buddy.' Her voice bounced off the neighbouring building as it carried down to him. 'Are you okay?'

Pausing, and looking up at her, he meowed. Then, nimble on his paws, he climbed and pounced until he was upon her windowsill. Gathering him into her arms, she cuddled him close and carried him into the kitchen, where she dumped her empty flask of vodka and packet of cigarettes into the bin, then busied herself taking care of him.

CHAPTER 2

Riverside Acres, Banshee Bay, Far North Queensland

The diehard countryman galloping like the wind upon his faithful stockhorse had learnt hard and fast, very early on in life, that danger lurked almost everywhere, and that you could trust no one.

But out here, in the beyond that was his backyard, surrounded by the beauty of Mother Nature, all he felt was …

Freedom, protection and euphoria.

On the one day of the year that was especially his, Jarrah King was in his happiest of places, enjoying his own company with nothing and nobody to hamper him. Rising as he always did to savour his usual extra-strong coffee, then saddling up before dawn, he'd spent a good part of the morning galloping the open landscape of Riverside Acres while witnessing another jaw-dropping sunrise. Not that he was about to let anyone know that on this very day thirty-eight years ago he'd come into this dog-eat-dog world. He didn't like a fuss being made over him, nor was he comfortable with being the centre of attention. He'd rather fade into the ebb and flow of everyday life, and allow others to stand in the limelight.

And for damn good reason.

With the life he'd lived, remaining a little mysterious, and extremely guarded, was a good thing. Nobody needed to know his business, because that could lead to them learning his secrets. And he couldn't risk that. The skeletons in his closet were ugly. He'd worked too hard to evolve into the man he now was, and he wanted to keep it that way. His past needed to stay dead and buried. There would be nothing gained from looking back at it. And that's what a birthday was essentially about, wasn't it? Looking back on where you'd come from, so you could celebrate surviving life up until that point. Although he was grateful, and somewhat surprised, that he'd survived his treacherous path. Now his present life was all about the present moment. And as for the future, well, that was the gift of tomorrow.

Right in this very moment, with the wide expanse of powdery blue above him and the open arms of Riverside Acres surrounding him, he felt at peace, and safe to be the man he truly was, down to his country-loving core. It was as if here – surrounded by the tropical rainforest on one side and the far-flung view of the ocean on the other, with the wind whipping past him, lush green pasture beneath him and the mid-morning sun beating down upon his back – time stood still, and all the bad that had happened, never did. He could almost imagine another life, where everything went as planned. Where his loved ones were still alive and well. The freedom of this allowed him to momentarily let go of the chains wrapped around his heart, and take the breath he felt he had to hold to get through each day.

Inheriting money while in prison, from a grandfather he'd sadly never met, had been his saving grace, and had helped him to buy Riverside Acres so he could finally put down roots. His professional bull riding had helped him to keep the initially failing property out of the bank's greasy fingers, as well as his tireless work painstakingly developing it into the fruitful business it was now – with horse agistment and training, along with a roadhouse breakfast café and eight studio-style motel rooms. That didn't mean he didn't have times of struggle, and times of self-doubt, but every drop of his blood, sweat and tears that had dripped into the fertile landscape had been worth it. To be able to call such a majestic place home was the greatest of blessings.

Riverside Acres was a far cry from the streets of Sydney he'd grown up on.

Silently bearing the scars of his past, both physical and emotional, Jarrah hadn't gone by his birth name of Luca Martino in seven years. His beloved mum would have turned in her grave, a hundred times over, if she'd known the unlawful things her husband had forced her two beloved sons to do. He missed her gentle ways and optimistic spirit so much, but in a way he was thankful for her early departure from this world, as it saved her the heartbreak of learning exactly who the man was that she had married way too young. Gazing through rose-coloured glasses at a man who knew the art of being devious like the back of his hand, an incredibly naïve Kate King had been given no reason to believe that her new husband was a ringleader of one of the biggest underground crime rings in New South Wales.

God rest her innocent, trusting soul.

No matter how angry it made him, Jarrah couldn't hold his turbulent childhood against his mother. Desperate to leave her strict, god-fearing parents and country lifestyle behind her, Kate had fallen for the flashy Carlo Martino in a heartbeat, moved to Sydney, and immediately cut ties with her disapproving parents and church group. Believing Carlo was the owner of a successful car dealership – it had been purely for money laundering – she'd happily fulfilled the role of wife and home-keeper, given birth to two healthy boys within the space of two years, and then died in a head-on collision five years later. Leaving Jarrah and his younger brother to be raised by a very bad man who resided in a very dark world.

A world he'd hated, and yet one his brother, Joey, had worshipped.

Chalk and cheese. Night and day. He and Joey were never alike. But Jarrah had loved his little brother. Unconditionally. After Luca had spent his teenage years trying to keep Joey out of harm's way, and out of prison, Joey and his wife had died from point-blank gunshots to the back of the head at their very own dining table. With their terrified eight-year-old son peering through the thin slats of a linen cupboard. This heart-crushing, soul-destroying knowledge was cruelly revealed to Jarrah while watching the nightly news from the confines of his prison cell. His father hadn't even had the decency to tell him. The son of a bitch. He hadn't even been able to attend Joey's funeral. His estranged father had made sure his paid connections at the prison had kept Jarrah in solitary confinement for an invented wrongdoing that very day. Just another thing that Jarrah would never, ever forgive him for. It was safe to say there was no love lost between father and son. For Jarrah, when it came to Carlo Martino, blood did not run thicker than water. In his mind, for him to be able to have any sort of a normal life, his father was dead and buried.

All Jarrah could pray for now was a safe and honest existence for his nephew. Becoming eleven-year-old Tommy's guardian the day after he'd walked out of prison had been a lifelong commitment that he took seriously. He'd made a solemn promise to Tommy's sick maternal grandmother that he would keep her beloved grandson away from the anarchy of Carlo's rule. So far, so good. He might not have been able to save his brother, but as long as he could keep Tommy away from his paternal grandfather, and Carlo's rotten world filled with rotten people, he believed that as well as doing right by Tommy, he might be able to find a way to live with the grief and guilt of Joey's horrendous death.

Slowing Waylon to a canter, then to an easy walk, Jarrah gave his horsey mate's neck a few hearty taps as he turned towards home. He'd started afresh, tried to make things right and get on with the life he wanted for himself and Tommy, but he knew his existence had inevitably become a complete lie. It was a crippling conflict for a man who had once prided himself on speaking the cold, hard truth. And in fact, still did when it was in his control to do so. But to be able to have any chance of redemption, what else was he meant to do? He hated knowing he'd become what he'd chosen not to be as a young boy – a storyteller, a fabricator of his past, present and future. The patriarchal Martino blood might run thick through his veins, but so did his maternal bloodline, rich with country traditions, so that was what he took pride in. His late grandfather, William King, was the man he aspired to be. But to do so, he had to leave everything behind him. It had been his grandfather's dying wish that he change his name and start afresh – it had been a prerequisite of his inheritance, and he'd been honoured to do it. And he would respect his grandfather's memory by upholding his fair and wise request.

Still, he sometimes wondered: if he was ever put in a position where he had to reveal his true identity for a greater cause, would he? It would have to be for a very significant reason. And even then, he wasn't sure he could. He'd slaved for way too long to shed the skin of Luca Martino – the convicted arsonist who'd been charged with taking three innocent lives. He'd stood wrongly accused in the courtroom, eyes facing the floor, while the courtroom had erupted in cheers and onlookers had called him every name under the sun as he'd been led away. He'd chosen to take the rap, for his brother's sake. At that point in time, he had nobody to love and nothing to live for. Joey, on the other hand, had a fiancée and a toddler. And after growing up without a mother, he didn't want his nephew to grow up without a father.

Being in the wrong place at the right time, with the best of intentions and the wrong kind of people, had seen him thrown in prison for eight long years, but given the chance to do it all over again, so he could protect his brother, he would, in a heartbeat. Try as he might, he hadn't been able to stop Joey and his gang of heavies starting the fire that wasn't meant to kill, but to warn the police officer who was threatening to expose Carlo's underground drug running and weapon sales in the Blue Mountains unless he paid him a bigger percentage of bribe money. But he'd saved her. At the very least, he had that to hold onto. The secrets he kept about the motives behind the tragedy were not so much for himself, or Joey, but for her. Amelia Price had been through enough. She'd suffered immeasurable loss. Immeasurable heartbreak. There was nothing to be gained from her knowing the truth about who her father really was – a crooked cop who was as bad as the men he worked for. In his heart of hearts, Jarrah believed he had to take that knowledge to his grave. She deserved that much from him. It was all he had to give her. If only he could turn back time and twist fate's arm, slap the hand of destiny away, he would.

But he couldn't.

Even after fifteen years, the guilt, frustration and torture he'd carried around in his heart had never left him, nor lessened. He'd just learnt to lug it around with him, wherever he went, as best he could. If only he could get back into bull riding, now that would give him a place to vent, to push himself to the limits, but even he knew he was getting a bit long in the tooth for challenging death. His doctor had warned him in no uncertain terms – one more fall and it could be the tumble he never got up from. And after racking up fifteen broken bones, countless bruises, sprains, hundreds if not thousands of stiches, five concussions and one near-death experience when a bull had decided to throw him around the arena like a rag doll, he'd finally listened to his doctor's hard-hitting advice and hung up his chaps and spurs. But that didn't mean he didn't miss it. One hell of a lot. The only thing he didn't miss was the attention that came with being a champion bull rider. That bit of it was not his cup of tea.

Passing the dam, with its glassy top and cool water that flowed in from the surrounding creeks, he couldn't resist the urge to stop for a quick dip, and he could tell Waylon felt the same. So he gave his four-legged mate the okay. He stayed in the saddle and they plunged into the water until it was up to his waist. His boots instantly filled with water and his jeans clung to him, but he didn't care – spontaneity was the spice of life, and with so much on his plate he didn't get enough of it lately. With his ears pricked, Waylon's powerful legs kicked, propelling them towards the bank on the opposite side. Jarrah laughed out loud at his equine mate, Waylon's excited whinnies music to his ears. Innocent, live-for-the-moment, free-spirited: animals were so much better company than humans. Which was why he chose to make horses his life, his living, the very reason he got out of bed each and every morning.

With a snort and a fart, Waylon clambered back onto dry land, and after he shook himself off like a dog, much to Jarrah's amusement, off they went on their adventures again. Eventually reaching the trickling stream that narrowed into a small waterfall, Jarrah urged his ten-year-old stockhorse onwards with a slight hand and heel. Waylon didn't need any more of an invitation as he dropped his head and accelerated towards home like a plane taxiing along a runway. With hoofs rhythmically pounding the earth, and a far-reaching bright sky above, man and horse rode hell for leather towards the one and only love of Jarrah's life.

His two-storey home pretty as a picture in the distance, Riverside Homestead shone like a beacon amid the lush, thick tropical landscape, and just beyond that the Riverside Roadhouse invited passers-by into its welcoming hospitality. Bright pops of colourful flowers adorned the perimeter, the pink hibiscus, orange birds of paradise, yellow frangipanis, red gingers and lobster claw heliconias he and Tommy had planted a few years ago in full bloom. Alongside the Queenslander-style building – sitting on one-metre-high stilts with cool, wide, wrap-around verandahs to while away the time with a beer or coffee in hand – the well-known truck stop's car park was jam-packed with campervans, semitrailers and road trains, some loaded with cattle. Some of the drivers would have slept in their trucks overnight and some would have pulled in that morning.

Over at the roadhouse the breakfast rush was in full swing, and it made Jarrah happy to know the customers would be enjoying their break in the air-conditioned dining room after being stationed behind the wheel. Some would then choose to use the paid showers, while others would be on their way after their bellies were sated, chasing the white lines so they could pick up or drop off their load. In Jarrah's mind, that part of Riverside Acres was the front of house, the bit that Tommy liked to manage on a day-to-day basis. As for Jarrah, the back of house was more his style; the training and feeding of the agisted horses, along with handling his small herd of cattle, was his role. The upkeep of the buildings and machinery was shared between them.

Slowing as he and Waylon neared the communal areas, Jarrah lifted his hat and wiped the sweat from his brow. He hoped the new cook's mind was on the job, and not on Tommy, like it had been of late. He didn't want any more complaints about the quality of food slipping. Since Mary had decided to retire from her kitchen duties two months earlier, after seven years of service, he had to admit the meals had taken a nosedive, but with the lack of people interested in the cook's position, he'd had to bite the bullet and hire the only half-decent person who'd stepped forward to take the reins of the kitchen. Who just so happened to be Tommy's biggest admirer, Jasmine Jasper. He hadn't caught them in the act, yet, but he wasn't stupid – the attraction between the two was evident. His own personal rule was ironclad: no relationships between staff. Every employee knew about it and Tommy certainly knew about it. If she was willing to break his trust in this way, he was not going to extend any further benefit of the doubt about the terrible meals, customer complaints, late-start early-finish shifts and insolent attitude.

Then he'd be strapping on the apron himself until he could find a replacement. Which might take a while. But he'd have to grin and bear it. The number one rule of Riverside Acres was no relations, physical or emotional, with the hired help. And Tommy knew that.

Standing at the back door of the kitchen, a smouldering cigarette in hand, Tommy turned to the sound of Waylon's hoofs. Locking eyes, he offered Jarrah a tip of his cap. Smiling, Jarrah tipped his wide-brimmed hat in return, noting there hadn't been a fragment of a smile on Tommy's face. He wasn't his usual self – friendly, albeit a little moody at times, since teen-aging was a tough gig – and Jarrah couldn't help but wonder what was going on with his nephew since he'd returned from a seven-day break. Tommy's hazy details about his camping trip were weird, because he'd always been forthcoming with his occasional trips away, usually relishing in telling Jarrah how big the fish were and how many mud crabs he'd caught and eaten. This time, Jarrah had heard nothing of the sort. Wasn't a holiday meant to relax a person, not wind them up like a two-bob watch? Jarrah could only put it down to the conversation they'd had the day Tommy had left, about steering clear of the very pretty, very flirty cook. Then again, it could just be a typical eighteen-year-old, flexing his adulthood muscles. Either way, Jarrah wasn't going to put up with it for much longer. Respect was everything. As was loyalty. He'd done a lot for Tommy and expected both from him.

After dismounting in the shade of the stables, it didn't take him long to get Waylon unsaddled, hosed down and back into his paddock with a bucket of hay topped with a treat of molasses. He crossed the paddock that led towards Riverside Roadhouse and the adjoining motel rooms, the long grass swaying around him as he made sure to shut both gates behind him. Still wet through to the skin, he chuckled at his squelching boots as he made his way up the pathway towards Tommy. A shower followed by bookwork and the weekly payroll was next on his agenda – he needed to get a move on if he wanted to make it into town before the bank shut. Friday afternoons were an early knock-off for the bank's staff – sometimes three, sometimes three-thirty, it all depended on how generous the manager felt. The joys of small-town living.

'Hey, Tommy, how's tricks mate?'

'Hey, can't complain.' Tommy looked him up and down. 'You've gone for a dunk in the dam again, I see?'

'Yeah, but it was worth it.' Jarrah couldn't help but frown as Jasmine stuck her head out the door, spotted him, then quickly ducked back out of sight to where she should have been focused on meal prep, and not chatting Tommy up. 'You better go see if everything's running smoothly, and I better go and get changed before getting stuck into some dreaded bookwork.'

'Yeah, righto, boss.' The screen door of the kitchen slapped shut as Tommy stepped away from it, and then stubbed his cigarette out beneath his boot.

Boss? What the hell? Tommy has never called me that. 'Make sure you pick up that cigarette butt.' Tommy's sarcasm had irked him.

'Yup, righto, boss.'

And there it was again. Jarrah had always seen them as a team, so this was new. He almost spun around to ask where in the heck Tommy's sarcastic statement had come from but refrained. There was an odd static energy between them, and he didn't want to provoke it. These days he liked to steer clear of drama. In his previous life he'd had enough of it to last him a lifetime.

Twenty minutes later, showered and sculling his lunch from a carton of milk he'd just shaken two heaped tablespoons of Milo into, a noise at the back door caught Jarrah's attention. He turned to see a snout planted against the flyscreen. 'Oh hey, Scruff, you're right on time for your lunch, as usual.'

Scruff pressed his snout in further, creating a bulge in the screen. 'Oi, you, stop that or you're going to bust it, again.' Eyeballing his mate as he tipped a bag of diced steak into a metal bowl shaped like a dog's paw, he frowned as he neared him. 'Far out, Scruff, would you look at the state of you.' His loyal companion had visibly lived up to his name. 'What in the heck have you been up to, or should I say, *into*, mate?'

Plonking onto his rump, soaked, matted and muddy, the mix-breed fluffball with big floppy ears that Jarrah had saved from a local farmer – one too many run-ins with the bloke's ducks as a mischievous puppy had pushed him over the line – replied with an enthusiastic woof.

'Is that so?' Jarrah shoved the screen door open with his socked toe. 'Don't even think about stepping a paw inside here mister.' He plonked the bowl of chuck steak down beside Scruff's hammock bed. 'Because you're a grot and you reek to high heaven.'

Scruff stayed put, and with his tail slapping the floorboards waited for his okay to tuck in. Jarrah toyed with him for a few seconds and then told him to tuck in. Scruff gulped down his meal in five seconds flat.

'Hungry then, buddy?' Folding his arms, he looked towards where the garden hose was. 'You know what's coming next, don't you?'

Following Jarrah's line of sight, Scruff's ears flattened and he dropped his head.

'Sorry, bud, but if you want to sleep inside tonight, you need a hose down and time to dry off before you do.'

After wrestling with the hose and Scruff, and succeeding in staying somewhat dry, Jarrah strode into the roadhouse, saying quick g'days to familiar faces in passing. The two local waitresses were ushering plates of food out, and piles of empty plates back into the kitchen. Tommy was busy making coffees and milkshakes, a tea towel tossed over his shoulder. Jarrah tried to keep out of everyone's way. He was pleased to see it was packed to the rafters despite the fact that the food was slipping. He'd have to try and make that right quick smart, or risk losing customers. If only Mary could come back, but she'd made it clear she'd only return if he was in a pinch, for a day or two. And after forty-eight years spent cooking wholesome food around Australia, she'd earned her retirement.

Clearing the takings from the till, he was pleased to see business was picking up again now that the monsoon season was almost over, which meant most of the trucks could get through again. The pile of twenty-dollar bills was nice and thick, as were the fifties, and there were quite a few credit-card receipts too. Shoving it all into the banking bag, he was about to make his way out back, to the safe in his office, when a familiar, unwelcome face drew his guarded attention to Ken Buller, who was making a direct line for Tommy. Tucking himself behind the segregating curtain, not far from Tommy, he decided to eavesdrop. Ken spelt trouble with a capital T. And he wanted none of that at Riverside Acres. Or for Tommy.

Tommy wiped his hands on the tea towel over his shoulder and then held one out. 'Hey, Buller.' Clasping hands, the men shook in greeting. 'How are things panning out?'

'Yeah, all good, King.' Shifting his beady gaze left to right, Ken dropped his voice. 'I've made some inquiries, and it looks like we can go ahead with our business idea.'

'Awesome.' Tommy dropped his voice too, as he leant into Ken's space. 'Go on.'

Jarrah had to really hone his hearing to be privy to their quiet conversation. There were only snippets, but enough to get the gist. Unregistered weapons. Ken was trying to sell them. Tommy was agreeing to talk to a possible supplier, and they'd both make a decent percentage. The exchange was so blatantly illegal Jarrah couldn't believe his ears, or the fact that Tommy would get himself involved. This was how it had all started for Joey. It was like history repeating. He thought he'd raised Tommy better. Jarrah's fury hit boiling point, and he took a breath. And another, before he trusted himself to be able to step in without throttling the pair of them.

What was Tommy thinking?

Having heard enough, he made his presence known. 'What are you doing in here, Ken?'

Ken fidgeted with his belt buckle, and then gestured to Tommy with a tip of his head. 'Just chatting to me mate.'

Jarrah liked the fact that he was almost twice the size of this little weasel. 'About what?' He leant forwards to accentuate his size.

'Nothing important,' Tommy swiftly replied from beside him.

Jarrah shot Tommy a look that spoke of his disappointment, and then fired his steely gaze back to Ken. 'I heard something about guns, and FYI, Buller, Tommy's not bloody interested.'

'Hey, don't speak for me.' There was no apology in Tommy's gaze, just utter defiance. 'This is private business between me and Ken.'

'Tommy, don't do this, especially in here.' Taking a slow, calming breath, before he said anything more in haste, Jarrah pinched the bridge of his nose, then shot both Tommy and Ken a warning glance. 'I'm not allowing illegal dealings to go on under my roof, and I'm certainly not going to step back and allow you to get yourself involved in something so reckless and stupid, Tommy.' He waved a hand towards the door. 'Now bugger off, Ken, before I drag you out myself.'

A couple of regular, burly truck drivers sitting at the breakfast bar seemed to catch on to the heated dispute and shifted in their seats to let Jarrah know they had his back, if needed. Jarrah offered a brisk nod in appreciation. The air shifted, thickened. Other people began to glance in their direction. Detecting he was very unwelcome, and very outnumbered, Ken couldn't hightail it out the front door fast enough on his short, stubby legs.

Jarrah huffed and shook his head, then placed a parental hand on Tommy's shoulder. 'What the hell are you thinking, getting yourself involved with that piece of scum?'

Tommy's lips pressed together, and with the insolent look he gave Jarrah in that moment, it was as if Joey had risen from the dead and taken over his son's body and mind, ready to fight Jarrah tooth and nail all over again on his decision to stay loyal to the Martino blood.

It shook Jarrah to his very core – history *could not* repeat itself. 'Tommy, talk to me.'

'It's all right for you, inheriting money from a grandfather you'd never even met.' Tommy shrugged Jarrah's hand off his shoulder. 'But some of us have to carve our own way in this world, and I'm honestly getting sick and tired of living here.' His face grew redder, his expression angrier. 'I want my own life and my own place, and my manager's wage isn't going to make that possible anytime soon.'

'You've got a pretty good deal going here, Tommy, with a decent wage, and now your own studio room seeing as you don't want to live in the homestead any longer.' The arrow Tommy had fired was lodged straight through the centre of Jarrah's heart, but he couldn't let it destroy him, or their relationship. 'And just so you know, I'm not apologising for my inheritance, not now, not ever.'

Tommy puffed out his chest, eyeing Jarrah like he was an enemy. 'I didn't ask you to say sorry.'

'Good, I'm glad that's sorted.' Put on the spot, Jarrah didn't know what else to say. He'd never seen Tommy like this.

'Good, fine, whatever, I need the loo.' And with that, Tommy stormed away, leaving Jarrah standing there, angry, hurt and confused, wondering what in the hell had just taken place, and where this new version of Tommy had come from.

Catching sight of Ken out the window, climbing behind the wheel of his four-wheel drive, it took every bit of resolve not to race after the scumbag, grab him by the collar, and teach him some good old-fashioned manners. His fists clenched at his sides; it was all he could do to remain glued to the spot. Jail had been tough. He'd had to fight to survive way too many times. And old habits didn't die easily. Ken didn't know who he was playing games with. And although he was a changed man in many ways, Jarrah still didn't play well with thugs or bullies – they were the scum of society. And Tommy had another think coming, if he thought associating with men like Ken Buller was okay. He simply wouldn't stand for it. Although he was of his father's blood, Tommy was not going to turn into Joey, God rest his soul.

CHAPTER 3

Millie's mobile phone bleeped annoyingly, waking her. The glow of her clock told her it was 2.35 am. Rolling over, she grabbed the phone from the bedside table, knocking the empty bottle of red wine to the floor, and quickly shut down the Facebook Messenger tone. Whoever it was, it wouldn't be important – she'd get back to them come daylight hours. Then she buried her face in the pillow and screamed. But before she succeeded in suffocating herself, she turned on her lamp, rolled onto her back and stared at the ceiling. The chipped, yellowing paint aggravated her, as did the broken wardrobe door she kept having to lift up to slide along the argumentative runners. She wanted, needed, to focus on the few good things in her life: like Ebony, and being able to stay here, and Felix the second, and … ah, um, there wasn't much else. Go figure! She huffed at her pessimism. It was time to face another day of feeling as if she was falling short of everything. Something had to eventually give, didn't it? Groaning, she tried to rub the hangover from her face. She shouldn't have drunk two entire bottles of cheap red wine, although it had seemed like a good idea at the time.

Hindsight was a royal pain in the you know what.

She heaved another heavy sigh. Was she just being too hard on herself, like Ebony told her all the time? Maybe. Maybe not. Groaning, she buried her face back into the pillow to stifle another scream. It usually helped a little bit, but today it wasn't doing a damn thing. After using one bottle of wine to numb the pain of her miscarriage, and then another to lure herself into something resembling sleep, she felt like death warmed up, and then some. The pounding in her head intensified as she tried to sit up. Looking to the offending bottle, now lying on the rug, she gave it the finger. Oh, how she wished she could quit using alcohol to anaesthetise her heartache.

Argh, she needed to stop obsessing and try and go back to sleep.

One sheep, two sheep, three sheep, four sheep …

She realised she must have drifted off when she woke to her text tone with her heart pounding. It was still dark, with not even a sliver of sunlight peeking through her curtains. At the foot of the bed, Felix stirred. Looking to her digital bedside clock, she grumbled beneath her breath. It was only 5.48 am. Who in the hell was texting at this time of the goddamn morning? Faceplanting in her bed at midnight, she'd now only succeeded in having five hours of fitful sleep. Her text tone resounded, and echoed around the bedroom. Snatching her phone from the bedside table, she glared at the glowing text.

Rise and shine, Millie! I'll be home from work in about fifteen minutes … I bet you went and forgot about our running rendezvous, didn't you? Eb xx ☺

Oops. Damn it. Sorry. Yes, I did. Raincheck? She was hopeful Ebony would say yes.

No way! Get your sorry arse up! We're doing this whether you like it or not! Love you xx

Groaning, Millie almost dug her heels into her tousled bed and bluntly refused, but then she remembered she was the one that had come up with the crazy idea of joining Ebony on her exercise routine in the first place.

Okay, bossy boots, see you soon, she stabbed back.

That's the spirit, my dear friend!

For goodness sake, where on earth did Ebony get her stamina?

Tossing her phone beside her, she flopped back onto her pillow. She needed a few more moments tucked up in bed before braving a brisk morning jog. She seriously couldn't remember the last time she'd tried to do anything so stupid. Running her hands through her chaotic bed hair, she considered having a quick shower, but then questioned why she should bother when she was going to get sweaty. So, commando rolling from the bed before she went back to sleep, she pulled on the activewear Ebony had loaned her the day before, then traipsed towards the bathroom, where she dragged her shock of blonde hair into a messy bun. Returning to the bedroom, she rifled through her drawers, grabbed a pair of socks and a jacket, and then made her way into the kitchen, where she downed a can of Red Bull. There was no time for her habitual cup of coffee today.

The front door opened and Ebony waltzed in.

'Morning, Ebs,' she said as brightly as she could muster.

Ebony greeted her with a smile so big it should have been illegal at that time of the morning. 'Morning, Millie.'

'You're full of beans, aren't you?' Millie's voice was so croaky she imagined she'd be attracting frogs for miles.

'I always try to be.' Ebony plonked her handbag onto the dining table. 'Once I get changed, are you ready to hit it?'

I'm ready to hit something, she thought. 'Uh-huh, ready as I'll ever be.'

Ten minutes later they were stepping onto the footpath.

Ebony clapped her hands together, making Millie jump as if a gun had just gone off. 'You right, Little Miss Jittery?'

Her hand on her chest, Millie chuckled. 'At the very least you've kickstarted my heart.'

'Sorry about that.' Ebony brushed a kiss on her cheek as she skipped past. 'Come on, Mills, you got this.'

'Woooh, yeah, I do,' Millie tried to say as enthusiastically as she could.

They hit the walkway at a brisk walk, chatting about Ebony's heavy workload, and Millie's lack of, followed by their latest television favourites and Ebony's upcoming two-month-long African safari. For the first little bit, with her lungs and legs playing nice, Millie could see the logic in this power-walking malarky, especially so early in the day. The lightening sky was pretty with the sun languidly rising, and there weren't too many people about. She had to admit that she felt a bubble of goodness, somewhere deep down in her belly, steadily rising, making her ready to face this athletic challenge with refreshing vigour.

'You know what, Ebs, I can't believe I'm about to say this out loud, but I think I like this exercise thingamajig.'

'Yay!' Grinning widely, Ebony looped an arm through Millie's as they power-walked onwards. 'This means that you can start joining me more often.'

Nodding, Millie matched her grin. 'Yeah, maybe, I mean,' she shrugged, 'stranger things have happened, hey?'

But a few kilometres in and her enthusiasm didn't last as they headed uphill, and she began to suck in tortured breaths, while Ebony was basically skipping beside her with her breath steady and even.

'Oh, my goodness, I didn't know I was this unfit.' Hands planted on her hips, Millie grimaced, but she pushed on.

'Oh, hon, do you want to stop for a bit?' Ebony offered a sympathetic glance. 'You're looking a bit red in the face.'

'Nope, it's all good in the hood, my friend, I got this.' She tried to sound convincing, if not for Ebony, then for herself. 'I reckon I'll be running before we know it.'

'That's the spirit.' Ebony punched the air. 'In that case, do you want to try and shuffle those feet of yours a little faster? Maybe work up to a jog?'

Was she kidding?

'I'm going to die anyway, so why the hell not?' Millie replied, ignoring her inner voice of reason that was mocking her stubborn stupidity.

'Woohoo, let's do this.' And off Ebony went, light as a feather on her feet.

Do her very best to keep up, Millie tragically put one foot in front of the other, feeling like a dog wearing shoes. With her lungs crying out for reprieve she tried to make herself believe this would do her the world of good. Then they turned a corner, and just when she was feeling like she might make it home alive, the road became steeper.

Oh lord have mercy on my oxygen-deprived soul!

'Come on, Millie, you got this, remember!' Ebony called from two metres in front. 'You'll feel on top of the world when you're finished.'

'I'm a-comin',' she called back, breathlessly. 'Eventually.'

As she began what felt like Mount Everest, there was a crack of thunder, and just off in the far-flung distance, grey clouds gathered with their bellies full of rain. She hoped they'd make it back before it rolled in and drenched them to the bone. You beauty! Maybe this was her excuse to go home.

No! she firmly told herself. *No excuses.*

Determined as hell now, she opened her mouth wider to try and draw in some much-needed oxygen. In the strangest of ways, the brisk air burnt her lungs, shockingly reminding her of a similar time her lungs had burnt, but she shook off the haunting sensation, pushed through and soldiered onwards. Harder. Stronger. Unwavering. Gritting her teeth, she looked up the narrow street, at a seemingly never-ending stretch with its vertical incline, hugged close by redbrick apartment blocks on either side, and with one almighty thrust she heaved her weary mind, body and soul upwards. As if in combat, the wind funnelled downwards, making her push even harder. She suddenly felt extremely light-headed, as though she was going to hurl at her jogger-clad feet. But onwards and upwards she went, doing her best to push through the nausea. This road, like her life, was just one big upward struggle, she thought as she put one cumbersome foot in front of the other. She could do this. She craved to prove it to herself, and Ebony.

'Come on, Millie, you're almost there,' Ebony called back from the top of the rise.

It looked as though her best friend hadn't even broken a sweat, whereas Millie felt as though she could wring her clothes out and fill a bucket. 'Yeah, yeah, I'm coming.' She waved her arms in the air and tried to smile.

Then, with three more steps, she was there. She'd made it. Bending over, she heaved in air, gasping as if she was asthmatic.

Ebony patted her back. 'Good job, hon!'

'Ha, thanks, Ebs.' She chuckled. 'My legs are shaking, and there's a weird clicking noise in my right knee, but I'm alive and kicking, so that's good.'

Ebony smiled kindly. 'You're way stronger than you give yourself credit for, Millie Price, in so many ways.'

'I'm glad you think so.' She tossed an arm over Ebony's shoulder. 'Sorry about my sweaty pits.'

'All good, mine are too,' Ebony chuckled.

Feeling on top of the world now she'd caught her runaway breath, Millie squinted as she gazed out and over the now roused city. 'Wowsers, the views from here are pretty darn awesome.'

'They are, hey.' Ebony drew in a few breaths and exhaled each away. 'Are you ready to head back home now?'

Millie nodded. 'Just knowing it's mainly downhill from here, damn straight I am.'

It was way easier on the homeward stretch with gravity on her side. When they arrived back at the apartment block, Millie paused to grab the pile of mail from their letterbox.

'Dibs for the shower, Mills.' Ebony raced ahead and started up the stairs.

'You go for it, Ebs, because I ain't running any more today.'

'I'll leave the door ajar for you,' she called over the banister.

Traipsing up the staircase, Millie had never been happier to reach the front door. Stepping inside, she kicked off her runners, and then moseying into the lounge room, flopped onto the couch with an almighty sigh. Sifting through the mail, she tossed the grocery store flyers to the floor, along with a couple of pizza coupons – the junk mail was going straight into the recycling bin. Almost at the bottom of the stack, her fingers froze. Wide-eyed, she stared at the yellow envelope with her name scrawled across the front in bold black letters. There was no address. The sender had clearly placed this envelope within the stack, and deliberately hidden it towards the bottom. How in the heck did whoever it was get into the apartment block in the first place? Jason came to mind, but then she shoved the thought away – he'd already be hunting down his next unsuspecting victim and wooing the poor woman with his narcissism hidden until he hooked her in. She shook her head to get rid of the painful memories of him doing exactly that to her. She felt foolish for having fallen for him. Blinking her tears away, she stared at the envelope with her heart hammering in her rib cage as if trying to break free.

'Amelia Price.' She whispered it, as though terrified to speak her name.

Nobody called her by her birth name anymore. Not even Ebony. And other than her best friend, no one knew she was living here, or so she had thought. She flipped it over, not surprised to see the back of the envelope was blank. A terrifying thought struck her. What if the person who'd put this in her letterbox, who had somehow let themselves in the building, had let themselves in here too? She shot to her feet, looking left to right. Without wanting to scare Ebony, who was singing at the top of her lungs from the shower, she tiptoed about the small apartment, checking cupboards, looking under beds and behind every nook and cranny. Satisfied she and Ebony were safe, she released the breath she'd been holding and made her way back to the couch, sat stiffly, then, slipping her index finger beneath the edge of the envelope, carefully unsealed it. She removed the folded bit of notepaper and opened it, and a photo fell out and onto the rug at her socked feet. Bending over, she snatched it up and stared at her six-year-old self, wrapped up in the loving arms of her father. The photo had been taken from afar, as if someone had been watching them, stalking them. It wasn't your usual happy family pic – there was malice behind this photo. Evil intentions. Fear snaked up her spine as another jolt of adrenaline shot through her.

What in the hell?

With quivering hands, she turned her attention to the note.

> *Hello Amelia. It's been a long time. You wouldn't remember me, so no need to fill you in on who I am. You'll work that out in time. I know your family died in a fire. I know someone saved you. I'm presuming you've never gotten over the grief of your loss, or the guilt of surviving. If you want to know the cold hard truth of exactly who your father was, and finally learn who it was that saved you, you need to go to Northern Queensland, to a place called Riverside Acres. Find a reason to stay there. It won't be hard, given the fact it's a motel. Don't tell a soul who you are. And in time, everything will be revealed. Because the truth always comes out, one way or another, especially when you're at the source of the secrets. I suppose I could just tell you straight out, save you a trip, but then where's the fun in that? Your father put me through hell. Now you're paying the price for that. And besides this very valid point, in my family, unlike many others, we don't rat on one another. Snitches die. Rats live in sewers. These are the mottos we live by. Now get a move on. Time's ticking.*

Her vision blurring, she felt the note flutter from her trembling fingertips and to the floor. With the room spinning in dizzying circles, she leant forwards and tried to catch her leaden breath. This couldn't be happening. She had to be having another nightmare. Squeezing her eyes shut, she began to count to one hundred as she rocked back and forth. Next thing she knew, Ebony was kneeling in front of her, wrapped in a towel. Millie wiped at her eyes and tried to focus. The note and photo were now in Ebony's hands, and the fearful look on her best friend's face matched the angst swirling like a whirlwind within her own stomach.

'Mills, look at me.' Ebony placed a gentle hand on her cheek. 'Do you have any idea who could have sent this?'

Still rocking back and forth, Millie shook her head.

'Okay.' She chewed her bottom lip as she re-read it, then locked her eyes with Millie's again. 'We should call the police and get them to investigate this.'

'No.' Millie took the note from Ebony's hand. 'You know damn well the police came up empty after all their investigating, and I don't want anything to ruin the possibility of me finally learning the truth about everything that happened that night.'

'Millie, don't be so foolish.' Ebony stood and then sat beside her, her hand once again steadying Millie's bouncing leg. 'Please tell me you aren't thinking about actually going there.'

Sucking in a breath, Millie tried to pull herself together, at least enough to speak. But her throat was so tight, and her mouth was so dry, she couldn't utter a word.

'Millie?' Ebony pronounced her name cautiously.

Millie finally sucked up courage from some place deep and dark. 'I have to go, Eb.' She whispered it, as if too afraid to hear herself say such a thing.

'No way, I won't let you go and do something so stupid.' Ebony grabbed both of Millie's hands and squeezed them. 'Listen to me, this is crazy talk.' Pausing, she cleared her throat. 'How do you know you're not walking into some kind of trap?'

'I know you're worried, and I am too.' Sitting up straight, and meeting Ebony's eyes, Millie took a moment to gather herself, and the right words. 'You of all people know just how much I've wanted answers to why it happened, to us, a family who lived in a tiny little town with hardly any crime.' She sucked in a shuddering breath. 'This might be the closure I need, to somehow get on with my life.'

With a myriad of emotions contorting her features, Ebony took a long while to reply. 'Well, in that case, if you need to do this, I'm cancelling my trip and coming with you.'

Millie shook her head. 'You can't, Eb, you've worked too hard for your dream holiday.'

'But, Mills,' Ebony was blinking now, and her lips trembled, as if she were holding back a flood of tears, 'I can't leave you to do something like this alone.'

'I'm not going into the middle of Timbuktu, Ebs. I'm going to a roadside motel, so I'm sure there'll be plenty of people around.' Although terrified, Millie wanted to protect Ebony from this worry, this pain. Her darling friend had been through enough, with her and because of her. 'I'll have my phone, and I'll make sure I call you, and you can call me, so you know I'm safe, okay?'

Nodding slowly, Ebony rested back against the couch. 'I know you, and I know there's no way I'll talk you out of doing this, so I'll just have to find the courage to support you.' She pointed a finger in Millie's direction. 'But you make sure you stick to your promise of staying in touch, no ifs, buts or maybes, and no excuses, you hear me?'

'Yes, loud and clear, and I promise.' Gobsmacked she was going to do this, Millie heaved an almighty sigh. 'Can you please make sure, while you're still here of course, that you take good care of Felix while I'm gone?'

'Trust you to think of that cat at a time like this.' Ebony smiled a little. 'Of course I will; he was kind of mine before he kind of became yours, remember?'

'Yeah, I know he was.' Nodding, she smiled a little now too. 'He's my buddy.'

'Yes, and you're mine.' Ebony hooked her arm into Millie's. 'So, you make damn sure you come back to me safe and sound. And if you get one whiff of trouble, you call the police, or even better still, get the hell out of there and call them on the way.'

Millie gave her a confirming nod. 'I most certainly will.'

Then they sat there, holding hands, in a shocked silence, both absorbing and trying to process what was about to unfold.

Millie just prayed to the powers that be that she wasn't making the biggest, and most dangerous, decision of her life. But without a job, or a love interest, or basically a life, what did she have to lose?

CHAPTER 4

His arm buried up to his elbow, and his lower half covered in blood and birth fluids, Jarrah couldn't believe his eyes as he briefly caught sight of Jasmine tiptoeing out of Tommy's place. Damn it! Tommy knew the number one rule was no cavorting with the employees. And she was meant to have started her shift ten minutes ago, too. The perks of sleeping with her boss weren't going to last long. Disappointed, irked and angry, he cursed beneath his breath. Tommy had been forewarned and forearmed. This was it, the very last straw. Tommy and Jasmine had left him no choice.

Focusing back on his present situation, Jarrah tried to keep a firm grip on the slippery calf as he encouraged the heifer to keep going. 'Come on, girl, just a couple more pushes I reckon, and then you can have that well-earned rest.'

The heifer bawled. Then bawled again. Moments later, the calf came into the world in a slick messy heap at Jarrah's equally messy boots. Chuffed to be witnessing this incredible moment, he stepped aside as the mother turned and began to lick its baby clean. The calf tried to stand, stumbled, and then tried again. Wobbling on shaky legs, it found the teat it was so desperate for, and suckled. Jarrah smiled at this miracle of life before heading over to the sink and grabbing the bar of soap to wash up. His job was done here. He'd come back later and check in with mum and her calf. For now, though, he needed to get changed and check in on the roadhouse. The breakfast rush wouldn't be far off. And something told him things wouldn't be running as smoothly as they should.

Thirty minutes later, he stepped into the buzz of the dining room and went straight over to his most loyal, and sometimes brutally honest, customer. 'Hey, Jacko, how's the grub?'

As he looked from his half-eaten plate of food to Jarrah, the bloke's bushy grey brows furrowed. 'I have to be honest, King.' He plonked his fork down and sat back, burly arms folding. 'It tastes like crap.'

'Oh, Jacko, I'm sorry, mate.' He went to take the plate from the table. 'Let me get you something else.'

Jacko shook his head and took his plate back. 'I don't have time to wait for something else, and it's filling the hole, so all good this time round.' He gestured towards the kitchen with a tip of his head. 'I get she's new and learning the ropes, but let's just hope she learns to cook while she's at it, hey.' He chuckled, extra loud. 'Us truck drivers might not be fussy, but we do like a good wholesome feed, like Mary's used to be.'

'Cheers for understanding, Jacko.' Peeved with Tommy and his newfound fling, or whatever the heck she was, Jarrah huffed. 'This one's on the house, and your next meal will be too.'

'Thanks, King, that's real nice of ya.' Jacko offered him a stern nod.

'It's the least I can do.' He gave Jacko a friendly slap on the back. 'Stay safe, and see you soon, yeah?'

'Yeah, I'll be coming back through in a couple of days.' His grimace was lighthearted. 'Hopefully for better fodder next time.'

'You have my word it will be.' Swallowing an entire sentence of expletives, Jarrah turned and thundered into the kitchen, where he plucked a full plate of food from the serving counter and carried it with him. 'You got a minute, Jasmine?'

'Yeah, I suppose so.' Glancing over her shoulder, she offered a fake smile. 'What's up?'

'This is what's up.' He held up the ghastly plate of overcooked corned beef and sloppy vegetables. 'I can't have you serving this.'

'Oh, for god's sake.' Her collection of cheap bangles jingled as she raised both hands into the air. 'Why the effing hell not?'

Jarrah was gobsmacked at her flippant response. 'Because it's inedible.' She had a mouth worthy of a bar of soap, and a temper that was way too quick to flare.

'The truckies aren't fussy, and the few travellers that call in seem happy with my food.' Her expression both taunting and smug, she shrugged at his look of disbelief. 'I mean, they all clear their plates, so what's the big problem?'

'They eat it because they're hungry, and most of them don't have time to send it back.' His temper rising, he plonked the plate, quite loudly, onto the stainless-steel bench. He was on a roll now, and it was time to end this. 'And as for Tommy, you know the number one rule of this place is not to have relations with staff.'

'Uh-huh, of course I do.' Her expression turned poker face, but her darting eyes couldn't hide the fact she knew she'd been busted.

'I know you were in Tommy's unit today, and I know what you were up to, so you can get your things and get out of my kitchen.'

'You're actually firing me?' She stabbed a finger into her chest.

'I actually am, yes.'

'Fine, it'll be my pleasure to get out of this shithole.' She ripped off her apron and threw it across the room, then stormed past him, grabbed her handbag from the hook and turned back to face him, her gaze fierce. 'I know there's nobody else willing to take on this job, so good luck managing all of this on your own.' She flapped her arms around, jangling her bangles again, then in a flurry of swear words, stomped out the back door of the kitchen.

One of the two waitresses stood in the doorway, a pile of dirty plates in her hands. 'Blimey, that was hectic.' Jenny's smile spread. 'But hallelujah she's gone.' Waltzing over to the sink, she plonked the plates down. 'My sister is going to be well pleased we don't have to work with her anymore.' Rinsing the dishes, she glanced over her shoulder. 'That Jasmine is a right cow.'

Jarrah had to agree. He almost fell to his knees and thanked god she was gone. But then he looked left to right, spotted the line of orders hanging from the serving window, and sighed. He needed to take over the reins in here, get the orders done as best he could with the food he had, and then tomorrow he was going to have to try and find another cook, one that could serve food he was proud of. Lord only knew where he was going to pluck one from at the very last minute. But he could only try his best.

Catching sight of Tommy, out the front of house, glaring at him from his station at the coffee counter, he groaned. That was a conversation, or disagreement, they'd be having later, and not within the hearing of the diners.

* * *

Looking to the faded photograph of her and her father that she'd placed strategically on her dashboard, while the letter was tucked up nice and safe beneath her seat, Millie swallowed down a lump of emotion. Her tears had all but dried up when it came to the unfathomable grief that came with losing both of her parents and her little brother, but the resounding heartbreak remained as strong as it had ever been. It was a harsh slap in the face to know that some sick individual had carried this photo around for all these years, when for her, all the memories up until this point were the ones she held dear in her mind and heart. As haunting as it was that someone had taken this picture without her father knowing, this photo was priceless – a rare treasure she would keep safe now it was in her possession.

Things are about to get a whole lot better, she told herself with an acknowledging nod. *You're finally going to get the answers you need, and at the very least, learn exactly who it was that saved you, so you can thank them.*

She rolled her eyes at her train of thought, which had been recklessly all over the place since she'd left Sydney. If she didn't get out of her old Jimny soon, her mind-train was going to run off its tracks. Idle hands, idle thoughts. If only she could wholeheartedly believe this trip up north was going to be the closure she'd needed for fifteen long years. But it was hard to deem plausible when she had no idea what she was about to walk into. And to hide who she was from whoever it was she was about to cross paths with was – well, it was out-and-out weird. Would she be able to figure out who'd been the one to send the note, if she came face to face with the writer of it? Then again, what if it was some cruel prankster sending her on some wild goose chase? Or what if she was about to be brutally murdered by the same underground organisation that had, for some unknown reason, killed her family?

What if. What if. What if …

Argh, stop it, Millie, before you drive yourself insane!

The highway stretched on, rising upwards and over the hazy horizon. Longing to be at the end of her journey but afraid of her destination, Millie stretched out her neck in a bid to ease the knots from her shoulders. Although nervous, she was keen to get to this place called Riverside Acres, which she'd discovered, after googling the heck out of it with Ebony, was in the small coastal township of Banshee Bay, a forty-minute drive north from Cairns. Leaving the morning of the day before, she had driven until the segmented white lines of the highway had turned into one long line. It was then, and only then, she'd decided to call Ebony and tell her she was pulling into a roadside motel for the night to get some much-needed shut-eye, to her friend's, and her own, relief. After devouring a greasy burger and over-salted chips from the takeaway store next door to the motel, she'd fallen into the firm motel bed and slept harder than she had in forever. Her alarm had woken her at 4 am sharp, and she'd been back on the road for almost twelve hours now.

Almost there.

With relentless North Queensland sunshine beating down upon her windscreen, and her air conditioner on its last legs, she turned it up as high as it would go and angled the air vents towards her face. Leaning forwards, she savoured the blast of coolish breeze while trying to ignore the trickle of sweat rolling down her back and between her breasts. Then, feeling somewhat cooler, she grabbed her water bottle and guzzled the last of it. Tossing the empty bottle to the passenger floor, amid Mintie wrappers, she kept her attention pinned to the increasingly winding road.

The rich green fields of sugar cane with pink fairy-floss tops that had been flashing past her for almost half an hour finally gave way to rugged mountainsides with sheer drops that appeared to dive into the frothy waves of the turquoise water beneath. It was hard to keep her eyes away from the unblemished beauty of it all. Then as she turned a sharp bend, a picture-perfect postcard-worthy panorama welcomed her from the wide frame of her windscreen. The sight of the secluded palm-fringed seashore with golden sand and aqua-green water lapping at the coastline stole her breath. This stretch of untainted paradise was even more stunning than the pictures her laptop had shown. She craved to pull up, race down to the shoreline, dive into the impossibly blue water and swim to her heart's content, but no way was she going to risk being eaten alive by a crocodile or stung by a jellyfish. There were so many things in Far North Queensland that were hell-bent on killing you and she wasn't going to be risking making the headlines of the local newspaper anytime soon.

Her navigation forewarned that she'd be turning left in three hundred and sixty-five metres. She eased off the accelerator, then reaching an intersection, turned off the highway and towards Banshee Bay. A few hundred metres down the road, a slight knocking noise caught her attention and she spotted a thin spiral of smoke coming from beneath the bonnet.

And where there was smoke …

Noooooooo!

After pulling to the side of the road as quickly as she could, she shoved her door open and leapt from the driver's side. Coupled with a hissing noise, the smoke intensified, thickened, quickened. With her panic rising, she tore over to the opposite side of the road, out of harm's way, one hand over her sprinting heart and the other covering her open mouth. Seconds passed into a minute, as her mind raced and her eyes blurred. She roughly wiped away two stubborn tears that had rolled down her cheeks. This was no time to be crying. She needed to pull herself together and make a game plan. Up above, Mother Nature appeared to be mimicking her nosediving spirits as the rumble of thunder sounded in the not-too-far distance. She noted that the sun was no longer beating down upon her, and shadows were quickly stretching across the tropical scenery surrounding her. There wasn't a house in sight. Nor had any cars rumbled past. She was broken down in the middle of nowhere, with nobody to ask for help, and to top it all off, it was going to pelt down with rain. Just her damn luck. Glaring at the darkening sky, she screamed out a myriad of swear words. A cow in the paddock nearest her lifted its head, eyeing her impassively while chewing its cud.

'What?' she called out to it, her hands in the air.

Of course she didn't receive a response.

Groaning, she turned back to her Jimny, and finally saw the problem for what it was. And she instantly felt like an idiot. It was steam, not smoke. The old beast had overheated. She wasn't defying death by standing here, yelling at a cow. She was just in her regular ongoing mess of a life, watching the next setback on her crazy agenda unfolding. She needed to do something other than standing here, feeling sorry for herself. Because soon, by the looks of the dark clouds eating up the last of the blue, she was going to add getting drenched through to the skin to her list of hindrances. So, stomping back to her Jimny with newfound determination, she tugged the bonnet open and stared into the steamy abyss of the unknown. Not mechanically minded in the slightest, she had no clue what to do next, but she'd just have to wing it. Otherwise, she may end up stuck out here all night. And after watching *Wolf Creek* too many times, there was no way in hell she wanted that.

* * *

With Tommy having disappeared bang on the 2 pm closing time, Jarrah and his two long-serving waitresses, twin sisters Jenny and Penny, had done the clearing up. It was four by the time they'd finished – an hour later than usual. Even though he was miffed Tommy hadn't done the right thing by staying to help with end-of-shift duties, he decided to leave his nephew to his sulking until later. Or maybe tomorrow. It was probably a good idea for him to calm down before what was going to be an uncomfortable conversation anyway. So, instead, he headed into town with Scruff as his happy passenger, to put up a notice at the local shop saying that he was looking for a new cook, pronto.

With the gloomy sky having split open half an hour earlier, the tropical storm hadn't eased, and the heavy downpour was making it hard for him to see the road. This trip into town was going to take him a little longer than expected. Slowing as he approached a cattle grid, he then turned right. Just up ahead, he spotted a little jeep-looking car with its hazard lights flashing. Turning the stereo down, he eased off the accelerator and went down a gear. Checking his rear-vision mirror, he made sure he didn't have anyone travelling too closely behind him. Indicating, he then began to pull to the side of the road. The older style Jimny four-wheel drive was parked up on the shoulder, and from what he could see, there was nobody inside. Rolling past the front end, he spotted a very nice butt captured in a pair of diamante-studded denim shorts, with the woman's head hidden beneath the open bonnet. It was all he could do to respectfully drag his eyes from the pleasant sight.

He looked to Scruff, who was getting antsy beside him. 'You stay put, mister, or there'll be trouble, okay.' Then he rolled his window down, copping a spray of raindrops to his face as he called out, 'Hey there, do you need a hand?'

Caught unawares, the petite woman bumped her head then unfurled from where she was tinkering. 'Ouch, damn it.' She spun to him while rubbing her head, a shifter clutched tightly in her hand. 'I didn't hear you pull up.' Not moving a muscle now, she stared him down.

With buttercream blonde hair, rosy full lips, and womanly curves in all the right places, her natural beauty momentarily struck Jarrah speechless. She was striking in a very ethereal kind of way. Then, before he had a chance to say a single word, a sense of familiarity whacked him fair and square in the chest, and he had to take a quick breath to recover. 'Sorry, I didn't mean to startle you.' Thank god he'd finally found words.

She half-smiled. 'Of course you didn't.' The blowing rain had drenched her to the skin, and her blue T-shirt clung to her.

'Engine troubles?' he said, unable to stop staring at her.

'Hmm …' With her half-smile turning a little cheeky, she wiped locks of long, wet hair from her face, succeeding in smearing grease all over her cheeks. 'Whatever gave you that idea?'

Well, hot damn, she had sass, and he liked it. 'Wild guess, I suppose.' Her hint of a smirk was both cute and challenging.

'Well then, you guessed right.' She threw a quick glance over her shoulder. 'And as much as I'd like to say I don't need any help,' she flung her reflective gaze back to him, 'I'll have to humble myself and say I do.'

'In that case, I'm at your service.' He offered her a smirk in return before grabbing his hat from the dashboard – it would help keep his face somewhat dry. He tugged it on, shoved his door open and stepped out. 'You can come too, buddy, if you don't mind getting wet.' Scruff didn't need any more of an invite to follow him.

It was only when Jarrah neared her that he caught sight of the mesmeric sea-green of her eyes – he'd never seen a shade so intensely yet calmingly beautiful. In an instant, she innocently dragged him into fond memories of swimming in the ocean off the glorious coastline of Western Australia, without a care in the world, and a twangy country song playing in his heart. And with his next intake of breath, it made him ponder what it would feel like, diving into all that made this stunning woman quintessentially her. Such a deep contemplation made him breathe a little faster and take a little longer to find any decipherable words. And that left them in a strange kind of silence, with him standing in the glow of her flashing hazard lights, with the rain slowing but still falling in a soft sheet. Time seemed to stumble, stall, then stand still. He sucked in a breath, and so did she. Her inquisitive yet cautious gaze went to the burn scar on his left cheek and loitered there. He understood it gave him a scary-looking edge, and he didn't want her to get the wrong impression of him, so he turned to the other side, blocking it from her view.

'So who's your friend?' Her voice broke through his thoughts and her gaze motioned to Scruff, now sitting on the toes of his boots.

'Ahhh.' He ruffled his best buddy's head. 'This here is Scruffball, or Scruff for short.'

'Scruffball hey? Cute name.' Her diamond-studded left brow lifted a little. 'Is he friendly?'

'Uh-huh, he sure is.' Glancing down at Scruff – who was now keen to doggy-welcome this new person, but unable to because Jarrah had his finger looped through his collar – he chuckled. 'Maybe a little too much for his own good at times, though.'

'Hey, buddy.' She crouched down to give Scruff a ruffle on his head, and he lapped it up. 'You're a sweetie pie, aren't you?'

His tail slapping the gravel by the side of the road, Scruff gave her a sneaky lick up the cheek.

Even though she didn't seem the least bit put off by dog slobber, Jarrah was quick to remind Scruff of his manners. 'Oi, you scallywag, you know that's not cool.' But too wrapped up in this pretty woman, Scruff didn't acknowledge his reprimand.

'Aw, all good, he's just saying hello, aren't you, buddy.' She chuckled as she straightened.

Jarrah noted that she didn't even bother to wipe her cheek. A person that loved dogs was his kind of human. Especially one as cutely packaged as this woman.

'So, let's see what's happened here, hey.' He peered beneath the bonnet, thankful for the reprieve from the intensity of her striking gaze. 'It looks to me like you've got yourself a cracked radiator.' He glanced to where she was standing closely at his side. She was short and petite, and he felt like a high-rise next to her. 'I'm afraid I don't think we're going to get this fixed here, or anytime over the next couple of days for that matter.' He grimaced at her pained expression. 'Sorry to be the bearer of bad news, but the local mechanic has gone on a fishing tournament for the weekend, and won't be back until Tuesday, at the earliest.'

'There's only one mechanic in Banshee Bay?'

'With just under four hundred and fifty residents around here, I'm afraid so.'

Her huff could have blown him to Timbuktu. 'Oh bloody hell.' Stomping left to right, she kicked the front tyre, and then planted her hands onto her hips. 'I seriously don't have time for this crap.'

Jarrah had to stifle a grin, now wasn't the time, but holy hell she was attractive when she was mad. 'You got something important to get to?'

'Yeah, something like that.' She bit her bottom lip and her brows furrowed in thought.

'Can I give you a lift to wherever it was you were going?' It was the least he could do. 'As long as it's not an age away, that is.'

'Oh, that's really kind of you, but …' She looked to her broken-down old beast, then back at him, blinking really fast.

Oh lord, was she about to cry. He couldn't stand here and witness that, especially not when he couldn't comfort her. Maybe she didn't have anywhere to be, or to go? He hadn't stopped to think of that. 'You can come back to my place and have a hot shower and a good couple of nights' sleep,' he said hurriedly, trying to somehow soothe her. 'And then, as soon as the mechanic gets back into town, we'll get him on the job as quickly as we can so you can be on your way again.'

Sniffing and squaring her shoulders, she folded her arms and assessed him through her piercing eyes. 'How do I know you're not going to take me back somewhere to have your way with me and then murder me?'

'You don't.' He chuckled, but then zipped it when he noted she was deadly serious.

Her suspicious eyes narrowed. 'That's not funny.'

'Sorry.' Grimacing, he held his hands up. 'I'm not trying to be.'

More thunder rumbled overhead, and a crack of iridescent lightning shot across the sky. She glanced upwards, into the soft pitter-patter of rain, cursing. 'Oh, for god's sake, really? Haven't you watered your garden enough already?'

'What did you just say?' He couldn't hide his chuckle now.

'Oh, that.' She looked a little embarrassed. 'My mum always told me that when it rained, it was God watering his garden.' Her shoulders lifted in a little shrug. 'Not that I believe in all of that religious stuff much these days.'

'I like her analogy, it's very sweet.' Jarrah noted she was talking about her mum in the past tense, and his heart squeezed for her loss. He knew all too well what that felt like, to lose a mother. 'I don't think this is the safest place for you to be camped out all night.' Grabbing his wallet from his back pocket, he plucked out a business card. 'Here, this might make you feel a little better about coming back to mine.'

Taking it from him, she read the front, and when she looked back at him, her eyes were wide. 'You own Riverside Acres?'

'I sure do.' He was a little thrown by her reaction, but shrugged it off.

'Okay, well, in that case, I'll gratefully accept your offer.' She motioned over her shoulder. 'Just let me go and grab my bag.'

Well that was a quick change of heart. 'I can get it for you.'

She shook her head. 'You could, but I don't need you to.' Going to the passenger side of her car, she fumbled about then hauled a duffel bag from the back seat and tossed it over her shoulder, along with a tasselled handbag. Going door to door, she made sure the car was locked up nice and tight, then turned to him with a determined look on her face. 'Will my Jimny be safe left here?'

'It will be, yes.' He hooked his thumbs into his belt loops. 'I'll come back tomorrow and tow it to the mechanics; we can leave it parked there until Macca gets back from fishing.'

'Sounds like a plan, thank you.' Rising to her tippy toes, she eyed him a little uneasily. 'Right then, let's do this then.'

'Yes, let's.' He completely understood how it would feel for a woman to be getting into a car with a stranger, and he hoped she'd relax in time, once she totally believed he wasn't a weirdo.

Although he'd come to her rescue, Jarrah knew without a doubt that she was the furthest thing from a damsel in distress. Sassy as hell, and obviously independent and strong-minded, this little package of captivating woman was a livewire. He led her around to the passenger side and opened the door for her. She thanked him with a smile as she climbed up and in. As he headed back to the driver's side, Scruff leapt up and planted his now wet rear in the middle of the bench-style seat.

Revving his four-wheel drive back to growling life, Jarrah waited for her to tug her seatbelt on, checked his mirrors, and then eased back onto the road, towards home. The ad for the cook would have to wait until tomorrow now. 'So where are you from, if you don't mind me asking?' He shifted up gears.

'Everywhere.' Her reply was a little distant as she stared out her window.

Jarrah found her air of mystery captivating. 'Okay, well, will you at least tell me your name?'

'Millie.' She turned to him now, and offered a tight smile.

'Nice to meet you, Millie, my name's Jarrah King.' He made sure his smile was warm and welcoming.

'I know, I read it on your business card.' She responded with another tight-lipped smile, and then looked back at the roadside flashing past.

He was about to turn the radio up, to drown out the sense of unease, but thought better of it. Conversation was the way forwards. 'So where you heading to, Miss Millie with no last name?'

Her shoulders lifted casually. 'Wherever my heart desires.'

'Wow, now that's freedom.' He chuckled. 'I have to say I'm jealous.'

'Jealous?' She finally turned all of her attention towards him. 'Of my freedom?'

His nod was exaggerated. 'Hell yes.'

'Trust me, freedom is not all it's cracked up to be.' She paused as if considering what to say next. 'Having a place to call home, somewhere that's yours and yours alone, now that's something to be jealous of, in my opinion.'

'Yes, I suppose so.' Rubbing his five o'clock shadow, he took a moment to choose his words wisely. This woman wasn't one for small talk, he knew that right off the bat. He got the gut feeling she was a drifter, with no fixed address, and no permanent job. 'You wouldn't be looking for work while you're around these parts, would you?' He was going out on a limb, but why not?

'I might be.' She shifted in her seat a little. 'Do you know of something?'

'I have a kitchen job up for grabs, if you're interested.' He held his breath, praying for her to say yes, for more reasons than the fact that he was desperate to fill the position.

She seemed to contemplate this. 'That seems very convenient, that I might be looking for work, and you suddenly have a job for me.'

'Convenient, yes, I suppose you could say that.' He deliberated. 'But I see it more as a wonderful coincidence.'

She regarded him thoughtfully. 'Fair play, Jarrah King.' She seemed to smile from the heart, and it suited her.

It made Jarrah happy to think he was the one to entice such a beautiful smile on such beautiful lips. 'So, you might be interested?'

'Maybe.' Even though she was clearly very interested, she also very clearly tried to act nonchalant. 'Can I think about it overnight and let you know in the morning?'

'Of course, but make it bright and early, otherwise I'll have to put up the ad I was on my way to post when I came across you on the side of the road.'

'Ha, what are the chances of that happening, hey?' She looked at him like she was trying to read him. 'Fancy that,' she added with a shrewd smile, like she was privy to something he wasn't.

A little confused as to what was going on in that pretty head of hers, he graced her with a small, but charming smile. 'Like I said, it was a wonderful coincidence.'

'Sounds like you're in a rush to fill the position.' Her tone was inquisitive.

'Yeah, you could say that.' He grimaced. 'My previous cook and I came to a mutual understanding earlier today that she should hang up her apron.'

'You mean you fired her?'

'Yeah, after she broke the number one rule when you're employed at Riverside Acres, by sleeping with my nephew.' He chuckled, shaking his head at her look of incredulity. 'And besides this candid bit of information, her food was crap.'

'Say it like it is, why don't you?' She chuckled, addictively so, enticing the same reaction from him. 'I really like people who are up-front and honest, you always know where you stand with them, so good on you, Jarrah, for doing what you had to.'

Liking how his name sounded rolling off her tongue, he almost blushed with her compliment. 'Thanks, Millie.'

They fell into a comfortable silence, and only then did he turn the radio up. Waylon Jennings was belting out the lyrics of 'Are You Sure Hank Done It This Way'. With her foot tapping and her fingertips drumming her leg, her lips moved ever so slightly to the words of the song, letting him know she liked her country music. And only a true country lover would know the words to this particular song. Another tick to his long list of attributes that he liked in a woman.

Dog lover. Tick. Country music lover. Tick. Gorgeous natural looks. Tick. Sassy. Tick. Independent. Tick. And all in a matter of less than an hour.

Thankfully, he'd made sure any woman he had the least bit of interest in had a lot to live up to: that way he always had a reason not to give in to his emotions. Because his emotions ran extremely deep, deep enough to drag him under if he wasn't careful. He had a lot of love to give, hidden within his shackled heart. That was why he kept it under lock and key.

Apart from what he already liked about her, he couldn't quite put his finger on it, but there was something special about Millie, something he needed to understand, to know more of. And although it felt bizarre, there was part of him that felt a strong need to protect her, to shield her from whatever, or whoever, she might be running from. In the strangest of ways, he almost wished she was his. And that floored him.

A relationship could spell disaster for him.

In so many ways.

He needed to be very, *very*, careful.

CHAPTER 5

Millie was glad for the scruffy dog that sat between them – in spite of the fact that its breath stank to high hell and its slobber was dripping onto her legs – and not only because she didn't know this tower of virile man from a bar of soap, but also because she felt like she did. It was an oddly conflicting sensation. One she didn't know what to make of. As the highway rolled away, she couldn't help but wonder if this rugged-looking bloke was the person behind her being here. If he'd been the one to put pen to paper. Or was he the one who would slip up and reveal the truth? There was an addictive air about him, suffused with mystery and determination and an unfathomable depth – a powerfully heady combination. Her heart quivered as she recalled turning to see him for the first time, the shifter in her hand her only means of protection. It was an intense moment, and she'd felt a magnetic attraction to him in that instant, as well as an intoxicating aura of safety within his presence. As if they'd already spent a lifetime together.

Or maybe a past one …

Giving Scruff a distracted scratch on his neck, which he was lapping up – shame the same couldn't be said about his slobber – she snuck curious, sideways glances at Jarrah. Something about him was niggling something deep inside of her. Maybe it was purely because he was easy on the eye. Maybe it was because her hormones had been all out of whack since her miscarriage. She could come up with a myriad of reasons, or excuses, depending how she looked at it, but if she were being completely honest with herself, with his shaggy light-brown hair, tinged with a bit of grey near his temples, and his angular jaw hardened even more by his five o'clock shadow, and the tattoos she was privy to on his forearms and one of his hands, he was a hell of a lot of man. One she needed to turn a blind eye to if this trip up north was going to prove successful. She had one goal, and one goal only – to know the truth. Besides, she knew the pain of wearing rose-coloured glasses all too well. Most men lied, almost all eventually cheated, and in one way or another members of the human race in general let down the people closest to them, the people who would do anything for them.

Slowing at an intersection, the four-wheel drive then veered left, and a little further down the road the tyres met with the crunch of a gravel road. Not long after, they rattled over two cattle grids, both making her teeth chatter. Scruff barked as he bounced in his seat. Jarrah laughed at his dog's antics, and she couldn't help but chuckle to herself too. Another kilometre or so down the road, Jarrah accelerated through a running creek bed, sending a spray of water over the bonnet, then, reaching the top of a steep rise, they met with bitumen again just as a packet of

Minties fell from the dash and upended in her lap. It appeared he liked the same lollies as she did.

Gathering the teeth-sticking mint-flavoured sweets and plonking what she'd been able to retrieve back into the bag, she looked to Jarrah. 'Gee whizz, your roadhouse is off the beaten track, isn't it?' Sitting ramrod straight, she braced herself for more surprise bumps.

'Ah, not really, sorry about the bush track, but I took a short cut through the back of my property.' He pointed up ahead. 'Other people usually come from that way.'

'Ahhh, okay, gotcha.' Her eyes widened as she inhaled the refreshing aroma of the lush tropical rainforest floating through the air vents of the LandCruiser. 'This is all yours?'

'It sure is, and isn't she beautiful.' He sighed, and dimples appeared on his cheeks as he smiled dreamily. 'I have to pinch myself every single day I'm lucky enough to wake up to it.'

Nodding in awe, she had to agree wholeheartedly. With thick shrubbery surrounding them, the deep green umbrella of the foliage above, and bright pops of colours from tropical flowers amid it all, the entirety of it was a multisensory overload, especially for a gal who had grown used to the big smoke of Sydney.

'You would never believe it, but this place is apparently over one hundred and thirty-five million years old,' he said, his tattooed hand rubbing his stubbled chin.

'Holy moly, really?' Handsome and intelligent, this man was growing on her way too quickly.

'Never a truer word spoken.' He nodded earnestly. 'David Attenborough said it's the most extraordinary place on earth, and I have to say I totally agree with him.'

'Yeah, me too.' Her words were more breathed than spoken, as her eyes gladly rested back on the view through the windscreen. Never in her life had she seen a place so lush and pure. It was utterly breathtaking.

'I'm glad you like it.' Jarrah's smile was gentle as his gaze briefly met with hers.

'I don't just like it, Jarrah, I love it.' And she meant it.

Slowing, he turned beneath a sign with *Riverside Acres* etched into the wood. Horse-dotted paddocks hugged either side of a driveway that curved its way towards a sprawling double-storey homestead with wide wraparound verandahs that she instantly craved to lounge upon, a good book in hand. The grand home appeared to stand proudly upon the flattened tip of the rise, and an air of warmth and openhearted hospitality beckoned for her to step through the front gates of the rustic timber fence line. The many windows, she presumed, would be spectacular viewing points over the lush expanse of tropical landscape, and she swore she could see the tiniest flicker of the ocean off in the far-flung distance. Budding rose bushes flanked the redbrick pathway that led up a few steps and towards the front door, and a huge water tank sat off to the left of the house. If not for all her emotional baggage, this place would be paradise to spend some time in, she was sure.

After pulling up beneath a towering gum tree that shaded one side of the homestead, Jarrah killed the engine. 'Well, here we are.'

'So it appears.' Her heart now in her throat, Millie sat forwards and, looking past the homestead, she spotted the roadhouse and a neighbouring row of motel rooms a few hundred metres away.

Was this it? The very place that held the answers to her past? Someone had to be callously toying with her, surely? The tropical panorama and well-kept outbuildings appeared so beautifully wholesome there was no way a dark past lingered here. She suddenly felt like a complete and utter fool, coming all this way, on a whim, all because a letter had told her to do so. But then there was the photograph that some nasty online keyboard warrior wouldn't have been able to provide. Whoever was behind this knew of her, and what had happened to her family that fateful night. It made her ask herself: if the person behind the words had told her to jump off a bridge, would she have done so? No. But if they'd told her the answers were at the bottom? Quite possibly. She was a desperate woman, with desperate questions. She had no idea how she was going to stay here indefinitely. No idea at all. But if her car breaking down was anything to go by, maybe the hands of fate were finally ushering her in the right direction. Maybe her destiny had been to arrive here, in this moment, all along.

'Millie, are you okay?'

She jumped so high her head almost hit the roof. 'Sorry, yes, I'm fine.' Her hand now pressed against her racing heart, she nodded to affirm this fabrication.

'Okay, let's get you settled then, hey.' Jarrah shoved his door open, then stepped out and hefted her bag from the back as Scruff leapt down behind him.

After drawing in a quick deep breath to try and bolster her courage, she stepped out and then followed closely behind him, her thongs flip-flopping and his boot heels clip-clopping along the pathway that led to the sweeping verandah adorned with trellises of rambling bougainvillea. Scruff quickly hightailed it to the front lawn and did his business as if he'd been busting.

Just as they reached the top of the steps, a thickset young bloke with dark hair pulled back into a ponytail appeared from around the far side of the house. Scruff raced to his side and he gave the dog's head a quick ruffle. Spotting her, his eyebrows sternly pulled together as he pushed past Scruff and took long strides towards them.

The intimidating-looking bloke caught her gaze. 'Who's that?' she murmured as she came to a stop at the front door. 'Correct me if I'm wrong, but he looks a little peeved.'

Pausing to kick off his boots at the welcome mat, Jarrah leant into her space. 'Oh, that's my nephew, Tommy, he looks big and tough but don't let that fool you. He might be a little on the moody side at times, being eighteen years old, but he can be a really good fella when he wants to be.' He gave a nod in greeting to the bloke, now coming up the steps two at a time. 'Hey there, Tommy.'

'Hey there, yourself.' The stench of cigarettes clung to Tommy's clothes. 'So, who's this?' His dark gaze narrowed while he looked her up and down, then folded his arms.

'This is Millie.' With a wave of his arm, Jarrah introduced her. 'She was broken down just outside of town, so I offered to give her a lift here, and tow her car to Macca's shop tomorrow, and he can hopefully fix it when he reopens on Tuesday morning.'

'Oh, bugger, that's a bit of bad luck, breaking down in the middle of Woop Woop.' His inquisitive gaze remained wary as he held out a hand. 'I'm Tommy, it's nice to meet you … Tillie, was it?'

'No, it's Millie, but close.' She could already sense that he didn't like her. Not that she cared. She wasn't here to make friends. 'Nice to meet you too.' She forced a smile as she lifted a hand to begrudgingly shake his.

With the hairs on the back of her neck bristling, she was taken aback by his grip. It was almost vice-like – as if he was trying to convey loud and clear that he was not someone she wanted to mess with. But she wasn't going to give him the satisfaction of knowing he intimidated her, so she squeezed back just as forcibly. Not that she was assured he sensed that, given their size difference.

'So, King, where's she going to be staying?' Tommy's unyielding gaze met with Jarrah's as he finally released her hand. 'Because all the motel rooms are full.'

'Yeah, I know. She can crash here, in one of the spare rooms.' Jarrah half-shrugged at Tommy. 'It's only for a couple of nights, or until her car is fixed, either, or.'

'Yeah, righto.' Tommy's response was clipped. 'Interesting.'

Jarrah didn't bite back or mention her possibly taking the cook's job, instead turning his focus to tugging the screen door open, revealing a pretty leadlight and timber door.

'I'll leave you to it,' Tommy said as he turned and took heavy steps away. 'I'm heading into town, to Jasmine's place.'

'Yeah, righto.' Hands on his hips, Jarrah watched Tommy vanish around the corner.

Millie could see, plain as day, that Jarrah's nephew was carrying a massive chip on his shoulder. And it wasn't anything to do with him being a moody eighteen-year-old, either. There was something about Tommy that was off, that threw her off kilter. She was going to be keeping a close eye on him, seeing as she'd be taking the cook's job, come morning, and staying here until she got what she came for. Which hopefully was going to be sooner rather than later.

All things going well …

'Come on in, Millie.' As he slipped off his boots, Jarrah's husky voice lured her undivided attention from Tommy, and in the opposite direction. 'And please, make yourself at home.'

Turning her regard back to the man who seemed to be the polar opposite of his nephew, her eyes went to the way his broad shoulders pulled his shirt taut as he stepped through the doorway. And when he turned to face her, as she flicked off her thongs and moved towards him, she was met with an equally broad chest. In this brief moment of arresting closeness, it made her want to lean all of herself against him, as if acutely aware that if she allowed herself to, Jarrah King would protect her from all the bad in this world. And as she'd learnt, there was a lot of it to be shielded from.

What in the heck is going on here?

She blinked, forcibly moving her gaze back to his soulful sky-blue eyes. They were striking against his tanned skin. For goodness sake, wasn't there anything about this man she didn't find attractive?

Stepping into the sundrenched lounge room with gleaming polished timber floors adorned with a huge cowskin rug, Jarrah waved her deeper into the heart of his home. 'Come on, follow me and I'll show you around the bachelor pad.'

She did as asked, and fell in step beside him. Her hands slipped into her pockets as she looked to the high ceiling with rustic open beams. It could have easily made the space feel hollow, but instead only added to the open-plan charm. Wandering through the comfy room, she noted the simple touches: a vase of fresh sunflowers on the side table, matching cushions and a throw rug on the modular couch, a rustic coffee table with a stack of *R.M. Williams Outback* magazines on top. The walls were painted a soft hue of eggshell blue, giving a sense that the outside was making its way in. The same could be said for the huge bay windows framed by lace curtains, where the view of the horse paddocks was to die for. Passing a tightly packed bookshelf – she liked the fact that he was a reader – she followed him into a long hallway, which passed a staircase, a bathroom and the laundry, then led into a spectacular rustic-themed kitchen with appliances to die for.

She couldn't hide her wonder, nor did she want to. 'Wow, Jarrah, this is …' She turned in a slow circle. 'Just wow.'

'I had it renovated last year.' He ran his gaze over the room, his smile stretching. 'I don't get much spare time, but when I do, I love to lock myself away in here, turn on some country tunes, and cook to my heart's content.'

Liking this man even more now, Millie nodded. 'I can see why.'

The open, light-filled space was a country cook's dream with classic cream cupboards, hard-wearing timber benchtops, a double porcelain farmhouse sink, a gorgeous stone island bench with copper pots and utensils hung above, and a six-burner Aga stove at the centre of it all. A bright red KitchenAid mixer, along with a matching kettle and toaster, added a pleasant pop of colour, as did the colour-coded barista-style coffee maker and double-door Smeg fridge. She could easily see herself in here, whiling away an entire weekend, making all the things she and her mum used to love to cook.

Blessed is the woman who gets to call this place her home.

Jarrah came around to face her from the opposite side of the breakfast bench. 'In my hour of need, I didn't even think to ask if you've had any experience in a commercial kitchen?'

His voice was deep, verging on the edge of husky, and those enchanting eyes of his – she felt as if she was tipping into them. 'No, not in the usual sense.'

His slight smile was a little cheeky. 'Hmm, righto, so what's "not in the usual sense" mean?'

'I spent my childhood in the kitchen with my mum, mixing, whipping, licking beaters, having my hand slapped away from hot things, and tasty things.' A rush of nostalgia had her blinking faster, in a bid to ward off a sudden urge to burst into tears. 'And my love for home-style cooking has continued on from there,' she added, quickly.

'Food is a magical thing that can bring people together.' Reaching across the bench, Jarrah offered reassurance with a gentle brush of his hand over hers. 'And leave lasting memories.'

His touch startled her, as did his ability to read her expression so accurately, and she had to take a moment to gather whatever it was he'd just stirred within her. 'Uh-huh, it sure can.' She stepped out of his reach. She couldn't risk feeling whatever that was again, or it might bring her crumbling into his big strong arms, where she would bare her soul.

A lengthy moment passed, followed by another, as he regarded her through deeply perceptive eyes. It made her feel exposed, vulnerable, giddy, and yet extraordinarily drawn to him.

'Your room is this way,' he finally said, walking past her.

Thankful for a reprieve from his undivided attention, she followed him back down the hallway and up the flight of steps. As she turned right, away from what she guessed to be the master bedroom, a corridor led her past two closed doors and what would be her very own bathroom, with a claw-foot bathtub and shower, and then they stopped.

Turning the handle, Jarrah pushed the door open. 'Here you go.' With a sweep of his arm he gestured for her to step past him. 'Home sweet home for a few days.'

Her breath caught as her gaze met the unmade queen-size bed with a plush-looking mattress and topper, flickered over the ornate timber headboard, and then travelled over the antique dressing table. It was so pretty, with just the right amount of sunshine filtering in through the wide windows. She could call this her bedroom for a lifetime.

Jarrah remained at the doorway, as if stepping in would be an invasion of her privacy. 'I'll grab you some fresh sheets, a couple of pillows and a doona. I hope you don't mind making it up yourself.' He glanced at his watch. 'I got a couple of things I need to do before sundown.'

'Yes, of course I don't mind. It would be the least I could do.' Although she wanted to, she failed to smile as she tucked a loose tendril of hair behind her ear. Rolling emotions were making it difficult to breathe, let alone talk, but she pressed on. 'Thank you, for being so kind and welcoming.'

'Hey, no worries, Millie.' He offered her a charming smile, filled with his equally charming dimples. 'Back in a minute with your bedding, and your bag.'

'Okay, thanks.' She swallowed, and then swallowed again, willing herself to hold it together as she watched him disappear down the corridor, his footfalls fading away as he traipsed down the staircase.

Her head in a spin, she couldn't deny that something had ignited between them the second she'd locked eyes with him on the deserted roadside. And that certain something came dangerously close to a primal kind of attraction. As if they'd been born for each other. But as real as that felt, it was all too sudden, all too demanding, and way too intense for it to be tangible. Her nerves were having a field day and getting the better of her. She really needed to get a firm grip on the situation, and on herself. She dragged in a slow deep breath. Her voice of reason sprang to life as she exhaled, warning her to steer clear of him, and to tread carefully if she didn't, because she had no idea if he was going to become an ally or an enemy.

For all she knew, he could be the one who had sent the photograph and the letter.

* * *

The tropical downpour had all but disappeared. As the sun began its descent behind the surrounding mountain ranges, painting a scattering of warm brush strokes across the vast stretch of cloudless blue, Jarrah did his best to keep his mind present, instead of on the very beautiful woman to whom he'd just offered a bedroom, and a job. He hoped to goodness he'd made a good judgement call, and not just landed himself into deeper water. Inevitably, if Millie took the job, time would most certainly tell. Worrying about it was futile. Predictably, Tommy had been annoyed when he'd told him they might have found their new cook, if she wanted the job. Aware it was because he'd fired Jasmine, Jarrah had chosen not to fuel the fire by reminding Tommy who the big boss was around here. Tommy may have the manager's role, when it came to the roadhouse and motel rooms, but his nephew was seriously becoming too big for his britches. It was as if the Martino blood ran strong through Tommy's veins, and no matter how much Jarrah tried to flush it out by immersing Tommy in all that was Riverside Acres, he had a sense that his past would come through Tommy to bite him on the butt.

When he least expected it, too.

But, for now, all he wanted to do was be in the present moment, for that's where peace could be found. So, lunge rope in hand, he continued to put his new mare through her paces as he kept the rope taut while turning in circles with her. He always found how the magnificent creatures could read body language so very remarkable. There was no need for heavy-handedness. The whip held in his other hand was merely for long lashes on the ground behind her, and never for her powerful body. Authority with a horse was all about the tone of his voice. Softly spoken words could slow the mare, and a few clicks of his tongue would get her to pick up the pace. Even though he was keen to get in the saddle, he knew groundwork was what built trust. He wanted her to be used to his touch, and voice, before putting anything on her back.

'Hey, Jarrah.' Millie's voice carried on the gentle late-afternoon breeze. 'Nice-looking horse you have there.'

'Isn't she a beauty?' He flashed a wide smile over his shoulder. 'And to think she was about to be sent to the abattoir.'

'Oh my gosh, really?' Stopping next to the railings, Millie rested her chin on one and her foot on the lowest. 'Why would someone want to do that to her?'

'Her previous owner thought that a heavy hand would train her, and she wasn't having a bar of it.' His jaw momentarily clenched with the anger that fired through him. 'And that, in my opinion, makes her a victorious survivor of animal cruelty.' He glanced towards Millie, loving the way she was looking at him, as if he was a hero. 'So you're all settled in?'

Nodding, she held her hand up to shade her gaze. 'Pretty much, yes.'

'Great.' Her slow smile warmed something deep within his soul. 'Make sure you let me know if there's anything else you need, okay?'

'I think you've done enough for me already, but thanks for the offer.' Her smile stretched wider. 'And I've decided to take the job, if that's still okay with you?'

Jarrah had to fight from fist-punching the air. 'Great, yes, of course it is,' he called back, as coolly as he could. 'I've got the ex-cook, Mary, ditching her retirement for a day and filling in for tomorrow, as a favour, and Sunday we're closed, so you can start on Monday if you like, give yourself a couple of days to settle in.'

'Great,' she echoed back to him. 'Monday it is then.'

She continued to watch him as he made use of the last ten minutes of daylight, before the sensor floodlights would kick into life and he'd put the mare to rest for the night. And he liked the fact that she remained at the railings of the house paddock, instead of wandering back across the drive to the homestead, because from where he stood, as the mare trotted past him, he caught glimpses of her dreamy face and wistful smile. If it were peacefulness she was feeling, it suited her. And if so, he valued that he had possibly played a part in that. Uniquely pretty, with delicate features, shambolic wavy blonde hair that hung past her shoulders, and a feisty personality, Millie, whoever she was, fascinated him. And the more he snuck secretive glances in her direction, the more he liked what he saw. But as much as that lit little fires inside him, it was also a hazardous place to be, because anything other than a platonic connection was the last thing on his agenda. Getting close to anyone meant his entire life could be unravelled. And in a small town like Banshee Bay, gossip spread like wildfire.

He had secrets to keep.

He couldn't afford the luxury of falling for this striking woman.

Steering clear of the temptation that was Millie would have to be a top priority.

CHAPTER 6

Listening intently to Ebony's fantastic advice, Millie looked to where she knew her bag was, wondering if she should find somewhere other than her secret compartment inside it for the letter and photograph. Once she got her Jimny back, she would pop both back beneath the driver's seat. Until then, she'd just have to wing it, like she was doing with everything else.

'So, it sounds to me like you've landed on your feet, Mills.' Ebony's voice carried down the line. 'Which I'm happy to hear.'

'Yes, for now.' Swapping her phone from one ear to the other, Millie made sure to keep her voice hushed. 'We'll see how the next week pans out.'

'And that Tommy guy, you really think he has something to do with the letter, huh?'

'I kind of do, yes.' Millie sighed. 'But who knows, it could be Jarrah for all I know.'

'Yes, true. Mills, just be super careful, okay? I'm so worried about you.'

'I promise I'm being careful, Ebs.'

'Good, I'm glad to hear it.' A beep echoed in the background. 'I'm sorry, hon, but I have to run, my microwaved scrambled eggs and baked beans are ready, and I only have ten minutes to eat it before I have to get back to work.'

'Yes, you go eat, and we will talk again soon.'

'We most certainly will. Love you, Mills.'

'Love you too, Ebs.'

Millie popped her phone back onto the bedside table. Propped up on her pillows with her nails almost chewed down to the quick, she felt restless, edgy and uncomfortable in her own skin as the new day entered the bedroom through the crack between the blackout curtains. Having retired in there not long after Jarrah had come home – her excuse being that she was feeling beat after a long drive – she'd lain awake half the night, worrying about what was going to come next. And with the dawning of her first day at Riverside Acres, reality was hitting, real hard. Coming here might have been a mistake of epic proportions. It could end up being a major disaster. But Ebony was right: she wasn't about to run back home with her tail between her legs, and not only because she was a strong-minded pain in the butt at times, but also because it would leave her forever wondering what she would've found out if she'd stayed. She may be closer than she'd ever been to discovering the truth of why she now roamed this earth without her family to share it with, so she wasn't about to throw in the towel.

You've got this!

Climbing from the bed, she straightened her skew-whiff pyjamas. She wandered over to the window and drew the curtains so she could take a few moments to admire the untainted views before heading downstairs for the hit of caffeine she was going to need to face the day. As she pushed open the bay windows, crisp fresh air greeted her, as did the lovely scent of recently mowed lawn. Her eyes followed the winding driveway that led to where a tractor trundled along the fence line of well-manicured horse paddocks. Her heart did a weird pitter-patter as she visualised the man behind the wheel of the green John Deere. Jarrah had mentioned he was going to be up early to start his day out yonder. From what she could tell, he worked hard and had a heart of gold. And she admired both traits. They made him even more believable, likeable, innocent of anything to do with her tainted past.

Turning her gaze to the warm-hued sky, she blinked into the absorbing hues of sunrise as she pondered the last twenty-four hours. Over their early dinner of leftover spaghetti and cheese toasted sandwiches, washed down with a glass of Coke, Jarrah had offered for her to move into one of the motel rooms with a kitchenette when one became available, seeing as she'd be staying on for the job. Apparently it was a perk of the position for anyone who was from out of town, and she hoped so, because she didn't want to owe him for any favours. He'd even agreed to pay her cash, when she'd told him she needed to stay untraceable for a private reason. He hadn't blinked an eyelid or asked for an explanation – it was as if he understood her request wholeheartedly. It was all just too easy. She still found it hard to believe how fate had brought her straight to the place she needed to be. To stay with a man that was as handsome and kind as Jarrah. But hey, she was going to run with it, because what other choice did she have?

Inhaling deeply, she stepped away from the window and tried to focus on the positives. She had a really nice place to stay. She'd finally scored a job she'd quite possibly enjoy, as short-lived as it would be. And, to top it all off, her boss was extremely easy on the eye. Today she was going to spend time familiarising herself with Riverside Acres and its surroundings. Sitting around the homestead twiddling her thumbs would do her no good. Her overactive mind would send her crazy. Heading into the great outdoors of tropical Far North Queensland would be a welcome distraction from her uncooperative internal thoughts about everything that could possibly go wrong. And the fresh air would do her the world of good, too. She hadn't had the pleasure of inhaling country breaths for way too long.

Pausing at the dresser mirror, she stripped off her pyjamas then dressed in denim shorts and a T-shirt. She grabbed her brush out of her bathroom bag, ran it through her long hair, and then twisted it into a bun at the nape of her neck. After padding to the bathroom, she cleaned her teeth and washed her face before heading downstairs in search of a coffee, which she made from instant granules, instead of using the espresso machine – she had no idea how to work it.

Heading out the back door and onto the verandah, she sank into the cushion-covered day bed located in prime position for the jaw-dropping views. Getting comfy, she tucked her legs up beneath her. Relishing each sip of her strong cuppa and the lushness of the surrounding tropical landscape, she felt her downtrodden spirit rising. Riverside Acres was so very different to the cityscape she'd grown accustomed to, and yet it gave her the sense that although it was a world away it was one that she belonged within. And that sense of familiarity, of belonging, brought her to ponder, for what felt like the umpteenth time, about the acquainted feeling Jarrah King roused in her. Who was he? And what made her feel so calm within his presence? She didn't like the fact that he'd been on her mind since she'd found herself snagged by his pensive gaze yesterday, nor did she like how her body responded to his presence when he was anywhere near her. It was as if her body had a mind of its own. She also wondered if the attraction she'd felt in that heart-swooning moment of laying her eyes on him for the very first time the day before had in fact been felt by him too. And if it had, what did she expect to come from it?

Nothing, that's what you expect to come from it.

Shaking her head, she grumbled at her train of thought. She didn't even know the bloke, and had no clue if it was him that had sent her the letter and photograph, and yet here she was, wasting precious time and energy worrying herself about him liking her, and vice versa. Sculling the last of her coffee, she hurried back inside, dumped her cup into the dishwasher then, after tugging on her socks and joggers, made her way out the front door, down the steps and out the front gate. Where she literally ran into Tommy while looking over her shoulder to make sure she'd shut the front door.

'Oh, crap, sorry, I wasn't watching where I was going.' Embarrassed, she stepped back from him. 'Morning, Tommy.' She offered him a friendly smile.

He only lightly returned the smile. 'Morning, Tillie.'

Grrrrrr, he's really taking the ... tell him!

'It's Millie, Tommy.'

'Oh, sorry, yup, my bad.'

She could tell he wasn't sorry. Not in the slightest. He was baiting her, but she wasn't biting. 'It looks like we'll be working together come Monday.'

'So, you took the job?' He eyed her curiously.

'Yes, I did.' This conversation was gaining in awkwardness by the second.

'Right.' He fumbled with his belt buckle as he shifted from foot to foot. 'I'll be sure to chat with Jarrah about this when I see him.'

'Okay, you do that.' She made steps in the opposite direction. 'I'll catch you later.'

Millie felt his gaze pinned to her back until she cleared the corner of the homestead and found shady solace beneath a blooming jacaranda tree. The blanket of purple flowers made for a pretty pathway as she strolled away from the buildings and into the lush heart of Mother Nature. She had no idea where she was heading, just as long as it was away from Tommy, for now. Her gut was telling her that he was somehow behind her being here, but to what extent she was yet to find out. He was too young to have been involved in the death of her family, but that didn't mean he wasn't the one who had lured her to Riverside Acres with the contents of the envelope. But then if that were the case, he certainly wasn't acting like he wanted her anywhere near the place, so that bit of her scenario didn't add up. Hopefully, soon enough, if she played it cool, she'd be able to piece it all together, and finally find the closure she'd been searching for, for fifteen long years. With all her heart she hoped Jarrah wasn't a part of that puzzle because she liked him and hoped her instincts were right when it came to him. For once, she'd like to be right about a person's humanity.

Her fingers pensively rolling the tourmaline pendant swinging from her necklace, she did her best to enjoy her casual morning stroll. The black stone had been her twenty-first birthday gift from Ebony. The handcrafted crystal was apparently meant to keep bad juju away. She wasn't sure she believed in such things, but it was a kind gesture, and one she held close to her heart. Literally. What she did want to believe, though, was that fate did have something magical, something amazing, in store for her, rather than leaving her living an existence where she was surviving from one catastrophic event to the next, barely having the time to dust herself off before the next tragedy had her falling to her knees.

Wandering along the earthen path, she glanced up at the far-flung mountain ranges adorned with lush green pockets of tropical forest, occasionally dotted with ragged outcroppings of rocks, and she couldn't help but ponder how the stone formations reminded her of tombstones. Tipping her head to the side, she wondered if people had been buried up there, and if so, when, how and who? Goosebumps rose and covered her skin. Maybe, if she got the time, and found the get-up-and-go, she'd hike up there and check it out. Ebony would be so proud of her if she returned back to Sydney with a thirst for exercise. *Ha, yeah, and pigs might fly too.*

Deep in her thoughts, a crack of twigs and the rustle of bushes stopped her dead in her tracks. Frozen to the spot, she honed her senses. She'd heard stories of roos and feral pigs attacking people up this way, and the recollection of such tales sent a shot of fear up her spine. Shielding her eyes from the bright sunshine, she looked left and right. There wasn't a soul, or dangerous creature, in sight, but she couldn't shake the sense that someone, or something, was following her. The hair on the back of her neck rose. Her mouth was abruptly dry. She spun around, her skin prickling. Turning in a full circle, she confirmed she was alone, and also that she had a very overactive mind. But then, just when she'd relaxed some, a creature exploded from the scrub, racing straight for her. She screamed, and went to run for her life, when she suddenly realised it was Scruff. Panting like billy-o, he pulled to a stop just shy of her, sat, and then eyed her with eager adoration, his tongue comically lolling out to one side.

'Gee whizz, Scruffball, you almost gave me a heart attack, boy.' Crouching, she came eye to eye with him, and gave his head a ruffle. 'Would you like to join me on my mooch about and keep me safe from wild creatures like you?' She chuckled at his goofy regard of her.

He lifted a paw and placed it on her knee. Her heart melted at the cute gesture. 'I gather that's a yes.' Then she got a whiff of something rotten. 'Bloody hell, Scruff, you reek to high heaven.' She wrinkled her nose. 'What in the hell have you gone and rolled in?'

Scruff sneezed, twice, then his lips lifted upwards until he looked like he was actually smiling at her.

'You really are a one-off, aren't you?' She tipped her head and smiled into his kind eyes. 'Come on then, stinky, let's get a move on, shall we?'

She straightened and spotted the tractor parked up ahead, with Jarrah nowhere in sight. Disappointment blinked in her heart. It would have been nice to say good morning to him. Maybe she'd be lucky enough to run into him somewhere along her wander.

Noticing Scruff wasn't at her side, she glanced over her shoulder. 'Come on then, slowcoach.' Her dishevelled sidekick chased his tail, before proceeding to join her. 'You're a nincompoop, Scruff.'

Laughing at his antics, she moseyed on with him wandering at her side. Enjoying his company and liking how his presence made her feel a little safer, she breathed in the sights, smells and sounds of the ancient tropical rainforest surrounding her. Everything felt so fresh, so alive. With the melody of trickling water luring her, she wandered down a little embankment and after gasping at how pretty it was, followed the meandering creek for a bit, enjoying the sun-spangled water rolling over the jutting stones. A little way along, with her arms outstretched for balance, she made her way over a purposely positioned tree trunk, quietly cheering to herself when she made it over the other side safe and sound.

The sound of horses whickering to one another caught her attention. Curious, she headed in the general direction of the roadhouse, towards the horsey chatter. Tucking the sweaty tendrils of hair sticking to her neck behind her ears, she turned left, past an old barn filled with farm equipment and then the very impressive stables flanked by the round yard where she'd watched Jarrah working the afternoon before. A quick glance to her right gave her her bearings when the homestead came back into her view. Off to her left was the motel, roadhouse and truck parking area. How Jarrah kept this place looking so pristine, and running so smoothly, was beyond her. It would be a full-time job. Seven days a week.

More whinnies snagged her attention. Just up ahead, an energetic Arabian was prancing triumphantly up and down a fence line, his trot magnificent and his silky tail and mane floating. His attention was focused wholly and solely on the neighbouring paddock and its gorgeous occupant. With her head lifted high, the palomino mare strutted along the other side with an equine sashay worthy of a catwalk. She was driving the Arabian wild, and evidently enjoying every second of it. Millie chuckled at her playful, flirty antics as she changed direction and headed towards where she hoped, with a flutter and a skip of her heartbeat, that Jarrah would be.

* * *

His phone pressed to his ear, Jarrah didn't realise just how hard he was gripping his desk until he noted his white knuckles. 'Are you sure it was him?' This information was mind-blowing and deeply heartbreaking. 'He was meant to be on a fishing trip out bush, not traipsing around Sydney.'

'*Si*, I'm one hundred percent certain, Luca, that it was him, your nephew. He looks just like his father did at eighteen, god rest his soul.' Vincenzo Lombardo's Sicilian accent was as thick as the ragu sauce his wonderful, feisty wife was known for. 'I followed him from the jail the second time he went there, to the apartment block, then watched him get out of the taxi at the Sydney airport.'

'I can't believe this is happening.' Jarrah wished his only friend in the Martino mob wouldn't refer to him by his birth name, but old habits died hard. 'Damn it.' Staring out the window at the rambling river as he paced, Jarrah blew a weighty breath. 'But if I'm going to confront Tommy about this, I need to know what was in the envelope and who in the hell lives there.' His words were desperately clipped. 'And I have to be certain he was up to no good.'

'*Mi dispiace*, but it's the best I can do. You know that your father's runners usually have no information on what's in the drop, so Tommy was likely none the wiser as to who it was that he was dispensing it to.' Vincenzo sucked in a quick breath. 'That apartment block has over one hundred tenants, and from my hiding spot outside, I didn't see which letterbox he put it into.' The big man's voice was low, as if he was worried about being overheard. 'I've gone out on a limb calling you, Luca, I can't go sniffing around any more than I already have.' The spark of a lighter sounded, followed by a sharp inhale of a cigarette. 'And be real careful bringing any of this up with Tommy, because you know what your father will do to me if he finds out I'm snitching, especially on his grandson, and to you of all people.'

'Yeah, I know all too well what that son of a bitch is capable of,' Jarrah huffed. 'I'll make sure not to say anything, unless there's a sure way to leave you out of this.'

'*Grazie*, this has to stay between you and me, unless, like you said, there's another way around it.'

'Agreed,' Jarrah nodded affirmatively, 'and understood.'

There was a short silence. 'I just thought you should know to keep an eye on Tommy, that's all.' A car horn sounded. The phone muffled. '*Aspetta*.' Vincenzo's booming voice echoed. '*Mi dispiace*, I'm back.'

'All good, and sorry if I'm being short, I just can't believe Tommy would go and do this after I've drummed into him how important it is to stay the hell away from his grandfather. God only knows what information Carlo leeched from him or what bullshit he fed him.' Sighing, Jarrah shook his head. 'What in the hell was he doing, going there in the first place, let alone delivering an envelope to someone.' He was on a rant now, but couldn't stop himself – this was his worst nightmare. 'Jesus, it's like father like son in Tommy's case, hey, Vinnie.'

'*Si*, maybe more like grandfather, like grandson, so be careful and watch your back.'

'That's a scary thought, my old friend.' Pacing the office, Jarrah paused and dropped his head into his hand. 'I appreciate you doing this for me, I really do.'

'*Va bene, prego*, Luca, after you saving my daughter's life, I owe you.'

Recalling the day that he'd saved Rosa Lombardo from being run over by her school bus, just in the nick of time, Jarrah shook away the memory of the broken ankle and twenty stitches he'd needed afterwards. 'After all the favours you've done for me over the years, you owe me nothing, Vinnie.' Besides, he didn't need to be paid back for doing what most would, but he knew people like Vincent Lombardo took such matters seriously.

'You're like family to me, Luca, so I'll always have your back.' Vincenzo cursed in Sicilian just beneath his breath. 'Your father hasn't been a good man to me, but it's not like I can leave his employment; that'd be like me asking for a knife in the back.'

Jarrah dropped his gaze to the floor. 'Yeah, I know.' He grabbed a pen and notebook. 'Can you at least give me the address of the apartment block?'

'*Si*, it's one hundred and seventy-six Johnson Road, Parramatta.'

Jarrah scribbled it down and then tossed his pen across the desk. He wasn't sure what he'd do with the address, but at least it was something to work with.

The car horn sounded again, and this time Vincenzo released an entire sentence of Sicilian expletives. 'I have to go. You take care, Luca, and I'll be sure to let you know if I happen to find out anything else.'

'I'd appreciate it, thanks, Vinnie, and you take care too.'

'*Si, arrivederci.*'

Hanging up, Jarrah dropped into his leather chair, spun it away from his desk, and looked out the window with views to die for. And die for them, he most certainly would. This place was all he had left of his grandfather's inheritance money, and he'd do everything in his power to keep it. That included asking Tommy to leave Riverside Acres if it became that dire. God, he hoped and prayed it didn't, because he loved that boy like he was his own. But he couldn't have Tommy dragging a past here that he'd done his utmost to leave behind. Was it just a case of his nephew wanting to meet the grandfather he'd left behind as a little kid, or was there more to it? Had his nephew succumbed to the same insatiable appetite his own brother had, for the power and money that only Carlo Martino could afford him? Was Tommy going to end up with the same path, and inevitably the same fate, as his own father?

Please, God, don't let it be so …

Placing his shaking hands on the armrests, Jarrah steadied the tremor in his fingers and his breath. It would do him no good, jumping to conclusions. Neither was it wise to dismiss the problem by coming up with convincing reasons and motives. But it wasn't like he could ask Tommy outright either. That would put Vincenzo's life in danger, and the lives of his wife and daughter. And Jarrah wasn't about to risk having their blood on his hands. No, this would be something he'd have to do on the quiet, carefully and meticulously. How he was going to find out the truth, he had no idea. All he could hope and pray for was the truth finding its own way to him. Until it did, in one way or another, he had to carry the knowledge and unanswered questions around in his already heavy heart. He had to put one boot in front of the other and carry on as best he could, as though nothing was amiss.

Tommy's lying to me …

Jarrah didn't want to believe it.

And just when he thought the past was all behind him, behind them.

Damn it all …

Jarrah's mind went into overdrive. Was everything as it appeared? Was Tommy here for the right reasons? Was his nephew now his father's puppet? Did he really have to watch his own back, in his very own backyard? He gritted his teeth against the notion that he was being played for a fool. Maybe he was right to not trust Tommy as much as he had. Just because he was his nephew wasn't reason to believe Tommy had his best interests at heart, or those of Riverside Acres for that matter. The information Vincenzo had just given him was proof that his instincts had been right about something feeling off about Tommy since he'd returned home from his apparent fishing trip.

Tommy's lying to me!

Jarrah shook his head, discharging the anger that rose hot and poisonous with the painfully confronting thoughts. There had to be a rational reason, or at the very least an explanation, that would dismiss his gravest concerns. All he needed was reassuring clarification, something feasible, believable, understandable, that would allow him to mentally put Tommy back on the pedestal he'd placed him upon when he'd become his guardian seven years earlier. Tommy was his brother's child, his very own nephew.

After all the love and care he'd shown Tommy over the years, surely his nephew wasn't turning his back on him for the evil ways of the Martino family?

Damn it!

Who was he bloody well trying to kid? He knew how persuasive Carlo could be – he'd witnessed his callous father's manipulative ways firsthand with Joey. And now he was doing it all over again with Tommy.

Red-hot rage fired shots of adrenaline through Jarrah as he spun back to his desk, flicked his laptop on, and then rested back in his office chair with his fingers clasped tightly behind his head. Although his hands were tied if he wanted to keep Vincenzo and his family safe, he had to do something, anything other than sit passively. The internet could tell a man almost anything he wanted to know, if he knew what to ask and where to look. Leaning forwards, he typed the address Vinnie had just given him into Google Maps. In seconds a blue dot pinpointed the high-rise apartment block. He honed in and brought the area up in finer detail. Nothing rang any bells or jumped out at him. He hit 'street view' and swirled in circles, looking up and down the long straight road and at building frontages. Taking a few virtual steps forwards, he reached the front gates that Tommy had apparently walked through a few days earlier. There was a security box near the front doors, with an intercom to let visitors in. Tommy must have waited around until someone had walked out, to sneak in there. Or maybe he knew the person he'd delivered the envelope to?

Drawing in a slow, deep breath, Jarrah sat back again. With nowhere else to virtually wander to, all he could do was sit and stare at the towering redbrick building, while trying to come up with some answers of his own. The people who lived there would be middle class, and more on the younger side, he guessed, given it was Parramatta. It certainly wasn't a place anyone from the dregs of society would call home. Who in the heck lived there? And what did Carlo want with them? Had it been a payoff for a job done, or was it a threat of what was to come? Did Tommy know anything about it, or was he just doing what he was told? A sudden, intense pounding at his temples had Jarrah pinching the bridge of his nose and squeezing his eyes shut. He needed to stop trying to hunt down answers, for now at least, because this wasn't getting him anywhere.

Reaching out, he slapped his laptop shut. Then, with sheer grit and determination, he steered his mind to a nicer place, with a much nicer face to contemplate. Within seconds, a smile itched the corners of his lips and his tightly wound muscles began to lose a little of the tension. Ahhh, Millie-no-last-name, she was a picture of natural beauty. Happening across her just when he needed a cook as soon as possible made him feel like the hands of fate were at play, and somewhat working in his favour. He actually couldn't believe his luck. Although he'd have to make sure he didn't cross any boundaries, especially now she'd taken the job. He had to be a role model and walk the talk that he preached to all his staff, especially Tommy. But it was going to be tough. With her long blonde hair, striking cat-like sea-green eyes set in her heart-shaped face, and that little dimple that appeared on her chin when she smiled, holy hell she was an absolute stunner. And that certain thing that he couldn't quite put his finger on, the thing that tempted him to break his own rules about being keen on a woman who worked for him, well, it both provoked and startled him.

Just as Jarrah found himself in a happier place than he'd been in five minutes earlier, Tommy's booming voice carried from the hall. 'Jarrah, are you in there?' Seconds later he strode through the doorway. 'I've been looking for you all over.'

Fairly certain he knew what this was going to be about, Jarrah bit back a huff. 'Is everything okay?'

'No, it's not.' Arriving at the desk, Tommy threw his hands in the air. 'Millie let me know she's starting on Monday and I can't believe you've hired someone you know nothing about.'

'We've hired other people we know nothing about, Tommy, so I don't get why you're so worked up about Millie.' Pushing his chair back, Jarrah then rose, but stood his ground. 'Does it have anything to do with the fact that I had to fire Jasmine?'

'No, I, it, she …' Tommy seemed to stumble over words until he found the right ones. 'I'm the one who has to work with her, so it should've been run past me first.'

'I did run it past you, Tommy, yesterday afternoon. I told you in no uncertain terms that I had offered her the job.' He came around the side of the desk and placed a hand on Tommy's tense shoulder. 'Please try and understand that I had to find someone fast.'

Other than a weighty sigh, Tommy remained silent.

His patience wearing mighty thin, Jarrah huffed at Tommy's indignation. 'Look, you're essentially her boss, so you can report back to me if she's not as good as she reckons she is, okay?' He made sure to keep his words professional and measured, leaving no room for an argument. 'Just give her a go, would you?'

Tommy's look of defiance spoke loud and clear that his bad attitude wasn't going anywhere soon. Jarrah was just about to pull him up for it when a knock at the door halted their conversation.

'Oh hey, Millie.' A blonde tendril had come loose from her bun and he longed to close the distance and sweep it behind her ear. 'You sleep good?'

'I'll leave you both to it,' Tommy grumbled as he turned and stomped past her, pausing briefly in the doorway. 'You start at six am, and the kitchen opens at seven sharp, six days a week, so make sure you're on time Monday.' His parting words hung heavily.

'Don't worry, I will be, Tommy.' Watching him disappear, Millie blew out a breath, chasing the lock of hair back into place as she turned her attention to Jarrah. 'And I slept pretty good, thank you.' She offered a tight-lipped smile. 'I overheard Tommy's not happy with me getting the job.' She grimaced and shrugged. 'Mind you, he's making it pretty clear to my face, too.'

'Try not to take it to heart. He's never happy lately, about anything.' Jarrah tried to wave off her concern. 'He'll get over it eventually.'

'I hope you're right, because it'll make things a lot more comfortable in the kitchen, but if he doesn't get over it, for whatever reason, I won't let him be a grumpy tyrant to me, either.'

Jarrah couldn't help his admiring grin. 'Good to know you're not a pushover.' She might have been tiny, but she was strong-willed, he had no doubt about it. 'Would you like to come and meet some of the regulars?'

She smiled, nodding. 'Yeah, why not.'

'Come on then.' He met her near the doorway. 'Follow me.'

Five minutes later and they stood on the opposite side of the packed breakfast bar. 'Hey there, you three larrikins, this is our new cook, Millie.' Jarrah noted their plates were almost licked clean. Mary was doing them a huge favour, covering the shift today. He owed her one.

'Hi.' Smiling sweetly at the three sets of bushy furrowed brows, Millie shoved her hands into her cute denim-shorts pockets. 'Nice to meet you all.'

For a few seconds, the three old-timers sized her up, and right before the stare-down became awkward, the eldest – nicknamed after his truck – dropped his fork then held out his weather-beaten hand. 'Howdy, Millie, I'm Mack, good to meet ya.'

Gripping his hand, Millie shook it. 'Hey, Mack.'

Mack thumbed to either side of him. 'And these two grumpy bastards sitting next to me are Tom and Graham.'

'Oi, fair play.' His skin like leather, Tom elbowed Mack in the ribs, and then gave her a nod. 'Don't listen to him, he's the biggest grump out of all of us.' A goofy grin surfaced, then shone.

'Out of the entirety of Queensland, you mean, don't ya, Tom?' The wrinkles around Graham's eyes deepened as he chuckled.

With the three men erupting into snorts of laughter, Jarrah couldn't help but chuckle along with them. Beside him, Millie's laughter was music to his ears.

'We might be three pains in the butt …' After wiping his lips with a paper napkin, Mack gave Jarrah's arm a friendly slap. 'But as for this bloke, Miss Millie, I vouch for the fact that he's the best of the best. You've made the right choice, working for him.'

'Ah, stop it.' Although he appreciated Mack's compliment, Jarrah didn't take well to praise. 'Or you're going to give me a big head.' Jokes were always a good way around the embarrassment.

'Going to give you a big head?' Mack's bushy brows rose high. 'Don't you mean you've already got one?'

'Ba ha, good one, Macka,' Graham chimed in.

'Oath!' Tom added.

'Stuff all three of you,' Jarrah said lightheartedly.

The banter was a daily occurrence, and Jarrah loved it, just like he loved the way Millie was finding the conversation funny. She was going to fit right in around here. 'Right, it was great to meet you lot.' Millie clapped her hands together. 'As for me, I'm going to have a wander about outside and get familiar with the place.'

'Sounds like a plan.' Fighting a sudden craving to lean in and kiss her smiling lips, Jarrah quickly shoved his hands deep into his pockets and took a step back, allowing her to mosey past him. 'Just make sure you keep a lookout for cassowaries; they can be nasty buggers if you cross paths with one.'

Her face crinkled with confusion and concern. 'Cassowaries attack people?'

'Bloody oath they do.' Mack's expression turned gravely serious. 'And by crikey they can run fast too, up to fifty kilometres an hour.'

Her eyes widened to the size of saucers. 'Wow. Righto.'

Graham nodded. 'I had one chase me last month, damn near gave me a heart attack.'

'Ha, you never told me about that,' Tom chortled. 'I would have paid top dollar to see that.'

Millie grimaced. 'Maybe I might give the wander about a miss.'

'Nah, don't let these buggers scare you.' Jarrah shook his head at their antics. 'You enjoy your walk, Millie, just keep your eyes peeled, that's all.'

She hesitated for a moment. 'Okay, will do.' She gave them a wave then headed out the door.

CHAPTER 7

Terrified for her life, Millie fought to breathe. The hooded man was gaining on her, closing the gap with each of his heavy strides. Her heart in her throat, she ran blindly down the thin, sodden leaf-strewn track, legs pumping and lungs burning. Mud squelched between her toes and spindly branches reached for her, scratching her arms and legs as she pushed through the dense tropical rainforest. Tripping then pitching forwards, she landed hard, the wind completely knocked out of her. Behind her, his footfalls quickly approached. Then, in two frantic heartbeats, he was upon her, grabbing for her. His hands went to her throat and tightened. She tried to scream, but no sound escaped her. She willed herself to wake up, to escape from this nightmare, but sleep would not release her from its grip.

An excited bark sounded from outside, thankfully rousing her from her bad dream. She jolted back to reality, her heart racing. Blinking, she looked to where a sliver of sunlight peeked beneath the bottom of the curtains. She looked to the bedside clock. *Six-thirty*. Too early for a Sunday morning. Groaning, she pulled the sheet up and over her head. She didn't want to be awake yet. But then again, she didn't want to tumble back into a nightmare again either. So, kicking off the sheet and doona, she planted her feet on the cool timber floorboards and padded over to where her bag lay open, in complete disarray. She wasn't about to unpack it, when she'd likely be moving into one of the motel rooms in the next couple of days. Crouching, then sorting through the tousled pile of clothes, she finally decided on a pair of shorts and a black singlet. She made sure the envelope was still tucked away in her hiding spot in the bottom zip inside the duffle bag. Her fingers met with it. Of course it was still there. She was being paranoid. Next up would be a shower, hopefully followed by a nice strong coffee, before her first Sunday at Riverside Acres began.

Standing beneath the warm shower, the lingering memory of her nightmare taunted her as she stepped aside, lathered up and then rinsed off the suds. With the images so vivid, and the sense of malevolent hands wrapped around her throat so real, she struggled to think of anything else while she stepped out, grabbed her towel and began drying off. In the mirror above the sink, her image was blurred by the steam. Wiping her hand over the fogged-up reflection, she paused to really look at herself, hoping she could somehow see the shadows of her past lurking within her gaze, so she could catch them, red-handed, and get rid of them once and for all. If only it were that easy to free herself of her demons.

Securing her towel around her, and then running her fingers through her shambolic tangle of hair, she pulled it into a messy bun at the nape of her neck. One of these days she might actually style it and put on a little make-up. For now, with nobody to impress, she couldn't be bothered. Wandering back down the hall, she entered her bedroom and closed the door just in case Jarrah was home, although that was doubtful after sun-up, and got herself dressed for her last day of being unemployed. She was thankful Jarrah had agreed to paying her cash under the table, because if she wanted to remain somewhat anonymous she wouldn't be able to provide him with her tax file number, let alone her real name. She just hoped Tommy didn't have a fit about it. That might make Jarrah reconsider. Then where would that leave her?

Heading out and into the sunshine soon after her coffee, it only took her half an hour to fall into the slow steady beat of her rainforest surroundings. The towering trees playing host to cascading ferns and colourful orchids provided dappled shade. Warm, humid air brushed against her. As she followed the narrow trail towards one of the winding veins of the river, the tropical rainforest closed in around her. Thick ferns, giant trees and the scent of damp earth had her senses dancing. She felt like she could literally tuck herself away here and forget that anything else existed. It gave her the sense of freedom, of safety, of being invigorated deep down in her soul – a contrasting sensation to what she'd felt upon opening her eyes that morning. A rare rush of optimism filled her. And a euphoric quiver chased away her usual sense of foreboding. Maybe this little spot of paradise could be her hide-out while she was at Riverside Acres when things got too much, a place where she could come to regather, to think, to settle her nerves.

The thick canopy gave way to a small sun-dappled clearing, with a riverbank begging to be rested upon. Taking a few more steps, she stopped short of the water's edge, and craving to be completely present, immersed herself in her serene surroundings. She breathed in slowly, deeply, purposefully. Then she exhaled just as consciously. Frogs croaked, dragonflies flittered, sweet birdsong echoed, and the wind played with the leaves overhead. She briefly closed her eyes and smiled softly as a nostalgic sensation teased the back of her heart, and a vague memory shimmered, wavered, then disappeared before she could grab hold of it. She contemplated the sensation and wondered where it had stemmed from. And then, like a key slipping into a lock, a door opened in her mind and the feeling of familiarity made sense. Something about the tranquillity of this place reminded her of the times she and her family would spend the day picnicking by a river. Her mum and dad would be cuddled up together on the blanket, and she and her brother would spend so many hours swimming their fingers resembled prunes when their parents would finally coax them out with promises of ice-cream on the way home. Those were the days when she believed in the good in people and the world around her. When her possibilities had felt endless and her happiness had remained unscathed.

The memories choked her up, as did the awareness she was no longer that confident, bright girl any longer, but she fought back the tears. She'd cried enough throughout her life. She didn't want to stumble back into her world of misery. Not here. Not now. She wanted to push through the pain and come out the other side of it. So, squaring her shoulders, she took a breath and then another while staring into the inviting water. Hmm. A swim might be just what the doctor ordered. After kicking off her shoes, she dipped in a toe, loving the feel as the cool freshness trickled over her foot. She looked left to right, craning her neck to see over her shoulders. Even though she wasn't wearing her bathers, her mind was quickly made up. Although she'd always wanted to she'd never dared to skinny-dip, but now she simply couldn't resist the urge to strip off and feel the water caress her bare skin. And with not a soul in sight, why not tick something off her bucket list?

Feeling risqué, she stripped off before she chickened out. Wrapping her arms around herself, she squealed a little while wiggling on the spot, and then made a mad run for it. Arms out wide, her breath caught when she splashed into the refreshingly brisk coolness. It took her a moment to catch it again. Wading into the deepest spot, she dived beneath the surface then tipped her head back as she rose, feeling like a goddess in some hair product advertisement as she re-emerged.

'As if, Millie,' she mumbled, chuckling to herself while dog paddling to the opposite side.

Picking a spot where she could touch the bottom, but making sure to keep her breasts beneath the water, her eye was caught by the glint of a roof, and she spun in a circle to catch sight of a little hut. As she stared towards the little ramshackle building a shiver ran down her spine. What if someone was in there? Watching her? She suddenly felt very alone and at the whim of some weirdo spying on her. She was just about to bail on her skinny-dipping escapade when rustling grass caught her attention. Panic fuelled her pulse and for a moment she considered ducking back under the water to the only safe spot she had right now. But then she'd risk drowning.

'Oh, Millie, hey.' There was a brief fleeting moment where Jarrah's eyes held hers captive before he must have realised that she was completely naked. He threw his hands up to shield his view. 'Shit, sorry, I swear I didn't see anything.' He kept his hands over his eyes, but his wicked smile was brazenly sexy, as was the fact that all he had on was a pair of board shorts and thongs. His tanned, tattooed, muscular chest was to die for.

Good lord, help me ...

Embarrassment twisted her tongue into a knot, preventing her from stringing two decipherable words together. She desperately tried to clear her cottonwooled mouth and throat, but while treading water accidentally sucked in a lungful of it, then coughed and spluttered before finding the courage to, at the very least, speak.

'You all good?' His hands were still over his eyes.

'Yes, thank you.' She could have walked on water to run and hide from the embarrassment, if she wasn't as naked as the day she was born. 'What are you doing here?' What a stupid question, but it was all she had right now.

'I, ahh ...' his shoulders lifted a little, 'live here.'

'Yes, I know that, I mean what are you doing all the way down here?' She watched Scruff meander in and settle on Jarrah's feet with a contented huff.

Jarrah turned his back to her and his hands dropped to his sides. 'Oh, Scruff and I were about to have a quick dip.'

'Oh, right, yes.' She started her swim of shame towards the embankment, towards him. 'I'll just get my clothes back on and get out of your hair.'

'All good, Millie, take your time getting dressed, but you don't have to leave once you're decent.' He chuckled. 'And I promise I'll keep looking this way while you do.'

'Thank you.' She reached the edge and clambered out ungracefully.

'FYI, some of the grey nomads come down here for picnics.' His voice caught on the breeze and carried over to her.

'Oh my god, they do?' She was tugging on her clothes as if she was competing for the Guinness World Record for the fastest dripping-wet, naked woman ever reclothed.

'Yes, they sure do.' His light tone was laced with amusement.

'Well, I'm kind of glad it was you that busted me, then.' She zipped up her shorts. 'And not some stranger.'

'Ha, yeah, me too.'

'Okay, it's safe to turn around now.' She hoped to goodness her cheeks weren't bright red.

He spun to face her. 'Go on then, buddy, off you go.' He waved Scruff towards the water.

Scruff barked excitedly then galloped like a bull at a gate, all four paws splayed as he flew through the air then landed with an almighty splash.

Thankful for the distraction, she laughed at Scruffball's enthusiasm. 'I think it's safe to say he likes the water.' She glanced to where Jarrah was now standing closely at her side.

'Where'd you get that idea?' He offered her a playful sideways glance.

'You're a smartarse.' She grinned, spiritedly shaking her head.

'I like to think so.' He turned all his attention to her now. 'You going to hang here for a bit longer?'

She had a mind to make a run for it, purely out of embarrassment, but then there was a huge part of her that longed to stay there with him. 'I'll hang for a little longer, but only if I'm not intruding.'

'Intruding?' He laughed. 'I think I was the intruder in this scenario, don't you think?'

'Oh hardy ha ha.' She loved the way his lightheartedness instantly put her at ease.

'Come on.' He tipped his head to the side. 'Let's pull up a bit of dirt while Scruff gets rid of some energy.'

They wandered over to a dry patch of ground and she planted herself down beside him, making sure to keep a little space between them. For a few moments they sat in a silence that seemed natural, comfortable, as they watched Scruff nipping at the water while he paddled. It was only when the most magnificent bright blue butterfly caught her attention that she broke the short, companionable quiet.

'Wowsers.' She looked to the fluttering brilliant blue wings that matched Jarrah's lethally blue eyes. 'That Ulysses butterfly is stunning.'

'Ain't it ever?' He followed the butterfly's path until it disappeared out of sight, then he looked to her. 'There's over two hundred and thirty species of butterflies in this rainforest.'

'Really?' She was gobsmacked.

'Truly.' He glanced around, as if taking in his surroundings for the very first time, the dreamy smile on his face contagious. 'And I've probably only seen about twenty different kinds of them over the years I've been here.'

'That's still pretty impressive.' She pulled a face to convey her awe. 'I'm lucky to see one butterfly, back in …' she stopped short of saying Sydney, but only just, '… where I come from.'

A small grin quirked the corners of his lips as he turned his curious regard of her back to the gorgeous scenery enveloping them. Pulling her legs to her chest, she rested her chin on her knees and watched him taking in their small part of this big wide world. She loved the sincerity in his gaze, as if he was filing all of Mother Nature's beauty into his soul, for safekeeping.

'What is it, Millie?' He didn't turn to her. 'I can feel your eyes on me.'

'Sorry.' Caught red-handed, she darted her gaze away from him. 'It's just, well, I really like the way you look at the world around you, like you're breathing it all in.'

'I really like how you noticed that, because I am.' His sincere gaze was upon hers now.

Caught up, captivated, charmed, she almost tumbled into all that he was. Time seemed to grind to a halt, hover, linger, crescendo, and then tick back into rhythm once again. And thankfully so, because she needed to catch the breath he'd just effortlessly stolen from her. She took the moment to untangle herself from him and instead looked above, where she spotted a fruit dangling from the branches of a tall shrub-like tree.

Pointing upwards, she turned to him. 'Can we eat that?'

'We sure can, but not in its natural form.' He stood, rose on his toes, then plucked one of the purple hairy-skinned fruit from the shrub and held it out to her.

Puzzled, she met his gaze as she took it from him. 'What is it?'

'That little beauty is a native Davidson plum.' His eyes were vibrant with enthusiasm. 'You don't want to eat it like that, though, because it'll have your tongue sticking to the roof of your mouth it's so sour.'

She sniffed it. 'What good are they then, if you can't eat them?'

'People mainly use it to make jam, and there's a really tasty wine too.'

'Ha.' She gently rolled it around in her hands. 'People will turn almost anything into alcohol, hey?'

'Uh-huh,' he nodded, 'if given half a chance.' Scruff emerged from the water, and Jarrah quickly held out his hand. 'You better get up, or Scruff's going to shake half the river all over you.'

Taking his hand, she allowed him to tug her to her feet, where his gaze met hers and stayed there. There was so much depth within the mirrors to his soul that she could almost feel the touch of his stare. His eyes were such a fathomless blue, she immersed herself so deeply within him, she was afraid she wouldn't be able to resurface. So, tearing her eyes from his, she quickly looked down at her feet, as though they were objects of deep fascination.

A metre separated them now, but she longed to close the gap.

No! she told herself. *Do not go there with him!*

'Sorry I was MIA last night. I've had a heap of dreaded paperwork to catch up on before my GST is due, but tonight I'm free, so would you like me to fire up the barbecue and we can have a couple of beers to wash dinner down?'

Longing to be in his company overcame her instinct to hide away in her bedroom. 'Okay, that sounds good.'

His smile told her just how happy her acceptance of his invitation made him. 'Come on then, Miss Millie, I'll give you a lift back.'

She looked past him and tipped her head. 'In what?'

'Not in what.' He chuckled at her look of confusion. 'On my horse.'

She pointed up the rise. 'You got your horse parked and waiting for you up there?'

'Ha ha, yes, kind of.' Taking steps, he glanced back over his shoulder at her. 'I'm not crazy enough to walk all the way down here.'

'Why not? I did.'

'Well then, you've made it official.' His deep laughter was addictive. 'You're now legitimately nuts.'

'I can be sometimes, I suppose.' She laughed along with him, and at herself too. 'But it's what makes me interesting, don't you reckon?'

He stopped at the top and turned to face her again. 'I reckon I'd have to agree with you.'

His cheeky smile all but bowled her head over feet, back down to the water's edge. 'I reckon you might also be one of my kind,' she said, by way of banter.

'And I'd have to agree with you on that one, too.' He stopped at his horse's side. 'This is Waylon. Ladies first.' He offered a hand to help her up and onto the gorgeous stockhorse.

With his assistance, she slipped her shoe into the stirrup, took hold of the saddle horn, and reefed herself up the rest of the way. Waylon proved his worth and didn't budge, just patiently waited for her to get settled. Sitting tall, she felt a rush of adrenaline, followed by an encompassing euphoria. It had been a long while since she'd been in the saddle, a little over fifteen years to be exact. The last time had been with her mum, a week before her entire world had been flipped upside down and inside out. But even the painful reminder of her loss, and the resounding echo of her crushing heartbreak, couldn't erase the ear-to-ear smile planted on her face. With a spring in his step and a sweep of his leg, Jarrah effortlessly followed suit and settled himself in front of her. Scruff circled the ground beside them, clearly eager to make the trek back home. Waylon tipped his head a little, briefly bringing his muzzle to Scruff's.

Reins now in his hands, Jarrah slowly turned Waylon towards home. 'You all good back there, Millie?'

'Yes, thanks.' Relishing the sound of the saddle and the casual clip-clop of hoofs, she was better than good.

Taking her hands, he wrapped her arms around him so she was nestled up against him. 'I'm going to gradually ease him into a gallop, so make sure you hold on nice and tight.'

Would she ever! 'Will do.' All bared flesh and rippling muscle, this hell of a man felt mind-blowingly awesome to be pressed up against.

Jarrah did as promised and eased his horse into a gentle trot, then a canter, and then they were off, galloping across the paddocks with the wind whipping past them. Finding her rhythm and tuning it with the magnificent gait of the stockhorse soaring towards home, she relaxed into the saddle, and also into Jarrah. Closing her eyes, she savoured the sounds and sensations that came with riding a horse. The liberating feelings swirling in her heart and soul took over as everything else faded away – all the worry, pain, grief and guilt. Leaving just her, Jarrah, Waylon and Scruff. Four souls bonded in this moment of bliss. She'd long forgotten, up until now, just how much spending time in the saddle meant to her, as did losing herself in Mother Nature's rawest of heartbeats. The past fifteen years she'd given up so much of what brought her joy, because she'd believed she didn't deserve any, as the only one that had lived. The immense pleasure she was experiencing right now was a potent reminder of what she'd given up. She needed to do more of what she loved. More of what made her smile. Just, more. And this moreish man she was leaning into was so warm, so welcoming, so comforting, so real, so darn sexy. This would be a shared moment in time that she was going to cherish forever, she was certain of it.

* * *

From the comfort of his camp chair, beneath the star-spangled velvet-black sky, with one of the most fascinating women he'd ever met sitting beside him and his third beer in hand, Jarrah suppressed an almighty grin as he thought back to that morning. Although awkward at the time, it had been the icebreaker that he and Millie had needed. There he'd been, taking a rare moment out of his day to slow down and catch a breath. And there she'd been, as naked as the day she'd been born, lost in her own little world while she'd enjoyed a dip in the river. He'd almost turned and crept away, left her in solitude, but this woman stirred something deep inside of him, something he liked the feel of, so before he could go and change his mind he'd stepped forwards, instead of retreating, and quickly made himself known. And now, in spite of her moment of embarrassment, he was glad that he had. It had given them time to draw a little closer, to be friends instead of awkward strangers.

The heat of the campfire warmed his skin, bringing him back into the present. Letting go of his contemplations, he found himself mesmerised by the twirls of the flames in the same way that Millie captivated him. He snuck a look in her direction, and she caught him. There was a flicker of apprehension in her green eyes before the glimmer of the flames was mirrored within them and she graced him with a soft, sleepy smile. He offered her one in return. Then stifled a yawn. As tired as he was, he wasn't going to be the first one to end what had been a lovely evening. They'd contentedly chatted while making a garden salad, buttering bread rolls and barbecuing sausages, and then sat in a comfy silence as they'd devoured everything. Then, after clearing up, they'd chatted some more, about trivial things, and although he'd enjoyed the free-flowing conversation, he was craving to dive deeper, to learn more about who she was, where she'd come from and what made her tick. He sensed he'd have to tread carefully, and choose his questions wisely; he didn't want to risk chasing her away to hide in her bedroom like she had the past couple of nights, because he was thoroughly enjoying every second with her. Maybe a little too much. But he couldn't help himself. She was enthralling.

'So, Millie, do you have any brothers or sisters?' He kept his tone casual.

Her lips parted ever so slightly, as if she was about to reply, but then she seemed to stop herself. 'Nope.'

He wished he could see the expression on her face, but she'd tilted her head away and her face was shadowed. 'An only child then, huh?'

'Mmm, you could say that.'

'Me too, I mean, since my brother passed away ten years ago.' He wasn't about to let her know how. What would she think of him, being the son of a mobster?

'I'm so sorry, Jarrah.' She turned to him now and smiled sadly. 'That makes us two peas in a pod, then.'

Unsure as to whether she meant she'd always been an only child, or that her brother had passed away too, he picked at his beer label, thankful she didn't ask how his had died, and wondering what to say next. 'How about your parents, are they still together?'

'My parents are both dead.' The punch of her words didn't match the monotone of her voice.

'Shit, I'm so sorry, Millie.' His stomach tightened – she'd clearly lived with the grief of their loss for a long while. 'How did it happen, if you don't mind me asking?'

'In an accident.' She sucked in a sharp breath and then turned to him, blinking faster. 'To be honest, I don't really like to talk about it.'

She'd clearly been through hell and back, and he was inadvertently dredging it all up. And was that the glimmer of tears he saw in her eyes? Oh god no, he'd rather be chained and whipped than witness her in such heartbreaking pain.

'Sorry,' she whispered in response to his momentary silence.

'Oh, please, don't apologise.' His instincts were to reach out to her, so he could pull her into his arms and soothe away the deep heartache written within her gaze. 'Trust me, I get it.' He heaved a weighty sigh as he fought to keep his hands to himself – it was way too soon in their newly formed friendship to embrace her. 'There's a lot I don't like to talk about either.'

'Yeah, I think everyone has their secrets.' Her voice was softly soothing.

He did his best to match her tender tone, wanting her to feel just as much at ease, and at peace, as she was making him feel right now. 'Of course they do, and they'd be lying if they said they didn't.'

'Truth.' She nodded while covering a yawn. 'I think it's time for me to head to bed, Jarrah, especially seeing as it's my first day in the kitchen tomorrow and I want to make a good impression on Tommy.' She stood. 'Thanks for a lovely evening.'

'You're very welcome. I really enjoyed getting to know you a little better.' He rose from his chair, liking the way she was now looking up at him from beneath her lashes. 'I'm going to hit the sack too, so I'll walk you in.'

'Always the gentleman, aren't you?'

'I don't know about always, but I try to be.'

Side by side, they wandered along the garden path, up the stairs, and with Scruff lumbering over to his hammock bed, into the homestead, where Jarrah bid her goodnight then headed off to his bedroom to hopefully spend the night dreaming of her.

CHAPTER 8

Up at sparrow's fart, as her dear mum would have said, with two coffees under her belt and a gritty determination to make the best of an awkward situation, Millie made sure she was twenty minutes early for her very first shift at the Riverside Roadhouse, with her ideas for what she would cook folded and in her pocket. Jarrah had explained they'd have an hour of prep before the breakfast rush would hit them when Tommy opened the doors at seven, and she was keen to make a good first impression on the young man who seemed to have had quite a bad one of her from the get-go. As for the reasons behind Tommy's judgement of her? Well, she couldn't shake the feeling that he was somehow behind her being there in the first place.

Striding through the back screen door, to the hum of the local radio station playing from the speakers hung in the corners of the roadhouse, she met with her nemesis. 'Morning, Tommy.' She smiled as brightly as she could.

He offered a tight smile in return. 'Morning, Millie.' Disappearing into the coldroom, he then reappeared with a box of fresh produce.

He'd gotten her name right, which was as good a start as any – it gave her hope that things could only get better. 'Would you like me to make a start with that lot?' She peered into the box as he passed her: the capsicums, tomatoes, avocados and fresh herbs looked divine. She was going to be able to make some lovely omelettes and frittatas to pop in the hotbox out front, for those that wanted breakfast on the run.

'That'd be good, but before you do …' He plonked the box on the stainless-steel bench, beside a mountain of packaged bacon and ham, and glanced over his shoulder. '… can you go and let the girls out of their pen, and grab their eggs while you're at it.'

'Yes, sure can.' He was being civil, nice, almost – maybe Jarrah had spoken with him? Or maybe he'd just gotten out of the right side of the bed, for once.

'We can add whatever bum nuggets you get to this lot.' Crouching down, he grabbed a few cartons of eggs from the lower shelf and then placed them on the counter. 'The collection bucket is hanging from the hook near the door.' He gestured to it with a tip of his head. 'I'm going to go and get the front of house sorted.'

'Right you are.' She made her way outside and, bucket in hand, hurried towards the chook pen to collect, as Tommy amusingly put it, bum nuggets. Clearly he did have a sense of humour in there, hiding somewhere.

She was excited to make a start on her hotbox menu, and after that, she was going to get baking and make some fresh cakes and muffins, too. Although she'd only been at Riverside Acres for three nights, she already felt as if she'd been there for three weeks. It was as if time seemed to stretch and loiter without the constant hubbub of the city to distract her from being able to live within each moment. The peace and tranquillity here had offered her that luxury, and she was extremely grateful.

Reaching the chicken coop, she greeted the huddle of cackling hens. 'Good morning, ladies.' Twenty-five chooks raced towards her and formed a scrum on the opposite side of the door.

Stepping aside, she unlatched the lock and flung the door wide, laughing at the frenzy of feathered sprinters as the chooks made their zigzagging ways to a full day of sunshine and insect pecking. With it now safe to enter, she plucked the eggs from the line of laying crates and carefully placed each one into the bucket. There were twenty-four all up. She'd use the cartons of eggs for scrambling and frying; these little beauties were going to make a very nice pavlova, a baked cheesecake, some mulberry muffins and a few jars of lemon butter.

Carefully making her way back to the commercial kitchen, she strapped on her apron, popped a hair net over her bun, washed her hands then got to work. Three hours zoomed past her in a flurry of chopping, frying, stirring, roasting, whipping and flipping. The scent of sizzling bacon wafted, as did the delicious aromas of her three-inch-high chorizo, potato and capsicum frittatas – the number-one seller for the morning. The hustle and bustle of the front of house had carried into the kitchen, as did the hurried footsteps of the fifty-something twin waitresses, Jenny and Penny, who dutifully collected plates, then returned them. Millie noted all the dishes were coming back empty, which hopefully meant that bellies were satisfyingly full.

Having cleaned up after breakfast, and with the lunch rush just around the corner, she was busy preparing large bowls of salads – there'd be no frozen veggies or packaged salads on her watch. Her chunky guacamole, creamy potato salad and zesty coleslaw, along with a large freshly prepared vegetable bake, would accompany her specials of lasagne or chicken pot pies. Humming to the Adam Brand song chiming from the radio, she slid the knife along the chopping board, adding the eighth avocado into the bowl, along with chopped red onion, quartered sweet cherry tomatoes, fresh coriander, the juice of three limes and a splash of jalapeño sauce. Placing the bowl alongside the others she'd already prepared, she tapped her bell to let the front of house know that she was ready for them, and then took a moment to mop her brow with some paper towel.

Tommy appeared, soon followed by Jenny and Penny, who she'd been told had been working there since the very first opening day.

'Wow, Millie, this is absolutely amazing.' Jenny's eyes devoured the line-up of food. 'It all looks so bright and fresh.' She regarded Millie with an appreciative smile. 'You're certainly raising the bar with this spread, love; it's about time someone actually cared about the food being served.'

'Hasn't she ever.' Popping her pen behind her ear, Penny saddled in beside her identical sister. 'You're going to win some customers' hearts today, Millie, that's for sure.'

'Oh, come on, you two, stop trying to win brownie points with the new cook, will you.' Tommy huffed at their looks of disbelief. 'What?' He shrugged. 'Anyone would think you've never seen good food before.'

'You're being a little snappy lately, Tommy.' Jenny scowled. 'What's gotten into you?'

'Nothing's gotten into me.' Put on the spot, and in his place, Tommy shot her a cautionary glance. 'I know you're good friends with Jarrah, and I may be way younger than you, but please don't step over the boundaries, Jenny, because I'm still your boss, and I can fire you for disrespecting me.'

Penny gasped. 'I will not stand here and let you speak to my sister like that, Tommy, no matter who you are. She works extremely hard, and you know that.' She sucked in a sharp breath and took a moment. 'We know you don't like the fact that Jasmine was fired, but it's not our fault, and you shouldn't be taking it out on your staff.' Penny's tone was unsympathetic. 'I think I might have to have a chat with Jarrah if this continues to be an issue.'

'You do that, Penny.' Tommy pushed the bowls of salad towards them. 'Best get these into the display fridge and get the hot food out of the oven and into the bain-marie, don't you think?'

'There'll be no need coming to talk to me, Penny, I've just heard enough, and I'm sorry to both of you for my nephew's behaviour.' Shifting his kind eyes from the twins, Jarrah stepped out of the doorway and cut a steely glance in Tommy's direction. 'Please come and see me after the lunch rush, Tommy.'

Tommy didn't respond. Millie swore she could see smoke coming from his ears as he stormed past them all and out of the kitchen. Grabbing the bowls, Jenny and Penny got back to work.

'That kind of behaviour is not acceptable. I'm so sorry, Millie.' Jarrah shook his head. 'I'm at my wits end with him, to be honest.'

'I don't know what I've done to make him dislike me so much.'

'You've done absolutely nothing.' He huffed out a breath. 'This is between me and him, and trust me when I say, come hell or high water, I'm going to get to the bottom of it.'

Unable to feel like this had nothing to do with her, Millie swallowed down her rising suspicions that Tommy was the author of her letter. 'Okay then.' Not wanting to appear like a nosey person, and needing to catch her anxious breath, she refrained from saying any more. 'Is it okay if I nip to the toilet before the lunch rush?'

'Of course, yes, go for it.' He stepped back to let her past. 'Oh, and Millie.' He waited for her to pause and look back at him. 'Thank you for the effort you've put in today. The food looks, and smells, amazing.'

'My pleasure.' She flashed him a smile then quickly made her way outside into the fresh air, where she gulped it down while trying to slow her racing heart.

Still deep within her thoughts while sitting on the loo, she felt something wet and sticky land on her back. Screaming blue murder, she shot from the confines of the toilet, stumbling sideways while still hitching up her pants. Spinning in circles, she tried to remove whatever had landed on her shoulder. But it wasn't budging. And there was no way in hell she was going to try and swipe it away. What if it was venomous and it bit her and she died? Oh. My. God. So, spinning in circles, she screamed, and then screamed some more. So strident were her pleas for help, it wouldn't have surprised her if the entire community of Banshee Bay came to her aid.

'Millie.' Jarrah came running from the kitchen, his face etched with concern. 'What's happened?'

'Please, help me.' Eyes as wide as saucers, she clutched his arm, terrified he would vanish into thin air. 'There's something on my back.'

'Okay, let me have a look.' Prying her fingers from his arm, he didn't let her go as he began to turn her around.

A breathless second passed her by. 'What is it?'

'You can relax, it's nothing that's going to harm you.' Jarrah's chuckle had her glowing a bright shade of red. 'Hey there, little buddy.' He chuckled some more. 'It's just a green tree frog, Millie, we get lots of them in the rainforest.'

With her humiliation and ick factor at their peak, she felt him peel the defenceless amphibian from her shoulder. Stepping away, and out of bounding reach, she willed herself to take a few deep breaths as she turned around and stared at the bright green frog staring back at her with its terrified eyes, its new perch now on the back of Jarrah's raised hand.

'See, he's harmless.' Jarrah regarded her with a boyish smile, as if he was in his element.

Grimacing, she nodded. 'Yes, I suppose he is kind of cute.'

'Kind of cute?' Jarrah looked to the frog, then back to her. 'Come on, Millie, he's adorable.' He tipped his head to the side as if waiting for her wholehearted agreement.

Grinning at his antics, she nodded. 'Okay, yes, he's adorable.'

And so are you, Mister King.

Gosh, Millie, stop it! Now!

Her grin broadened while she still kept her eye on the stationary creature. The frog looked at her as if considering if it was going to pounce and land on her again. She took a cautionary step back.

Regarding his new little mate, Jarrah held his hand up to eye level. 'I better go and run him under some water, because the oils from my skin can burn his.' He glanced at her over the frog. 'And we don't want that.'

'No, we most certainly do not.' Her grin became more of an admiring smile – this big manly man with his broad shoulders and tribal tattoos could be so sweetly endearing. 'I didn't know our oils could hurt him, but mind you, I don't go around touching frogs.'

His dimples deepened. 'Ha, no, after your reaction, I didn't think you did.' Offering her cheeky raised brows above eyes sparkling with playfulness, he turned and headed towards the hose at the end of the building. 'Catch you a bit later, Millie.'

'Okey dokely.'

Okey dokely? Huh? Price, what the heck is wrong with you?

What language was she suddenly speaking? And how could such a cute little harmless frog have frightened her so much? Gee whizz, her mum would roll over in her grave if she knew what had become of her country-loving, free-spirited daughter. A daughter she'd raised to be a wildflower, just like her, and she wanted with all her citified heart to be like her brave, strong-willed, hippy-hearted mum. Wrapping her arms around herself, she sighed sadly as she headed back towards the roadhouse. The little girl who'd run through the countryside with twigs and leaves in her knotty hair, mud on her clothes and not a care in her heart, had died in the fire that night. Leaving an empty shell of herself. But Millie wanted her back to stay for the rest of her days. This citified version of her was half-arsed and half-hearted – she wanted the real Amelia Price back. The one who lived for each moment, believed in the good, and trusted that God had her future in his capable hands. Something told her that just by being here at Riverside Acres she was going to be able to grab hold of that buried part of her, drag her to the surface, and never let her go.

* * *

'For the love of god, you need to learn to show some respect, Tommy, to me, and to the staff.' Pacing behind his desk, Jarrah paused and shot a glance at his nephew, now seated in the chair opposite, his fists in his lap and jaw clenched as if wired shut. 'Well, do you have anything to say for yourself?'

Tommy arched a sly brow. '*You* want me to show *you* respect?' Meeting Jarrah's stare, he grunted. 'How about you do the same for me?'

'I do show you respect, Tommy, all the time.'

'No, you don't.' Tommy's eyes burned with hatred.

Baffled, confused, hurt, Jarrah wished he could throw the towel into the ring, but he wasn't about to give up on the one person in this world who deserved his love. 'I seriously don't understand why you feel this way.'

Tommy shrugged indifferently. 'Yeah, well, I'm not going to waste my breath trying to explain it.'

Jarrah gritted his teeth against a momentary lapse of better judgement – now wasn't the time to lose it. 'Tommy.' He made sure his next words were measured, steady. 'We're not going to get anywhere unless you're up-front and honest with me, about everything that's going on in that head of yours.'

Remaining silent, Tommy shrugged indifferently.

Yanking his office chair out, Jarrah sat then clasped his hands atop the desk, his gaze now pinned to his nephew. 'Refresh my memory, will you, Tommy. Whereabouts did you go fishing?'

Tommy turned his attention out the window. 'Up the Cape, why?'

Jarrah watched the rise and fall of Tommy's chest quicken. 'Where, exactly, up the Cape were you?'

'What's the deal with all the questions?' Tommy brought his darting gaze back to Jarrah's, but only momentarily.

'What's the deal with your elusive answers, Tommy, huh?' Jarrah gave as good as he got.

Tommy's Adam's apple bobbed in his throat as he shifted uneasily. 'One of the motel rooms is free for Millie now, so I'll let her know she can move in when her shift is done.' He cleared his throat, as if steadying himself. 'Having her in your homestead is not a good look, Uncle.' He stood and finally met Jarrah's eyes. 'And as for where I go in my free time, I reckon that's none of your business.' He turned and took strides towards the closed door.

'Tommy, stop.' Jarrah shot to his feet and came around his desk, but by the time he'd reached the door, Tommy had yanked it open and was storming down the hallway.

Watching Tommy slip away from him, in more ways than one, Jarrah chastised himself for being so … stupid. What was he thinking, putting his headstrong nephew on the spot? Yes, he was desperate to know the truth, to hear Tommy admit he'd gone to see his corrupt grandfather, but he wasn't going to achieve that by confronting him. Tommy was so much like his father, and Joey hadn't ever been forthcoming in giving anything away. No matter how much he'd begged his brother to open up, so he could somehow save him from what fate had in store for Joey Martino all along, Joey's lips had remained zipped shut. Jarrah knew he needed to take a breath and think with a level head, and not with his breaking heart, if he was to learn exactly what his horrible father had said to Tommy to make him so angry, so bitter. Because this couldn't all be to do with him firing Jasmine. As for the delivery of the envelope, and the recipient, that too would have to sit like a ton of lead upon his shoulders until he could hopefully find a way to discover the truth. Vinnie was his best chance. And Vinnie needed time and space to uncover anything else. So, for now, he needed to get the hell out of his office and into the great outdoors, where he could throw himself into some hard yakka and take his stress and anger out on something tangible.

Four hours later – with country tunes playing from the LandCruiser's stereo, the bright blue sky without a cloud in sight, and the mid-afternoon sun beating down relentlessly – Jarrah soldiered on, desperately hot as he was. His scruffy sidekick, on the other hand, was doing his usual trick when it was sweltering, and sleeping beneath the LandCruiser. Even the chooks had given up their hunting and taken shelter beneath the old gum tree. Shovel in hand, he stopped, wiped his brow, grabbed his flask of icy cold water, and drank deeply until there wasn't a drop left. He'd have to head back to the homestead at some point to grab some more, but for now he had to get back to work if he wanted this job done by sundown. Before he did, he stripped off his wet-to-the-skin shirt and tossed it over the timber railings. The little puffs of breeze cooled him, making his awkwardness at being a little exposed worth it. He rarely worked shirtless, but today was hotter than hot, so much so he wished he could strip off and get the job done while stark naked. Ha, wouldn't that be a sight for sore eyes, he thought with a chuckle.

Continuing his backbreaking task of digging holes for the new fence line, in ground that was proving as obstinate as Tommy, he ignored the burn of his muscles while he sang to the tune of Johnny Cash's 'Ring of Fire'. His boot toe tapped in time with the catchy tempo. Doing his best to reach the low baritones, he felt chuffed when he harmonised with Cash's unmistakable voice. Next along was Waylon Jennings, with his hit 'Are You Sure Hank Done It This Way'. Knowing every word like the back of his hand, Jarrah sung his heart out. He was so caught up that he didn't hear the footsteps coming up behind him.

'I reckon you could actually give up your day job, Jarrah.'

Millie's sweet voice had him spinning to face her, and the grin on her kissable lips made his insides tumble and flip. 'Geez, thanks, Millie.' He dragged an arm over his sweaty forehead as he spotted a tall, icy glass of something in her outstretched hand.

'I thought you might need a thirst-quencher.' She passed it over as Scruff plonked himself down at her feet. 'Hey, buddy, how goes it?' She ruffled his head.

Jarrah couldn't help but love how the two had bonded so quickly. 'Thanks for this, Millie, it was really thoughtful of you.' He took a thirsty guzzle, and the lip-smacking flavour was nothing like he'd ever tasted before. 'Wow, what is this stuff?'

'It's lemon and ginger kefir water.'

'It's what?' He sculled the rest of it.

'I didn't think you would've heard of it.' Her sweet smile was relaxed. 'It's made by fermenting little grains with a mixture of water, sugar, lemon, ginger, salt and a sprinkling of bicarb soda, then, after one to two days, depending on how warm the weather is, you get bubbly water that's really good for your belly.'

He held his empty glass up and nodded in appreciation. 'I reckon it's delicious, and very clever at the same time.'

As are you, sweet Millie …

Her cheeks flushed as if she'd heard his internal compliment, and he wasn't sure if it was from the sun or him. He liked to think it was all to do with the latter. 'Where did you get this kefir water stuff from around here?'

'Oh, I didn't, I brought the grains with me and made them up yesterday morning. The tropical heat makes it brew super-fast. Speaking of which …' She fanned her heated face with her hands. 'It's bloody hot today.'

'Damn straight it is.' So her flushed cheeks weren't from him. Bugger. 'How'd the rest of your shift go?'

'Yeah, really good.'

'So, despite Tommy being an arse, you liked your first day?'

'Other than being terrified out of my wits by a frog, I loved it.' Her laughter carried, and caressed him. 'Sorry for making you race to my rescue.'

'All good, any time.' He chuckled. 'I'm just happy you're still alive to tell the tale.'

'Oi,' she playfully slapped his arm, 'that'll be enough cheek from you.'

'Never,' he breathed, his expression playful. 'Banter is the way of Riverside Acres, if you haven't already noticed.'

'Ha, yeah, I actually have.'

Her grin was sassy and her arresting gaze caught his and held it. Scruff snapping at the air broke their fleeting moment of magnetism, and then the buzzing of a blowfly grew louder. Swatting it away from his face, Jarrah burst out laughing when Scruff finally caught his adversary and swallowed it whole.

Millie's eyes widened, as did her grin. 'Did I really just see that?'

'You sure did.' He ruffled Scruff's head. 'You hate those pesky little buggers, don't you, buddy?'

Scruff replied with one short sharp bark, licked his lips, and then headed back to the shade beneath the LandCruiser.

Millie watched him settle, then sighed. 'Well, I'm going to head back to the homestead so I can finish packing my things, then I'll make myself comfortable over at the motel.'

'Oh, yeah, Tommy mentioned a studio room had become available.' He felt saddened by the fact that he was going to return home to an empty house. Millie had somehow made it feel so full. 'You don't have to move over there right now, I mean, seeing as it was your first day, surely you'd be knackered.' He wondered if he sounded a little desperate for her to stay, so he shrugged as though it was no big deal. 'Feel free to camp out another night at the homestead, if it helps.'

'Thanks, Jarrah, but given the fact I'm staff, and Tommy's on the warpath, I reckon it's best if I make myself at home in my new abode.'

'Righto.' He swallowed down his disappointment. 'I better let you get moving, then, and I better get back to it before I run out of daylight.' He held up the empty glass. 'Thanks again for the tasty drink.'

'You're welcome.' She took it from his hand. 'I'll catch you tomorrow.'

'You will.' He tipped his hat. 'And I'll be sure to give the mechanic a call first thing, see if he can look at your Jimny first up.'

'Thank you, and thanks for towing it in there too. Let's just hope he can fix it easily.' She turned and sashayed away.

Jarrah couldn't help but watch Millie until she disappeared around the corner of the machinery shed. Then he worked until the sun had faded to a golden-orange glow as it slipped behind the mountain ranges. Shrugging his shirt back on, he dumped his tools into the tray of his LandCruiser, gestured for Scruff to jump in the passenger side, climbed behind the steering wheel, and after revving the engine to life, turned the air-conditioning to high. Leaning forwards, he enjoyed the blast of icy air for a few moments before straightening and turning the four-wheel drive back towards where Millie no longer was. And the very thought made his already downtrodden heart sink deeper.

CHAPTER 9

The sound of a car revving its engine just outside her motel room woke Millie. Momentarily confused about where she was, whether it was night or day, today or tomorrow, she sat up, turned her lamp on, rubbed her eyes to life and surveyed her surroundings. The flickering of the television caught her attention, as did the room she'd called home for three days now. A pizza box lay open on the little two-seater dining table beside the kitchenette, with half its contents gone, and beside it sat a half-empty, or half-full, depending on how she looked at it, hipflask of vodka. She really needed to stop trying to drink her loneliness away. It was going to do her no favours. A drunken conversation at midnight with Ebony had hammered that nail on the head.

She flopped backwards and stared at the ceiling, hoping she had the luxury of a few more hours where she could hopefully catch some decent sleep before she had to head to work. Groaning at the sudden onslaught of a hangover-infused headache, and the realisation that she was still in yesterday's clothes, she rolled onto her side and looked to where the glint of sunlight peeked beneath the curtains. Oh crap, what time was it? Grabbing her mobile and igniting the screen to glowing life, she noted the time, and the few text messages from Ebony, then shot to her feet and ran for the bathroom. She was going to be late. Not a good look on what was only her fourth day. Her self-induced tardiness reverberated through her weary mind as she angrily stripped off, dived beneath the shower while brushing her teeth, half-dried, tugged on some fresh clothes, dragged her hair into a ponytail at her nape, then raced towards the roadhouse. Chillaxing right in the middle of the walkway, Scruff eyed her as she leapt over the top of him.

'Morning, buddy.' She didn't have the time to give him his usual pat.

His short sharp bark of good morning echoed behind her.

Skidding into the kitchen, twenty minutes late, she quickly grabbed her apron and tugged it on. 'Hey,' she said in passing. 'Sorry but I must have slept through my alarm.' She wasn't about to admit she'd likely faceplanted the bed at some ungodly hour, too drunk to set it.

Tommy made a scoffing noise. 'Yeah, about that.' He turned and scowled at her. 'That's one strike against your name.' He shook his head scornfully. 'Two more and I'll have good reason to fire you.'

Blinking back the haze of rage his intimidation caused, she stole a moment to steady her voice before responding. 'I'll be sure to keep that in mind.'

'You do that, otherwise you might find yourself out of a job.' His tone was icy sharp. 'And Jarrah won't have a leg to stand on if he tries to overturn my decision, because it's his own bloody rule that there'll be no consorting between staff, and also being late is not acceptable.'

She was so gobsmacked by his assertive authority that she found herself lost for anything to say. And here she'd thought, with so much fantastic feedback from the customers, that she'd proven herself as the cook. Before today, she'd been almost half an hour early to every shift, and she'd even stayed late, without asking for anything extra, to make sure the kitchen was sparkling clean and the menu for the next day was well and truly ready to go. Tommy was an outright spoilt brat. Actually, no, he was an outright arsehole. Her nails dug into the fleshy part of her palm and she welcomed the pain while she fought to remain composed. One breath, two breaths, three … By the time she'd gathered herself enough to speak respectfully and calmly, he'd vanished out the door. So she did her best to shake off the feeling of dread as she endeavoured to turn her wholehearted attention to her love of food. But try as she might, her mind wasn't having it as ominous thoughts whirled through her head. If her instincts were right, and Tommy was the one who'd sent her the letter and photo, what was he planning? Why had he brought her here, only to treat her like this? Was it to seek revenge, for something she knew nothing of? Was he going to hurt her, or worse?

Her vision blurred and she blinked faster. Placing the knife in her hand down, she grabbed hold of the bench. She felt so torn between wanting to get the hell out of this place and staying put to hopefully discover whatever it was that she'd come here to find out. Feeling light-headed, then as if the walls were closing in on her, she knew she needed to get some fresh air. She hurried towards the back screen door and it slapped shut behind her as she rushed through it. Outside, she gripped the railings in both hands, breathing in deeply. The suffocating feeling gradually subsided, and once it did, she straightened, reminded herself she had to push through this, and then went back inside.

Hours later, breakfast had come and gone, the roadhouse was packed with lunchgoers, Tommy was nowhere to be seen, and Penny and Jenny were run off their feet, as was she.

Taking steps to deliver the order that had been sitting a little longer than she would have liked, Millie reminded herself over and over to breathe as she scooted out of the kitchen and towards a table. 'You got this,' she muttered to herself as she passed two huge plates of cottage pie and fresh steamed veggies over to the two equally hefty truck drivers that she'd met with Jarrah on her first day there.

'Thanks, Millie, this looks bloody delicious,' Mack said with a wide smile.

'Damn straight it does, much better than the last cook's muck,' Graham added.

She accepted their compliments with a smile. 'Thanks, guys, enjoy, won't you.' She liked the way they remembered her name.

His knife and fork at the ready, Mack grinned. 'Oh, trust me, I most certainly will.'

Heading back into the kitchen, with no more orders left to fill, she cleaned up and then got to work on the sweet treats for the next day – always a day ahead of herself when it came to the dessert fridge, she valued this precious time when she could focus on baking. Whipping cream into oblivion, by hand, she did her best to try and push aside her unsettling morning. The scent of the pumpkin scones baking in the oven wafted, taking her back to happier times, when she would spend precious time with her mother and Ebony in the kitchen – scones had always been Ebony's favourites. She drew in a few deep inhalations, making sure to slowly sigh each one away with the thought that her exhaled breath was taking some of her stress with it. She was so lost in her mediative breathing that the chime of her phone from her back pocket made her jump so high she almost hit the roof.

'Ebs, oh my goodness, I was just thinking about you.' Securing her phone between her shoulder and ear, she cracked an egg, separating the white from the yolk.

'Hey, hon, are you handling what I'd expect to be a bit of a hangover?'

'Yes, I am, while feeling a little sorry for myself.' She huffed at herself. 'I'm so sorry I called you when I was drunk.'

'Like I always tell you, I'm here any time, no matter what state you're in.' Ebony sighed. 'I'm worried about you, lovely, I just wish you'd take better care of yourself.'

'I know, and I promise I'm trying to.' Deciding to take a quick break, Millie ducked outside, out of earshot of Jenny and Penny, and Tommy. 'Last night was a bit of a lapse of judgement. It won't happen again while I'm here, that's for sure.'

'I know you're under a lot of pressure, so I get it, but alcohol isn't going to make things right. Nor is it going to help you sleep. And I know you said you think you can trust Jarrah, and that's a good thing, but I'm really concerned about this Tommy bloke, so just please be super careful, okay?' she pleaded.

For the life of her, Millie couldn't remember much of what she'd told her best friend about Tommy. 'I promise I am being careful, and I'll continue to be.' She knew she wouldn't have said anything good about her moody boss.

'Even though I'm going to be over the other side of the world in a few days' time, I'm only at the other end of a phone call, when I'm in service that is, okay, Mills?'

'I know you are, and will be while you're in Africa.' Millie's heart squeezed tight – she was going to miss Ebony like crazy. 'Have you seen much of Felix the second?'

'He's popped in a few times for some food and a nap, the scallywag.'

'That's good, at least I know he's keeping out of trouble.' Not having realised until this very second just how much she missed the feral ball of ginger fur, she choked back a sob. 'Now go and enjoy that holiday you've worked so bloody hard for, Ebs, and I'll see you at home when you get back in two months' time.'

'Okay, love you lots, Mills.'

'Ditto, my beautiful friend.' Ending the call, Millie slipped her phone back into her pocket.

As she wandered back towards the kitchen, a resounding thump caught her attention. Pausing at the doorway, she rose up on her tippy toes and spotted Jarrah over near the stables, bashing a fence post into the ground with a massive sledgehammer. Holy moly, he was ripped, and very easy on the eye. Other than his external attributes, she also admired how he was a man that seemed to accomplish everything he set out to do. Dropping the sledgehammer, he strode towards the back of the LandCruiser. His gait was strong but at the same time easygoing, giving off the aura of a man who would take the shirt off his back to help a mate in need, but in a heartbeat hurt anyone that hurt a person he loved. Getting the sense that he was a bit of a loner, she wondered if there was a person, other than Tommy, that he loved, and the thought that it could be a female fired a shot of jealousy through her. Mentally slapping herself for thinking, and feeling, such a silly way, she stepped back into the coolness of the kitchen and totally immersed herself in the therapeutic benefits of cooking to her heart's content.

Hours later, the sound of footfalls entering through the back door had her reluctantly turning, expecting to see Tommy. But to her delight, it was Jarrah. With his shaggy light-brown hair in disarray, piercing blue eyes, and a dark shadow of stubble across his chiselled jawline, she had to take a beat. Why did he have to be so damn sexy? All the damn time.

Blinking as if trying to rid the sunshine from his fetching eyes, he regarded her with a wide smile. 'Oh, hey, Millie, why are you still working at this time of the day?'

'What time is it?' She glanced up at the clock above the stove, answering her own question before Jarrah did. 'Oh, wow, I think it's safe to say I lost track of time.' She looked back to him. 'Don't worry. I won't put the last hour down. It's just a case of me being a bit extra when it comes to the choice of baked goodies for tomorrow.'

'Oh yes you will.' He looked, wide-eyed, at the baked goods covering the benchtop. 'You're an absolute blessing to this place, Millie.'

'Thank you.' The scent of horse and hay had followed him in, and she couldn't help but take another breath of him as she wandered past him and over to the sink. 'I meant it when I told you I love to cook.'

'I can see that.' Grabbing a glass from the overhead cupboard, he then crossed the room, heading straight for her. 'Thank you for caring so much about your job; it's a refreshing change from the last cook we had here.'

She shifted a little to the side, allowing him space to fill his glass from the tap. He did so, and sculled it. Then filled it up with more. 'Don't mind me, you just keep on doing whatever it is that you very clearly do with all your heart.' He turned and leant against the bench, taking tentative sips of water while he watched her over the top of the glass.

Although a little uncomfortable at being his centre of attention, she couldn't help but feel drawn to him as she iced the chocolate cake that had now cooled enough. 'So,' she said, desperately needing to talk or sing, anything other than be in this room, in an intimate silence, with a man who filled every nook and cranny of the kitchen with his charismatic presence. 'How's your day been?'

'Yeah, good, thanks.' The corners of his mouth inched ever so slightly into the hint of a smile, and a teeny ache gripped her heart. 'Would you like to come over for a bite to eat tonight?'

'Oh, um, I, ah …' *Find your words, Millie.* 'I don't want to give people the wrong impression.'

'It's all good.' His smile deepened and stretched into his eyes, tilting her world a little off its axis. 'Two adults can have dinner together without it being a date, can't they?'

'Yes, I suppose.' She was far too aware of his nearness, of his scent, of his captivating persona.

'And you have to eat, don't you?'

His easygoing smile, reaching across the room and resting upon her, had a calming effect. 'Yes, I suppose I do.'

'Good, that's settled then.' He drank the last of his water, popped his cup into the dishwasher, and then strode past her. 'See you at the homestead around six-thirty-ish, sound good?'

'Uh-huh, perfect, see you then.' She only dared a tiny glance in his direction as he paused, fleetingly, a wide smile on his fetching face, before he tugged down the brim of his hat and disappeared back into the bright late-afternoon sunshine now seeping through the windows of the kitchen.

Millie busied herself by placing all the baked goods into the dessert fridge for the next day, all the while telling her libido to rack off and her voice of recklessness to shut the hell up. Yes, she was single. And from what she gathered, so was he. She was becoming more and more attracted to him as each day passed. But no matter how handsome he was, or how charismatic he might be, or how much she wanted to do very naughty things with him, she'd do whatever she had to, to keep her feet planted very firmly on solid ground. She untied her apron, hung it on the hook near the door, surveyed the kitchen one last time to make sure everything was shipshape, then flicked the overhead light off. An hour later and she'd showered and changed into a pair of jeans and a T-shirt; nothing fancy. She didn't want to go giving Jarrah the wrong idea.

But holy moly if he could read her mind …

Crossing the gravel road over to his place, she smiled when she heard the distant lowing of cattle coupled with the sound of the breeze stirring the leaves of the towering paperbarks stretching overhead. Turning the corner towards the back verandah, she followed the garden pathway then met with the man who always succeeded in sending butterflies flurrying in her stomach and her heart.

'Hey, Millie.' Unshaved, wearing blue board shorts and a white T-shirt that hugged his biceps and chest, with his hair still damp and smelling of shampoo, it was all she could do to not lean into all that was him. 'You look lovely.' His marvellous eyes danced over her.

'Thanks.' Her smile was a little coy as she bit her bottom lip. 'You've scrubbed up pretty good yourself, King.'

'Why, thankya.' He bowed, waving the tongs in his hands as he did, cracking her up completely.

Once they'd both recovered from their moment of mirth, he ushered her over to the day bed and told her to put her feet up and stay put while he waited on her after her long day cooking up a storm. A little reluctant at first, she did as he asked. It didn't take her long to relax into the casual vibe of the evening. Watching Jarrah as he manned the billowing smoker barbecue, while taking sips from her beer, she felt herself slipping further into him. The voices of the Highwaymen serenaded her from the speakers hung at the corners of the verandah and she hummed in tune to the song, all the while laughing at Scruff dashing around the floodlit backyard, his nose to the ground and his tail spinning like helicopter blades.

'Would you stop chasing the toads, Scruff, or I'll have to wash your mouth out with the hose again, buddy.' Jarrah's deep voice carried as he glanced over his shoulder, his smile nonchalantly sexy. 'I reckon he likes getting high off the blasted things, the silly bugger.'

'I wondered what he was doing.' She chuckled then shook her head. 'You crazy goof, Scruffball.'

Lifting his head to the sound of her voice, Scruff dashed across the lawn, up the stairs, then with one flying leap landed in a panting heap beside her on the day bed. Successfully avoiding his slobbery kisses, but only just, she wrapped her arms around his neck and gave him a cuddle.

'I think it's safe to say he really likes you, Millie.' Wandering past with a delicious-smelling plate of grilled steak, rare for him and medium to well for her, and charred corncobs, Jarrah flashed her an admiring smile. 'Dinner's ready.'

Her stomach growling, she eagerly joined him. Helping herself to the garden salad, she poured a little smoky barbecue sauce beside her steak, then after waiting for Jarrah to do the same, they tucked in. She liked the way they fell into comfortable silences so easily. It said a lot for the person he was.

'Enjoying?' Jarrah garbled while munching the kernels off his corncob.

'I am, it's all so delicious.' Spearing a cherry tomato, and then enjoying the sweetness as it popped in her mouth, she grinned. 'I seriously don't know how you eat your meat still kicking like that, though.'

'It's easy.' Smirking playfully, he cut another piece of the basically still-mooing steak and shoved it in his mouth. 'Just like this.' He pointed to his mouth with his fork. 'Yum.' His grin was charmingly goofy.

Chuckling, she dropped her gaze back to her salad, and they chowed down until they had finished off every morsel.

'Shall I go inside and grab us a bottle of vino, and then we can retire over yonder?' He pointed to the alfresco chairs, saddled up against the banister.

'Sounds good, but let me help you clean up first.' She stood and went to gather the plates, but he placed a hand over hers, stopping both her movement and her heart. Then, a breath later, her heart was galloping, as if trying to reach his.

'Leave it, Mills, I'll clean up later.'

Mills? Ebony was the only person who'd ever called her that, and she liked hearing him say it. 'Are you sure you don't want me to help, two sets of hands are better than one?' Her heart felt so completely comforted right now.

'I'm absolutely positive.' Standing, he waved her towards the chairs, and she was glad for the moment's reprieve from his captive gaze. 'I'll be back in a minute.' The flyscreen door slapped closed behind him.

Back before the minute was up, he poured red wine into stemless glasses, passed one to her, sat, and then placed his feet on the banister as he pushed onto the back two legs of the chair. Keen to do the same, Millie plonked her feet up near his and precariously balanced backwards. She marvelled at the silvery brightness of the full moon in the inky-black sky, and how it lit up the landscape as if a million candles had been lit in the heavens. And the stars, they sparkled so much brighter here, as if rejoicing in the lack of city lights that inevitably dulled their shine – she could relate.

Jarrah sighed softly. 'I will never ever tire of this view.' He tilted his head to the side. 'This place is everything I'd always dreamt of having, and more.'

The joy written all over his face was unmistakable. 'You're a very lucky man, being able to call Riverside Acres home.' She met his soft smile, his soft gaze, and matched it.

He regarded her for a few seconds. 'You're calling it home too, for now.'

His simple statement stroked some deep dark part of her heart and stirred it to fluttering life. 'Yes, I suppose I am, for now.'

'Hmm' was all he said in response.

Millie felt like a moth drawn to the silvery moonlight reflected upon his face. The blueness of his eyes pierced right through her, caressing places she didn't know still existed. The pain of her miscarriage felt as if it was a million miles away. Gone, almost forgotten, just by being near him. She knew she should put the brakes on right then and there, but for whatever reason it was out of her control. A flutter rose, grew, spread, filling her with a rush of endorphins, as if she'd just jumped off a cliff and was flying. His lips moved ever so slightly, as if there were words that he was weighing up whether to free or muffle. She so desperately wanted to hear what he had to say. And she felt a longing to reach out and touch him, to run her fingertips over the hard planes of his chest as she traced his tattoos, to be wrapped up in his arms, pressed up against him, so she could feel the heat of his longing and the hunger of his kiss. Her stomach flipped with the sensual images as her emotions swirled into a heady concoction of fear, curiosity, ache and lust. As she watched him take an unhurried sip of his wine, with his gaze still joined to hers, she imagined him reacting to her want, her need, her craving for him and only him. He was looking at her as if she was a rarity – no one had ever looked at her like this before. It made her long to tear every shred of clothing from his towering body, so she could make real, pure love for the very first time in her life. Because everything else she'd experienced up until this very moment had been empty, hollow, soulless … loveless.

Desire, hot and sweet and dangerous – unlike anything she'd ever felt – overcame her. The entirety of the world faded away, and she could almost feel his breath on her cheek as she imagined him sweeping her into his arms, pressing her up against the wall, possessing her but at the same time protecting her. A shiver ran all the way through her and flames burst from a place she'd long ago thought had broken beyond repair. What in the hell was he doing to her, without laying a finger upon her skin? She really needed to get the hell away from him before she did something reckless.

Now!

'Well, I best be off.' She shot to her feet. 'Big day tomorrow.' She glanced at her watch. 'Far out, I mean, today.'

'Oh.' Jarrah stood, and raked his gaze down to hers. 'What time is it?'

'Twelve-thirty.' She grimaced.

'Oh, wow.' His smile turned from sweet to sexy. 'Looks like time got away from us.'

'Well, as they say, time flies when …' He was looking at her in that earth-giving-way-beneath-her-feet way again. She tried to clear the butterflies from where they'd landed in her throat. 'I better try and get what sleep I can, before my alarm goes off at five-fifty-five am.'

'Five-fifty-five hey, why not six?' His expression was delightfully playful.

'I like to take five minutes to wake up, before my feet hit the floor.'

'Nice.' He arched a brow. 'Me, on the other hand, I half wake up when my feet hit the floor, and then an extra-strong coffee gives me the boot up the butt I need to get out the door before sun-up.'

She grinned, nodding. 'I have to agree that caffeine is a much-needed boot up my butt in the morning too.'

'Like you said, Miss Millie, we're two peas in a pod, you and me.' He placed his hand in the curve of her back and joined her on the short walk across the back verandah and to the foot of the stairs.

Millie didn't want him to take his hand away, nor did she want to leave. But if she didn't extract herself from this situation, there'd be some deep regrets come sun-up. 'I can take it from here, Jarrah, no need to chaperone me.' Before she could chicken out, she reached up on her tippy toes and pecked his cheek. There was no harm in a friendly kiss. 'Thank you for a lovely night, and great company.'

'My pleasure, anytime.' He dropped his hand from her back and tucked it into his pocket.

The magnetism she felt in that moment, the impulse to throw caution to the wind, was almost unstoppable. And for an out breath, and an in breath, she almost gave in to her desires, gave in to him.

Almost …

'Night.' She squeezed the word past those damn fluttering butterflies, not only lodged in her throat, but now also inhabiting the entirety of her body.

One second stretched into another, then another. They lingered in between each one. Holding onto whatever this was between them.

Should I kiss him?

Would he kiss me back?

Jarrah lowered his head a little, meeting her gaze head on. 'Night, Millie, sleep sweet, won't you.'

Find that voice of yours, Amelia!

'I'll try to.' Heavens, she sounded like a pipsqueak. 'You too.'

Turning, she forcibly took steps away from the temptation of him, towards her motel room, where she would climb beneath the covers, close her eyes, and hopefully dream of him all night long.

Well, at least for the next five hours.

CHAPTER 10

The rest of the week flew by, and Sunday arrived in glorious tropical fashion, with a gentle breeze and powdery blue sky. It was her first day off since starting on Monday, and Millie was determined to make the most of it. Her motel room was being repainted, along with a few of the others, so she was calling the homestead home for the day, and possibly even the night if the fumes were too strong. Curled up on the day bed on Jarrah's back verandah, with a paperback from his bookshelf in her hands, she decided to read one last page of the edge-of-her-seat thriller before heading inside to make a coffee.

She'd awoken after an early bedtime, feeling rested – in spite of the fact that her monthlies had arrived two days early – and ravenous; and not only for the sustenance of food. However, not wanting her attraction to Jarrah to be obvious, she'd pushed her longing to the side, and done her best to get on with her morning by stuffing her face with way too many carbs. She'd had to do something to deter one half of her cravings. The other half, she'd never satisfy – Jarrah King was way out of bounds. She was well aware of the number one rule of Riverside Acres, and she wasn't about to step over any threshold to break it. She needed to be here. Getting herself fired by Tommy was not an option. She knew he wouldn't blink an eyelid if he had to. In fact, he'd likely enjoy every second of it. She wasn't going to give the brooding, and in her firm opinion spoilt-brat eighteen-year-old the chance, or the satisfaction.

Placing the colourful feather that she'd found on her way over there between the pages she was up to, she closed the novel and glanced up at the picturesque view. Jarrah hadn't been there when she'd arrived just after eight, which she'd expected, but she still had him within her sights, just up the rise, working in the top paddock with one of the agisted horses. He'd mentioned this particular gelding had been mistreated, and its new owner was paying to have him learn that some humans could be trusted. Jarrah was certainly the right man for the job – it hadn't taken her, a woman who trusted almost no one, long to trust him. Even though she couldn't make out his handsome face from her vantage point, she identified his broad-shouldered frame and soaring height. And the way he moved, so confidently, so patiently, she knew it was him. But she couldn't just sit here and perv all day. She needed to stretch her legs, and a double-shot espresso wasn't going to go astray either.

Crossing the back verandah, past where Scruff was having a kip on his hammock bed, she felt the cool floorboards creak beneath her bare feet as she stepped into the homestead. As she passed through the laundry and padded down the hallway, the sense that she didn't belong in here crashed over her. But then she'd never felt as though she belonged anywhere else, either. The big old house felt different when she was spending time in there with Jarrah. He always made her feel more than welcome and while this made her feel special, she reminded herself that he'd likely make anyone he invited into his home feel comfortable, special, looked after.

Sweet notes of native birdsong floated through the open window of the kitchen as she made use of Jarrah's coffee machine. His couple of lessons had taught her well. Within minutes the delicious scent of dark roasted beans filled the room, and she breathed in deep. Ahhh, coffee, it was her lifeblood. Next she frothed the milk, then added it to her double shot. The clinking of her teaspoon as she stirred in a teaspoon of raw sugar mingled with an approaching melodic whistling to a familiar Hank Williams tune. A quick glance out the window made her belly flip-flop. It looked as if Jarrah was making his way home for lunch. With her. She almost danced on the spot as she watched him stride through the gate to his enthusiastic welcome-home committee of one – Scruffball. Crouching down, Jarrah appreciated his doggy mate's warm greeting with a wide smile and a ruffle of his floppy ears, and as he straightened, he looked straight in her direction. And bam, caught red-handed ogling him, she returned a shamed smile. Not realising she'd been holding her breath, she released it with a sigh. With her lips still curled ever so slightly, she felt a little giddy as she dragged her gaze from the window.

Bugger, she should have thought to make a nice lunch, but then she hadn't known he was going to be coming back to the homestead around midday. It was the least she could do after everything he'd done for her, including putting the wind up the mechanic the day before about getting her car fixed by sometime next week. Apparently, the part he needed had been delayed in transport, but it was going to be here Monday, or Tuesday at the latest. Fingers and toes crossed he was right. She missed having transport. There was so much more of Banshee Bay she wanted to explore. Deciding to at least make Jarrah a coffee, she quickly retraced her steps, grinding beans, infusing the coffee and then frothing more milk. All the while she contemplated how he was proving more than just handsome, in just a little over a week. And not only that, he was intriguing her. How she was meant to fight off such a beautiful fascination, she hadn't a clue. But she had to give it her best shot, for the cause. So, demanding her voice of reason step to the forefront, it did so just as the object of her fantasies moseyed into the kitchen and made her forget what she was thinking.

'Howdy, Mills, how goes it?'

Mills, aww. 'Howdy yourself, King.' His husky tone had her turning to offer him the sweetest of smiles. 'And it goes pretty well, thanks. How's your day panning out?' Their eyes met, and locked, and he offered her a charming smile, one that reached deep inside her chest and caressed her heartstrings.

'It's panning out fabulously, thanks for asking.' He sniffed, and then rolled his eyes in pleasure. 'I smell caffeine.'

'Oh, yes, here you go.' She held out his cup. 'I took the liberty of making you one.'

'Oh, awesome, just what the doctor ordered, thanks.' He took a sip. 'Ahhh, it always tastes better when someone else makes it.'

The slap of the front door, followed by heavy footfalls, halted their conversation. 'Jarrah, you home?' Tommy appeared before Jarrah got the chance to reply.

'There you are.' Tommy looked to the paperwork held in his hands. 'I need to run a couple of things …' As he caught sight of Millie, hostility glinted in his steadfast gaze.

'Go on, I'm listening.' Jarrah's brows bumped together.

'It can wait until we're in private.' Tommy eyed Jarrah while tipping his head a little to the side. 'What's going on with you pair, huh?'

'Nothing at all.' Jarrah gave him a withering stare. 'Why do you feel the need to ask?'

'Correct me if I'm wrong, Uncle, but any kind of,' he shrugged coolly, yet conceitedly, 'let's say, cosy relationship between staff means instant dismissal here at Riverside Acres, doesn't it?'

'Yes, as you know all too well it does, but that's not the case here. Millie and I are just good friends.' Jarrah offered an apologetic glance in her direction, and then frowned as he looked back at his scowling nephew. 'Although, thanks for being thoughtful enough to remind me, Tommy.'

Tommy took a lengthy moment to respond, and when he did, his steely focus was fired at Millie. 'You're well aware of the number one rule too, Millie, aren't you?' He offered a sly smile. 'Because from where I'm standing, you appear quite smitten with my uncle.'

Jarrah went to speak, but she held up her hand. 'Please, Jarrah, let me have my say, because to be quite honest, I've been biting my tongue all week.' She was a big girl, and she could have her own back. 'I think that's way out of line of you to say something like that, Tommy.' Her face burned red hot, and her stomach flip-flopped sickeningly. 'And I take offence to it.' Blinking quicker, she bit back the sudden urge to cry.

'Well, I'm sorry to state the obvious.' Tommy didn't look apologetic in the slightest. 'But hey, I say things like I see them.'

'Like you *think* you see them, more like it.' Her unwavering gaze was as icy as her tone of voice. 'I've seriously had enough of your bad moods and your bullying tactics. I may work for you, but you don't have the right to treat me like you do.' Man it felt good to stand up for herself – after the past couple of years, it had been a long time coming.

'My bad mood is partly because of you waltzing in and taking Jasmine's place.' Tommy's red face articulated just how hot his blood was boiling, too. 'And for the record I ain't no bully, I'm just getting real sick of all the crap that goes on around here.' He hurled a rage-fuelled glance in Jarrah's direction. 'Especially all the underhanded BS and lies.'

'Tommy, what in the hell are you on about?' Jarrah stepped forwards, shaking his head. 'Jasmine, and you, crossing the line and getting her fired is not Millie's fault in the slightest, nor mine, and what lies are you talking about?'

'Are you seriously going to stand there and keep lying to me about my parents' deaths?'

His face paling and eyes wide, Jarrah looked as though he'd been king hit in the chest, but he recovered quickly. 'What exactly have I lied about, Tommy?'

Tommy laughed cynically. 'You know exactly what.' He chucked a sideways glance to Millie. 'Lying makes a person a fraud, wouldn't you agree, Millie?'

Alarm flooding her stomach, she stiffened, intentionally lifted her chin and did her very best to save face, desperate to change the direction this was heading. 'I'm sorry if my presence bothers you, Tommy, but I like my job here, and I'm doing my best to prove that to you, and Jarrah, and the customers.'

'Well aren't you just the best little cook this side of Sydney.' Tommy's arms folded tightly as he waited for her reaction.

How did he know she was from Sydney? Had she let it slip? Maybe. It was possible.

Jarrah stepped in the middle, his gaze burning with anger. 'I think you've said enough now, Tommy.' He pointed towards the doorway. 'Please, let yourself out, before I say something I might regret.'

His hands clenching at his sides, Tommy did the opposite and took a step closer to Jarrah.

Jarrah didn't move a muscle as they stared each other down.

Worried a fistfight was about to ensue, Millie stepped back a little and held her breath. This prickly situation was a hard-hitting reminder that nothing mattered other than surviving here, getting what she needed, and then getting the hell out of Banshee Bay. She needed to stop liking Jarrah so much. She needed to get a damn grip on her priorities.

Tommy finally backed off, turned and flung his hate-filled gaze at her. 'You better watch your back.' Every word was whispered. 'Because I'm keeping an eye on you, little miss turn up out of the blue, with no last name.'

He's enjoying this …

As quiet as they'd been, his words had hit their mark mighty hard, sending a trickling of fear down her spine. She turned her back to him in a bid to try and hide what she was feeling.

'Tommy!' Jarrah roared. 'Enough!'

With an almighty huff, Tommy stormed out of the kitchen. His stomping footfalls echoed down the hallway, a door slammed loud enough to come off its hinges, and then he was gone.

'Bastard,' she muttered as she tried to catch her breath.

'I'm so sorry, Millie.' Jarrah's hand came to rest protectively upon her shoulder.

'It's not your fault, Jarrah.' She turned to face him. 'You and Tommy need to sort this out between the two of you. I don't want any part of it.'

'I know, you don't deserve to be stuck in the middle of our drama.' His gaze dropped to the floor. 'I'll get to the bottom of this mess, I promise.'

'No need to make promises to me.' She cleared the emotion from her tight throat. 'I won't be around long enough for it to affect me.'

His eyes found hers, and the waves of despondency in their profound blue deepened. 'You're not planning on staying around for long?'

'It's not likely I'll be here any longer than a month, no.' His evident sadness was breaking her in two. 'I'm sorry to disappoint you.' She was fighting to keep this relationship businesslike.

'No, please, you don't need to apologise.' He nodded very slowly as he stepped away from her. 'You're a wayward wanderer with a free spirit.' He paused, drew in a breath, as if waiting for a response. 'Don't worry, I get it, Millie, you blew in and you'll blow away, it's as simple as that. I was foolish to think otherwise.'

Blindsided by his skewed perception of her, and hurt by the look of scepticism now within his gaze, she wished she could blurt out the real reason she was here, and why she wouldn't be here any longer than necessary, but she bit her tongue. Jarrah regarded her shrewdly, as if her silence confirmed whatever he was thinking, then he offered her a sad smile before disappearing in the same direction as Tommy had. Releasing the breath she'd been holding, she couldn't believe she'd even considered telling him the real reason she was here. No matter how strong the urge to open her true self up to him had been, it was dangerous to even tread on such shaky ground.

Left with turbulent, tumbling emotions, she bit back a sob as she wrapped her arms around her middle. Poor Jarrah. He meant well, and he was a good, decent man, she was sure of it. The last thing she wanted was to hurt him. Then again, she didn't want to leave here with a broken heart and none the wiser about her family's deaths either. So she needed to be more careful with her feelings, and with her actions. Tommy wasn't going to break her or chase her away from here. In the grand scheme of things, even if he'd been the one behind the letter, he was nothing to her. His opinion didn't mean a thing. She didn't need him in her corner. She just needed to discover what an eighteen-year-old short-tempered guy had to do with a past he hadn't even been old enough to understand, let alone be involved in. Who did he know that had been involved in her family's deaths? God, she hoped Jarrah's hands were clean. She wasn't sure how she was going to cope if she found out he'd played a hand in the night she'd lost everything that had mattered to her.

* * *

Swiping the paintbrush left to right while balanced on the top step of the ladder, Jarrah tried to focus on anything but the elephant that had been roaming Riverside Acres since his nephew had returned from his trip. He'd spent enough of his life trying to drag his brother out of trouble and danger, and now he felt as if he was doing that all over again with Tommy, when all he wanted was to settle into this peaceful life he'd built for both of them. But witnessing just how quickly his father's grimy fingers had dug into Tommy's innocence, and how easily Carlo Martino was turning his grandson in the wrong direction, Jarrah couldn't help but wonder if he was dodging a bullet by trying to keep Tommy out of harm's way, or taking one. He wished he could confront Tommy and hear the truth straight from the horse's mouth, but lives were at stake if he went and did something so reckless. No, he needed to find another way to raise the subject, and hopefully, somehow, some way, talk sense into his nephew before it was too late.

Admitting defeat for the time being, he shook his head sadly as he fought the stab of uneasiness from his chest. Unanswerable questions plagued him. A sense of helplessness overwhelmed him. Was he fighting a losing battle? Was Tommy going to turn out exactly as Joey had been – stubborn, money-hungry, and quite often ruthless in getting what he wanted? Was it in his nephew's blood to be corrupt? Had the toxicity of greed been bred into him from birth? And finally, could he really do this all over again, only to watch Tommy meet his own demise?

God forbid.

Grabbing hold of the handle on the paint tin, he carefully descended the ladder, plonked his tools down on the drop cloth, and then sat on an upturned drum to admire his handiwork. The lick of gleaming white paint had done wonders for the weather-beaten balustrades and gutters of the front of the homestead, but as much as he wanted to focus on how he'd finally got around to doing it, he couldn't drag his mind from Tommy's deceitfulness, or the way he'd treated Millie that morning, or Jenny and Penny the week before. For the very first time since becoming his nephew's guardian, he was tempted to share with Tommy just how tough it had been, raising him when he, himself, had been so young, so inexperienced with children. And also how, when he was trying to make ends meet, he had gone without food so Tommy didn't have to. But what was that going to achieve? He wasn't a martyr, nor was he going to pull the poor-me card. He liked to believe he was better than using guilt to bribe Tommy into being the best version of himself. In his opinion, the true worth of a man was measured by the impact he had on others. If only Tommy could see this, and live by it.

Standing and doing his best to let go of his deliberations as he tidied up a little, he noticed two things concurrently. One, he had skipped breakfast and lunch so he was starving, and two, something smelled utterly delectable. Turning in a circle, he followed the mouth-watering aroma with his nose, and smiled when he worked out it was coming from the back of the homestead. Millie was clearly making use of the kitchen and he liked the thought of her tucked away inside, cooking to her heart's content. His stomach growled in anticipation of a quick smoko break and he considered gatecrashing her culinary affair. Should he? Would she mind? The second coat of paint was about an hour away, so he had time. And he needed to eat before he passed out. But he wasn't sure she'd want his company after what had gone down a few hours earlier.

As if sensing his master's hesitancy, Scruff scooted in beside him and his tail smacked Jarrah's leg with anticipation. 'Does this mean you want to head inside for a break too, buddy?'

Scruff replied with a short sharp woof.

'Righto then, that's settled, let's go see what Millie's cooking, hey.' Jarrah felt silly, but having Scruff at his side made him feel more comfortable about heading in.

After kicking his boots off at the front door, he moseyed down the hall and into the kitchen. 'Hey, Millie, the house smells bloody amazing thanks to you.' He wanted to keep the conversation light, happy. 'What's cooking?'

'Oh, hey, Jarrah.' Millie's smiling face met him as she flicked the release valve on the pressure cooker and tossed a tea towel over her shoulder. 'I was wondering when you'd be back for that lunch you missed out on,' she said over the hissing of the steam being released. 'You'd be ravenous, considering it's almost three-thirty.'

'Yeah, tell me about it, I started painting and lost track of time, but I'm pretty bloody hungry now.' The unmistakable scent of corned beef filled the heart of the house, making his stomach dance with delight. And the KitchenAid mixer was plugged in, so she must have done some baking too. 'So, what have you whipped up?'

'I've made us corned beef, a fresh loaf of bread, and some of my mum's famous Anzacs.' Oven mitts now in hand, she plucked a tray of the legendary Aussie biscuits from the stove and placed it on the sink. 'As always, when I let myself loose in the kitchen, I get a little bit carried away.' She glanced over her shoulder, a playful grimace on her face. 'I hope you don't mind me helping myself to the ingredients?'

'Of course not.' Her presence was overwhelmingly comforting. Knowing she wasn't going to be around much longer, he made sure to capture the sensation and store it away for when she was long gone. 'I get to reap the rewards of your gastronomic cook-fest, so it's a win-win.'

'Ha, yes, good call.' Slicing the fresh loaf of bread, she then buttered four pieces. 'Would you like one corned beef and salad sanga, or two?'

'Two please.' He watched her owning the kitchen from the other side of the centre island. 'Can I do something to help?'

'No thanks, you'll just get in the way.' Her grin was cheeky as she buttered another two slices.

'Oi, fair play.' Jarrah jumped at the chance to banter. 'I'll have you know that I'm a pretty good kitchen hand.'

'Is that so?' She offered him a light-hearted glance. 'I'll just take your word for it while you pull up a seat, sit your butt down, and take a well-earned rest.'

'Well, okay then.' He did as he was told, unable to stop his smile from spreading as she bustled about the kitchen like it was her own, and it suited her. Very much.

Going to the fridge, she grabbed the butter, a tomato, a red onion, an iceberg lettuce and a jar of hot mustard. 'I think this will do.' Balancing everything, she carried it back to the centre island and dumped it down. 'I'll just go and grab the corned beef out. Fingers crossed it's nice and tender.'

'I have no doubt it will be.' Jarrah couldn't just sit and watch her do everything, so from his post at the bench, he slid the chopping board towards him and started slicing the tomato and onion.

'I know you're not putting your feet up over there.' She'd seemed to be focused on getting the corned beef out of the cooker; it was like she had eyes in the back of her head. 'You can't help yourself, can you?'

'Nope, I can't just sit here twiddling my thumbs when you're racing around, doing it all.' This salt-of-the-earth woman was like an enigma to him. A puzzle he craved to piece together, so he could understand what made her, *her*.

You're not going to get the time to, King …

'Oh my goodness, it's perfect.' Gliding across the kitchen, she proudly plonked the steaming serving platter in front of him. 'Just look at it.'

'I am, and I have to agree.' He looked just past her, where drool hung in one long string from Scruff's mouth. 'And I reckon our four-legged mate is in agreement with my opinion too.'

'Would you like some too, buddy?' Millie's eyes crinkled in the corners as she fondly regarded Scruffball. 'Here. Let me get you a bit.' Taking the carving knife and a fork, she sliced a chunk off the corner, blew on it a little to cool it down, and then held it out.

His paws slipping then regaining traction, Scruff couldn't get to her quick enough. Basically inhaling the piece of meat, he then spun in dizzying circles, chasing his tail like a loon.

'Ha, by the looks of you, I'm going to take a wild guess and say you liked it, Scruff.' She turned her attention to Jarrah. 'What say you?'

'I say a big hell yes to that.' As her smile broadened and brightened, Jarrah marvelled at how beautiful she was. 'And I also say, why does muggins over there get first dibs on this delicious feast?'

'Because he's wayyyyy cuter than you.' Her cheeky grin was overflowing with sass.

'Hmmm.' Jarrah regarded Scruff, who was now watching them both with eager eyes. 'I beg to differ.'

'Hmmm.' Millie pouted playfully. 'We will agree to disagree.'

Both chuckling, they worked together like a well-oiled machine, making their sandwiches. After popping the butter and lettuce back into the fridge, Millie pulled up a stool and sat opposite him, then they tucked in, lost in their mmms and ahhs as they devoured every last crumb. All the while, Jarrah clamped down on his thoughts of ravishing her, firmly reminding himself that his baggage could cause her a world of trouble, and he didn't want that for her. Painting himself as the bad guy in his own head was all he could do to stop himself from giving in to his desires.

But she was so disarmingly captivating, without even trying, without even knowing what she was doing to him, or the power she had over him. And that made her all the more tempting, all the more intriguing. He liked the way her mouth curved ever so slightly when she was trying to keep a straight face. He admired how tenacious she was. He loved the sound of her laughter. And he admired the woman she was proving to be – hardworking, caring, thoughtful, intense. Without even trying, she'd caught him off-guard, in so many ways.

Too. Many. Ways.

Pushing aside the way her fierce independence enticed him, there was also the glimpses of vulnerability in her eyes that catapulted him right into her. That made him desperate to protect her. To, dare he think it – love her like she deserved to be loved. She mystified him. Confused him. Intrigued him. She was an epiphany and a mystery, all rolled into one enthralling package. He couldn't help but wonder: what had brought her here? And what, or who, was she in a rush to get to, after here? He got how she wanted everyone to believe she was tough, capable and fiercely independent, and certainly not in need of *anyone*. But then there was that agonising sadness in her glorious green eyes which told him just how much she needed someone to hold her close, to tell her that life didn't need to be heartbreaking and hard, that, if she let her guard down to the right person, her future could be all she hoped it to be, and then some.

He wanted to be that person for her, to have the freedom to put his arm around her burdened shoulders and pull her close, so he could hold her against him for a little while, so she could lean on him and allow the strain of whatever was bearing down upon her to be lightened. But it was a bad idea to try and be her knight in shining armour. He knew deep down in his bones that would send her running for the hills. And he wanted what precious time he had left with her to not be cut short. So he kept what little distance he could between them as they began to clean up after their tasty feast. They, he, couldn't cross any boundaries, for many reasons.

Too. Many. Reasons.

'Do you have time for a cuppa and an Anzac or two before you head back out?' She rinsed the dishes and he stacked them into the dishwasher as she passed each one over.

'I don't know, I'm pretty full.' She looked saddened, and he quickly retraced his rebuttal. 'But seeing as you've gone to so much effort, I reckon I could squeeze a couple in.'

'Oh, no, all good, we can enjoy a few later; it's not like they're going anywhere.' She waved a hand through the air. 'I'll let you get back to it.'

Jarrah sensed the change in the air instantly and regretted his decision to not mention what had gone down just hours earlier with Tommy. Maybe it made him seem hard-hearted. 'Do you want to talk about what happened here this morning, Millie?'

Busy wiping the bench down with the wet cloth, she swung her gaze back to him. 'I'd rather not, if that's okay with you.'

'Yeah, of course.' Respecting her decision, he offered her a kind smile. 'How about a hug then, would that help?'

Shrugging, she tossed the cloth back to the sink. 'Probably not.'

Her response stumped him. Wounded him. He desperately wanted to leave here on much better footing than earlier on. 'Oh, fair play, Mills, my hugs are bloody awesome.'

Her smile was small, but sassy. 'Talking yourself up a bit, aren't you, King?'

He grinned. 'There's only one way to find out.'

'Go on then, show me what you speak of, or forever hold your tongue.' Her attempt at a posh accent failed miserably, cracking both of them up.

As he recovered from his moment of mirth, he didn't waste another second before seizing her and pulling her into his arms. There was only the slightest hesitation before she rested her cheek against his chest, and then her arms came around him. And just as he'd imagined, she fitted into him perfectly. As if they'd been made for each other. He heard her gentle sigh, felt it flutter against his heart. Then something inside him melted and disappeared. He somehow felt lighter, unshakable, grounded, as if he'd just discovered the quintessential meaning of life. His reason for living. And it was Millie. And although that awareness shocked him, he didn't want to overthink anything right now. He just wanted to enjoy this, her, them. It stunned and delighted him that she didn't feel the slightest bit tense in his arms. He wondered how long it had been since someone had engulfed her in a genuine, warm hug. Then, without his consent, his mind started to wander to places it shouldn't and his body began to respond to her closeness. Thankfully, at the same time she untangled from him and stepped back a little, her gaze coy and her bottom lip between her teeth.

'So, out of ten, for the hug?' He had to step away just a little too, as he regathered the pieces of himself she'd unravelled.

'I'm going to be generous here,' she smiled now, so big, so beautifully, 'and give you a nine out of ten.'

'See, I told you my hugs were awesome.' He frowned lightheartedly. 'But why wasn't it a ten?'

'There always has to be a little wriggle room, just for improvement.' Her smile turned sassy again. 'Don't go getting a big head on the high score, though, will you?'

'Ha, too late.' He managed close enough to a deadpan expression. 'Because according to Mack, Tom and Graham, I already have one.'

Her confused frown gave way to a sudden look of comprehension. 'Ah, yeah, that's right ... they're funny, those three old buggers.'

'They sure are. I couldn't imagine this place without them.' Before he could think better of it, he jumped the gun and added what he felt shouldn't be left unsaid. 'The same as I can't imagine this place without you around, Millie.'

Blinking faster, she swallowed, and squared her shoulders. 'I'll miss here, and you too, Jarrah.' A flicker of regret crossed her face. 'It's going to suck, leaving.'

'Then please, stay, Millie.' He sounded desperate, but he didn't care, because he was.

She hesitated, inhaled deeply, seemed to consider her response. 'I think we both know, for whatever reason, Tommy begrudges me, and that's not ideal working conditions, for me, or for him.'

'Yeah, about that.' His heart was galloping, so he took a breath. 'Like I told you, I'm going to get to the bottom of it.'

'The bottom of what, exactly, Jarrah?' Along with the shimmer of tears, her green eyes filled with questions that he didn't have the answers to.

He didn't want to lie, so he remained silent.

Brushing past him, she offered a small, sad smile. 'I'll be gone before you get to the bottom of whatever is going on with your nephew, I'm one hundred percent sure of it.'

Before he could find the right words, any words, to reassure her, she padded out of the kitchen, and he was left standing there, wanting nothing more than to follow her so he could show her just how deeply he was falling for her.

CHAPTER 11

Monday came around way too quickly. Once the lunch rush had been and gone, things slowed down considerably. Almost finished with tidying up the kitchen, and looking forward to the public holiday the next day, Millie heard footsteps coming up behind her. She spun, expecting it to be Tommy, which meant she'd likely be defending herself from one thing or another, only to find Jarrah staring back at her. His eyes seemed to light up at the sight of her and it made her feel attractive, liked, cared for.

And then stupid for feeling all these things …

'Hey, there.' His North Queensland drawl was sexy as.

'Hey there, yourself,' she replied, with as much nonchalance as she could muster.

He filled a glass from the tap and sculled it. 'Is everything okay, because you look like you're about to batter me to death with that wooden spoon.' His slow and sexy grin sent a surge of longing through her.

'Ha, not likely, the only thing this spoon is good for,' she held up her apparent weapon of choice, 'is stirring batter.'

'Fair enough,' he chuckled. 'So what's on your agenda for the rest of the day?'

'I'm not sure yet.' As he brushed past her, her pulse raced in reaction. It made her step back in a bid to stop from reaching out for more of that heady feeling that she'd felt when he'd hugged her the day before. 'Without a car, there are not a lot of options, really.'

'I have an idea.' He studied her with a gentleness that had the power to undo all the part of herself she had tied up nice and tight, so nobody could see through her. 'How about we meet up when I'm finished, say,' he glanced at his watch, 'around five, and enjoy a couple of beers the good old-fashioned way.'

'What do you mean by …' There was a little twinge in the veiled areas of her heart. '… the good old-fashioned way?'

He waggled his brows. 'Camped out on the back of the LandCruiser, watching the sun bow out to the moon, from the best vantage point of Riverside Acres.'

This sounded very much like a date. 'Ah.' She had to force herself to look away, because if she stared into his eyes a second longer, who knew what might happen.

'Come on, Mills, you'll love it,' he insisted softly.

How could she say no to a man as wonderful as him? 'Okay, sounds good, I'll see you at five.'

'Awesome, look forward to it.' His smile was slow and sexy as he tugged on his hat and headed back outside.

Three and a half hours later, sitting on his tailgate with the landscape unfolding all around her, Millie swung her legs to and fro while taking tentative sips from her icy cold beer. Beside her,

Jarrah was doing the same. He'd been right in saying she'd love it. With awesome views, awesome company, and awesome country tunes playing from the stereo, what wasn't to love? Feeling relaxed and at peace, she breathed in deeply, and softly sighed it away. The numbness she'd lived with since losing her family had splintered since being here, allowing shards of Jarrah's mesmerising light into places she wasn't sure she wanted awakened, although she was helpless to stop it. The sensation was both frightening and stimulating, like jumping off a cliff and not knowing whether she'd fly or fall. But something told her, if it were the latter, that Jarrah would be there to catch her if needed.

'Hey, Miss Millie.' Jarrah gave her a little nudge with his elbow. 'What's going through that head of yours?'

She shrugged, and offered him a small smile. 'A whole lot of nothing and a little bit of something.'

He eyed her like she was an intricate puzzle, and said nothing.

Ha, yes, I am a puzzle, with a few missing pieces too …

Growing anxious beneath his unwavering gaze, she shifted. 'What's with the staring, King?'

As if briefly considering her question, his shoulders lifted ever so slightly. 'You never give too much away, do you?' He took a casual swill from his beer.

She shrugged a little too. 'Why should I, when I can keep someone guessing?' She was enjoying their banter as much as his smile was revealing he was too.

'Why would you want to keep me guessing?' He chuckled and waved her words away. 'Are you worried I might get bored of your company if you don't remain a little mysterious?'

'Ha, fair play, I could say the same about you, Jarrah King,' she said matter-of-factly.

His gentle smile was filled with overwhelming understanding. 'Two peas in a pod, hey.'

'Kind of, yeah.' Her laugh was a little rueful as she nodded. 'I actually reckon we're more like what Pink Floyd sang, and we're two lost souls swimming in a fish bowl, maybe?'

He drew in a deep breath, and she liked the way he relished it before sighing it away.

Jarrah nodded. 'Hmmm, I know the song well, and we're that too, I suppose.'

She liked the way he'd seen them as kindred souls – it made her wonder if this man was what she'd been missing all her life. And she continued to quietly ponder this as they sat, side by side, with their gazes pinned to the sunset-hued horizon with the hint of ocean beyond it. If only things could be different, if only she wasn't here to unravel the secrets of Riverside Acres, she knew, without a shadow of doubt, that she'd fall mighty hard for him.

* * *

The following morning she woke in the pre-dawn darkness of the homestead with the overwhelming sensation of wanting with all her heart to stay there, so she could explore the feelings she had for Jarrah, and also so she could call Riverside Acres her forever home. Of course she knew she was being ridiculous, but something about this place, about him, stirred a sense of familiarity, of belonging, as if she'd finally found where she was meant to be. It was as if there was a glimmer of hope for a brighter future if she stayed there, especially with him by her side. But forever felt like a long time, especially when she considered her nomadic past.

Rolling onto her side and cuddling her pillow to her, she huffed a weighty breath. She knew she was allowing her mind to wander to places she shouldn't be venturing into. But when it came to Jarrah King, and Riverside Acres, she couldn't help herself. Maybe her instinctive feeling was to do with her quest to find answers, and had nothing to do with her future. Maybe she was closer than she'd ever been to discovering the truth, to learning exactly who it was that had saved her from the fire, and why her parents and brother had died. She was almost one hundred percent certain Tommy had something to do with that night, in one way or another. But then what in the hell did this place, or Jarrah, or both, have to do with her family's deaths? Banshee Bay was so far away from the Blue Mountains. Almost another world. Or was it only Tommy who was the missing link to her past, to her questions? She hoped so, because she hated to think of the possibility that it had something to do with Jarrah and nothing to do with Tommy.

God forbid such heartbreak …

Lying beneath her doona until the first sliver of light peeked around the corners of her curtains, she turned off her alarm before it had time to demand she start her day. A small thing, but she wanted to do it on her terms. Throwing back the covers, she got up, tugged on her robe, made her bed, then made her way out of the room, turned right and then down the hallway. The floorboards were cool against her bare feet, as were the steps as she made her way downstairs and to the kitchen. She flicked on the overhead light, and her heart swelled when she spotted a cup, atop a yellow sticky note, right beside the coffee machine. Padding over, she picked it up and whispered Jarrah's words to herself.

Good morning, Mills, I hope you had a great sleep and enjoy an amazing day! Please make yourself at home, because your motel room still isn't ready. It'll be another night before it's all painted. And FYI, it's my turn to cook dinner.

Jarrah xx

He'd ended with two kisses, how about that. With a wispy smile on her lips, she brought the note to her chest and pressed it against her cantering heartbeat. Where had this man been all her life? And why did she have to meet him in the exact place she'd been summoned to? If only she could indulge in learning him and loving him. Wouldn't that be a dream come true? But life didn't work like that. There was never an easy road. Not for her, anyway. So she slipped the note into her robe pocket, forgot all about making herself a coffee, and instead enveloped herself in the warm and fuzzy feeling, as if she was floating, as she made her way out of the kitchen and in search of a dose of sunshine before it was time to tuck herself away in the roadhouse kitchen again.

As she stepped outside, the scent of the white and pink frangipanis wrapped around her, as did the crisp coolness of dawn. The sun had just begun to crest the surrounding mountain ranges and the tropical landscape spread out before her, encouraging her to tumble into the soothing heart and soul of it. Early-morning fog blanketed the paddocks where the silhouettes of horses with their heads down and tails swishing created a vista that stole her breath. Settling on the top step, she hugged her knees to her chest, rested her chin on top of them, and waited for the end finale of the sunrise. In an ovation-worthy spectacle, the blazing sun rose above the lush green and spilt glorious golden sunshine over the countryside beneath. And in those few minutes, once the fog had all but dissipated, leaving the view with a whisper of what was to come, she slipped into the present moment like she never had before. With no traffic whooshing past, no sirens, no horns blaring, no high-rises blocking the view and no apartment blocks shoulder to shoulder, there was just so much to appreciate in the vastness of Riverside Acres. And before she knew it, tears were slipping down her cheeks, and there was an evocative pitter-patter of her heart as the power of Mother Nature's heartbeat moved her beyond anything she'd ever felt or imagined while existing in her claustrophobic world with the burdens of city life looming over her. Warmth spread through her chest, giving rise to goosebumps, as she sucked in a shuddering breath with the powerful realisation that she could be at peace, and happy, and settled, without having the closure she'd been seeking since losing her family. She just needed a place like this, where she could sit quietly, at one with the gentle in and out breaths of untainted land. Drowning in her grief and guilt, she'd all but forgotten just how much she had loved living rurally. How was she ever meant to go back to a place that had encouraged her to take such shallow breaths for almost half of her life? Ebony and Felix the second were the only things drawing her back into a lifestyle suppressed by cityscape suffocation.

'Beautiful, isn't it, Millie?'

Jarrah's husky voice made her jump, and a rush of euphoria at his presence left her bewildered. 'Hey, you, how long have you been standing there?' She quickly wiped at her cheeks, feeling silly for being so emotional.

Leant against the doorframe, one boot crossed over the other, and his face shaded by his battered Akubra, he lifted his shoulders casually. ‘Long enough.’ He strode towards her and held out the cup that he’d left beside the espresso machine. ‘I made you a coffee; white, one sugar, right?’

‘Yes.’ She nodded. ‘Thank you.’

‘I see you got my note.’ He took a sip from his mug.

‘Uh-huh.’ She gazed up at him through the steam rising from her cup. ‘Thanks for letting me stay another night, and I look forward to whatever it is that you’re making us for dinner.’ She took a sip and savoured both the flavour and the fact that he’d made her a coffee just the way she liked it.

‘I took some chicken breasts out of the freezer, I’m just not sure what I’m going to do with them yet.’ He sat down beside her, smiling at her nod of approval as he stretched out his long legs. ‘How long has it been since you’ve ridden a horse, Mills?’

‘Other than being doubled by you the other day, too long for my liking.’ She blinked into the glimmering sunshine now bathing the back verandah. ‘Why’s that?’

‘I was just wondering if you’d like to go for a bit of a gallivant around the place?’

Excitement had her sitting up straight. ‘I’d love to.’

‘Great.’ His charming smile deepened his dimples. ‘Seeing as it’s a public holiday, I’m going to give myself the day off too, so you and me can head out to the dam for a swim and maybe even a picnic.’

Smirking at his audaciousness, she tipped her head a little to the side. ‘Oh, we will, will we?’

‘Yes, we will.’ The playful sparkle in his eyes was heightened by the sunlight.

A hunky man, with a big, beautiful heart, on a horse, wanting to whisk her off – ahh, her heart was beating a little faster. ‘Okay, I think that sounds lovely.' She smiled softly as butterflies fluttered in her belly.

'Righto, well.' Standing, he shadowed the sunlight from her eyes. 'I'll just go and saddle up the horses and meet you back here in an hour or so.'

'Okay, I'll just finish my cuppa, have a piece of toast, then go grab a quick shower.' She gestured to his empty cup now sitting on the banister. 'Just leave that there, I'll pop it into the dishwasher.'

'Cheers, Millie.' He headed down the steps then took long-legged strides across the back lawn. 'See you soon, cowgirl.'

Cowgirl? She liked the sound of that. If only she could be *his* cowgirl, now that would be the icing on the cake. Picturing what the day had in store, she could almost feel the wind against her cheeks, tugging at wisps of her hair, and the horse's powerful body carrying her as if she were as light as a feather, towards the glistening dam, while she watched Jarrah take steps away. Just as he was about to disappear around the corner of the machinery barn, he paused and looked back, and her soaring spirit flew skywards.

Jarrah King liked her.

And she liked him.

But what was she meant to do with such a revelation?

Nothing, Millie, that's what you should do; remember why you're here …

Giving her voice of reason a little mental slap, she stood and made her way back inside to eat, shower and dress for the day ahead.

* * *

Two and a half hours later, colourful lorikeets heralded the sunshine glinting off the dam's glassy surface from their perches within the towering paperbark tree. With Millie standing before him in her cute little denim shorts, frayed at the bottoms, a white boho shirt that shared a peek of her pink swimmers beneath, and a smile sweet enough to attract bees for miles, but sassy enough to bring most men to their knees, it was all Jarrah could do not to grab her right then and there so he could do wild, pleasure-filled things to her. And her beautiful green eyes, they seemed so much brighter, filled with life. He liked – no, loved – to think he'd heartened her to feel such a way.

Turning from where she was watching blue and red dragonflies flittering above the glistening water, she smiled dreamily at him. 'It's so pretty here, Jarrah.'

You're pretty, Millie ... Oh god help him, he wanted to kiss her so badly. 'It's a stunner of a place, hey.' He got up from the picnic blanket and joined her by the water's edge. 'You ready for a dip, now we've let our lunch settle?'

'Damn straight I am.' She tugged her blouse over her head, and in what felt like mere seconds had stripped down to her bright pink bikini.

Jarrah's imagination took off into uncharted territory, and he barely reined it back in before it got hold of him.

'Last one in is a loser.' She squealed as she ran, jumped and then landed with an almighty splash.

'Hey, no fair, you got a head start.' Chuckling, he stripped down to his board shorts and, taking a running leap, dived in beside her.

Paddling on the spot, Millie shivered. 'It's a little chillier in here than I expected.'

'It can be a bit cold when we've had a bit of rain.' He felt a little cheeky, and ran with it. 'Do you want another of my awesome nine out of ten hugs to warm you up?'

Her teeth chattered as she shook her head. 'Nope, I reckon a good old-fashioned water fight would do the trick.' She shoved a surge of water in his direction.

The spray hit him fair and square in the face.

'Ha, shot or what, King!' Grinning, she spun and swam in the opposite direction.

Laughing, he took off after her and submerged – he could swim faster beneath the surface. But Millie got the upper hand, and as he resurfaced, her aim was perfect. He tried to duck the incoming splashes, but every one of them hit their mark. Hooting and spluttering, he lunged for her, but she was faster, nimbler, and got out of his reach just in the nick of time. But he didn't give up the energetic chase, and it was only when she was tiring that he finally got his hands on her. At first it was extremely playful, but then, before he knew it, they were wrapped around one another, Millie with her arms entwined around his neck and her legs tight around his waist as she tried to drag him beneath the water in an all-out tussle. Their laughter echoed and his longing for her intensified. And in that impassioned moment, with her beautiful body pressed up against his, he couldn't help the way she made every inch of his body harden for her. To his surprise, she didn't let go straight away, and instead stayed wrapped around him. With their jollity quickly subsiding, their gazes met and locked and the air around them shifted, intensified. Her lips parted ever so slightly, as if she wanted to say something, or tell him something. He craved to know exactly what it was, and more importantly, if he needed to be concerned about it. Or was she about to declare her feelings for him, so he could declare his for her? Could he? Would he? Should he?

'Millie.' He whispered her name and was about to say more when she brought a fingertip to his lips.

'Shhh, don't let words ruin this.'

He tried to read her thoughts. 'I don't understand.'

'Neither do I.' She glanced at the ripples on the surface of the water, then back at him.

Her breath quickening, she regarded him as if she could see his most hidden thoughts. And she allowed him to do the same as the connection he already felt with her amplified, strengthened, merged. It was as if they'd each torn down their walls and their hearts and souls were now bared to the other's. It made him feel vulnerable, but at the same time safe, because it was with her. There was a profound knowingness in her eyes, and a hunger that echoed his. His breath caught as flames of longing shot through her sultry, sensual regard of him. Why was he so hell-bent on holding back from her? She was what he'd always wanted, though he'd tried to make himself believe it would never happen. And right now, in their shared dreamlike moment, he craved her more than anything he'd ever desired in all his life. But just as he was about to go and do something really reckless, and kiss her like he damn well meant it, she loosened her arms and legs and swam away from him. Then, reaching the water's edge, she went one step further and climbed out, sashayed over to her bag, grabbed a towel from its depths and dried off.

Following suit, Jarrah made sure to keep a little over an arm's length from her. He didn't want to risk any rash behaviour on his part, because right now, he didn't trust himself. There was way too much unbridled heat coursing through his veins to be able to resist a brush of her skin, a whisper of her breath, or a simple touch as she spoke to him. But then she closed the distance and, stopping just short of him, she looked at him now, *really* looked at him, as if searching for the connection they'd both just undeniably felt. But why? What was she going to do with such a powerful connection? Likewise, what was *he* going to do with such a powerful connection?

Nothing, King, that's what you need to do …

So he pretended to cough, and then rub something from his eyes.

'Are you okay, Jarrah?' She gently touched his arm.

'Yeah, it's just my hay fever playing up.' He used the excuse to grab his towel from the ground so he could step away from her. 'There must be something in the air.' Unable to meet her eyes for fear of tumbling back into her, he rubbed the towel over his face.

She didn't say anything, just got dressed, rolled up her towel, shoved it back into her bag, and then slung the backpack over her shoulder. 'You want to head back to the homestead now?' she finally said, breaking the awkward silence.

Oh god, he didn't want this weird energy between them, but what was he meant to do? 'Yeah, sure, and then I can start whipping us up some dinner.'

'Sounds good, what's on the menu, chef?' Her smile was friendly, relaxed.

She was clearly trying to ease the apprehension from the air, and he appreciated it from the bottom of the heart she now had a big piece of. 'I'm thinking a creamy chicken, mushroom and bacon casserole, with buttery garlic mash and steamed green beans.'

'Oh my gosh, yum, Jarrah!' She jiggled on the spot, her hands clasped beneath her chin. 'I haven't had mashed potatoes in I don't know how long.'

And there it was, they were back to normal, just like that. Wow, he liked her, so much. 'That's sacrilege, Millie, a true-blue Aussie should have mashed potato at least once a week.' He began packing the picnic gear into the saddlebag. 'And Vegemite at least once a week too.'

'Agreed.' She passed him the folded picnic blanket. 'And Tim Tams,' she added with a giggle. 'Bitten from the end and used as a straw with a nice hot chocolate or coffee.'

'Yes!' he hurrahed. 'I haven't done that in I don't know how long.'

'Two peas and all of that.' She allowed him to help her up and into the saddle of his palomino mare, Sasha.

'Yes, we most certainly are,' he said, looking up at her.

As Jarrah settled himself atop his horse, Waylon fidgeted a little and he settled him with a light tug on the reins. Setting off, he rode closely beside Millie, the jaw-dropping tropical landscape demanding their silent absorption. When they did speak, their conversation was easy and free-flowing, and when they fell silent again, those moments were ones that didn't carry the need to be filled. Their saddles creaking, both the horses' breaths were slow and steady, their clip-clops rhythmic, mesmerising.

When they reached the stables, his gaze evaluated hers. 'Did you enjoy your day off?'

Her smile was coy, sweet, and a little bit suggestive. 'I sure did, thanks, Jarrah.' She leant in and gave Sasha's neck a rub. 'And this mare is a beauty to ride too, so attentive and with such an easy gait.'

'Yes, Sasha is one of my top horses here; I'm glad you enjoyed riding her.' He guided Waylon through the round-yard gate. 'Now let's get these two unsaddled, brushed, hosed down and back into their paddocks, so we can enjoy an icy cold one or two.'

Her eyes shone with enthusiasm as they worked together, doing just that. Then, side by side, they walked Waylon and Sasha from the stables and to their paddocks. At the sight of their feed buckets, both horses hurried through, and he and Millie undid the lead ropes from their halters. Closing the gate, he made sure to latch it shut behind them.

With her hands slipping into her pockets, Millie fell into step beside him. 'Thanks for a great day, Jarrah.'

Unexpected warmth flowed through him. 'My pleasure, Mills, but it's not over yet.'

They wandered up the gentle rise towards the homestead. Gratitude for this wonderful woman flooded his lonely, locked-up heart. It was as if she held the key and, little by little, she was turning it clockwise. He'd kept his guard up for so long; this was foreign, and invigorating, and downright scary. Should he let her in? Could he? Heck, he hardly knew anything about her. And she sure as hell knew nothing about him. And there was a reason for that. He had to remember the horrible path that had led him here, to Riverside Acres, and hold on tightly to the future he'd worked so painstakingly to have.

CHAPTER 12

Her legs folded up beneath her, Millie rested her head back and enjoyed the stillness of night from the camp chair she'd gratefully accepted from Jarrah and parked out the front of her motel room. The scent of fresh paint still lingered inside, not strong enough to bring on a headache, but enough to make her only want to be in there when she slept. The pitch-black sky sparkled with hundreds upon thousands of stars, but she pulled her gaze from the wonder of it and towards the soft glow of the homestead just up the rise. It had been four whole days since she and Jarrah had shared that incredible moment in the dam, and yet she couldn't shake the intensity of the feelings she'd carried in her heart ever since. If anything, her sentiments were only growing stronger, and she didn't know what to do with such overwhelming emotions. She'd tried to ignore them, avoid them, make light of them, heck, she'd even tried to boss them away, but try as she might, and as much as she didn't want to admit it, she had fallen for Jarrah King. Which was why she was avoiding spending any time with him outside of work, at all costs. Because, if she didn't, she wasn't sure she'd be able to contain herself a second time round. And the same went for him too, she suspected. They'd both almost crossed the line, and she didn't want to step that dangerously close again. Her job depended on her willpower.

But may the good lord help her. Because she was going to need all the help she could get to keep her hands off him. Jarrah was so prodigiously masculine, in every single way, and yet there was a gentleness to him that made her want to collapse against him, so he could hold her and make everything right in her mixed-up, muddled-up world. Every single time she gazed into his eyes, she felt that peculiar tug of recognition, the very one that had hooked and heated her while she was wrapped around him as the icy coolness of the dam thankfully kept her from being careless. It was as if they'd known each other before, in another lifetime perhaps. It felt idiotic, silly, way too crazy for her rational way of thinking. But the sense of familiarity was there, swirling with the other myriad of emotions he evoked, especially whenever he was near her. How could she feel him so deeply, as if he was inside of her, a part of her, when she'd only known him for a matter of weeks? And what was she going to do if she discovered he had something to do with her family's deaths? She almost wanted to give up the hope of learning the truth right now, so she didn't find out such heart-crushing information.

With all these crazy feelings bubbling at the surface of her consciousness, she didn't know if she had the self-control necessary to maintain a platonic friendship, if put in an intimate situation with him again. Tommy would have a field day if he got wind of her feelings. She couldn't, wouldn't, allow Jarrah's mean nephew to get a hint of just how much she liked his uncle. Her trek here would end up a disaster. She hoped something revealed itself to her soon, because she wasn't sure how much longer she could wait for whatever it was the conniving author of her letter was insinuating.

Suffocated by her roiling thoughts, she huffed and rubbed her weary eyes. At the very least, she'd be getting her Jimny back the next day, and about time after almost two weeks of patiently waiting. Then, if she chose to, or if the burning need arose, she could hit the road and head back to Sydney so she could get on with her mediocre life. Not that the big smoke appealed to her in the slightest. The only things she looked forward to were hugging Ebony, when she eventually arrived home from her trip overseas, and cuddling Felix when he decided to drop in for an impromptu visit. The little things were what needed to matter. Otherwise, she might never go back there.

Yawning, she glanced at her watch. It was nearing seven pm. With a five am start on the agenda for the next day, it was time for her to make something to eat, have a shower, and then hit the sack. Stirring from where he'd been crashed out on a blanket that she'd put down for him, Scruff hauled himself to his feet, and with his tail swishing casually from side to side, followed her into the studio-style motel room. Hearing his claws pitter-pattering closely behind her made her heart nice and warm. She loved animals and the unconditional love they gave. It was often way better than any human.

Squatting down, she looked into his kind eyes. 'You're an old soul, aren't you, boy?' she said gently. 'You know I adore you so very much, right?'

Scruff's tail slapped the floor as she straightened and made a beeline for the fridge. Scrounging through, she jiggled on the spot when she spotted the two steaks she'd taken out of the freezer a few days earlier. Along with some oven chips and a fried egg, they would make an absolutely divine dinner.

Carrying everything over to the sink, she looked to Scruff. 'How about you and me have ourselves a cook-up?' She giggled at the tip of his head. 'Actually, I reckon you'd prefer your steak blue. Right?'

Taking it out of the plastic bag, she held it up for him to see. 'Would you like it now, buddy?' Spinning in circles, he almost twirled out of his fur with excitement. 'I thought as much.' Plonking it onto a side plate, she placed it down on the floor. Scruff eagerly waited for her to tell him to eat it. 'Go on, tuck in, buddy.'

By the time she turned around to grab a frypan for hers, his piece was long gone. Sated, Scruff settled himself at the corner of the room by the door, as if protecting her, while she made her dinner. Half an hour later, she was sitting at her little two-seater dining table, dunking her last oven chip into the soft gooey yolk of her egg, when a rotten stench smacked her in the face.

'Oh my god, Scruff, was that you?' She leapt to her feet. 'Far out, boy, what in the heck have you been eating?' Turning the ceiling fan to full blast, she dared only little breaths until a good minute had passed.

After dumping her dishes into the sink to soak – she'd wash them up tomorrow – she made her way into her ensuite bathroom. Growing sleepier by the minute, she kept her shower short. She wanted to take advantage of her unusually lethargic mind and climb beneath the covers before she started overthinking everything again. Bundled up in her robe, she padded back into the bedroom, only to find Scruffball curled up on the end of her bed.

'Oi, you, scallywag, what are you doing up there?'

Scruff languorously lifted his head and opened one eye.

'Okay, all right, you can stay.' She grabbed her mobile from the bedside table. 'I'll just let Jarrah know where you are, so he doesn't worry.'

Not wanting to succumb to Jarrah's husky voice, she wrote a quick text message. *Scruff is with me, I'll let him sleep over because he's comfortable and he's too adorable to boot outside.* ☺ Pausing to re-read it, she pressed send. Less than a minute later, a reply dinged.

My boy is a charmer. He certainly has you wrapped around his paw. Thanks for letting me know where he is. Sweet dreams, Mills. ☺

Refraining from writing anything else, she forcibly placed her phone back on the bedside table. Settling beneath the covers, with one leg out and one leg in – her form of temperature control – she nestled her head into her pillow. After fidgeting for a few seconds, Scruff placed his chin on her leg and was sound asleep in seconds.

'Night, buddy,' she whispered, before turning off the lamp and drifting into sleep almost as quickly as Scruffball had.

* * *

Swearing beneath his breath, Jarrah jammed his phone into his back pocket. The call from Vincent had been startling and deeply disturbing – the reality of what Tommy had gone and done was really sinking in. Carlo Martino was up to his old tricks, using Tommy's age and naïvety about the underworld, and likely his eagerness to please his grandfather, to his advantage. The news that he'd delivered a letter to the address of the girl Amelia Price had grown up with angered and baffled him. What in the hell was his meddling father up to, and what did he expect to get by contacting Ebony Strathmore? Did Amelia live with her best friend? Had the envelope been for her and not Ebony? Or both of them? Surely there wasn't any more revenge Carlo could wreak on the man he'd had killed fifteen years ago, by Joey's hand. Hadn't Amelia endured enough, losing her family in such a horrific way? And the confirmation from Vincent, that Tommy hadn't a clue about what was in the envelope, or who he was transporting it to, only thickened the plot. He knew without a shadow of a doubt that money would have been involved. Likely a good chunk of it, and the fact that money talked in Tommy's world saddened him. He truly believed he'd taught him otherwise. Like grandfather, like father, like son. History repeating.

As his footsteps pounded up the walkway of the roadhouse, thunder exploded overhead and a crack of iridescent lightning shot across the foreboding sky. Just like the cantankerous weather, there was another kind of storm brewing, and it was going to discharge under his roof at some point. He was certain of it. Falling out with Tommy was the last thing he wanted, but he wasn't going to allow criminal activity, or criminals, to call Riverside Acres home. Thank Christ he hadn't seen hide nor hair of Ken Buller since telling him to rack off. That was a plus. But he was going to have to pick the timing of the battle with Tommy wisely.

So, with an achingly heavy heart, he strode purposefully across the verandah and into the roadhouse just as the sky opened and heavy raindrops drummed deafeningly against the tin roof. Rubbing the bridge of his nose in a bid to make his throbbing headache ease, he tried to shake off the prickly sensation. He wasn't in the mood for dramas today. Or any day. But Tommy had returned home from staying at Jasmine's the night before – at the very least his nephew had been up-front about that – and drama always seemed to find a way to follow Tommy home.

'Hey, Tommy, how goes it?' he called out as jovially as he could as he traipsed past the side door that led to the commercial kitchen.

But there was no response.

His jaw tightened, as did his gut. Hesitating for a second, he changed course and took steps towards a very nonchalant Tommy. 'I gather you're still not talking to me?' Given it was near four, he was glad that everyone had now gone home for the day.

Shrugging, Tommy helped himself to the last biscuit from the packet of Kingstons and dunked it into his coffee.

'Tommy, please don't ignore me.' Sighing, Jarrah ran a hand through his hair. 'This silent treatment is going to fix nothing.'

To his growing frustration, Tommy continued to play ignorant. God how he wished he could confront him, head on, and get the truth from him, but he had to tread very carefully, not only for Vincent and his family's lives, but for Tommy's too. Until he could get to the bottom of this mess, and have the proof he needed to be able to raise such a difficult topic with his nephew, he had to remain tight-lipped, as hard as that was going to be.

'Tommy!'

'What do you want me to say, Jarrah?' Tommy shrugged indifferently.

Foreboding snaked down Jarrah's spine – if he gave in to his irritation, this wasn't going to end well. 'How about trying to be less angry and a little more grateful for your life here; that'd be as good a start as any.'

'It's not that easy.' Tommy's gaze burned with resentment. 'I can't pretend I'm not angry that you went and fired my girlfriend and then hired some random chick from the side of the road that we know nothing about.'

'Forget about Millie for now. You know the number one rule here, Tommy, and you and Jasmine disrespected me by breaking it.' Shifting from foot to foot, Jarrah shook his head. 'Wait, she's actually your girlfriend now?'

'Yes, she is.'

'Well, that's even more reason for her not to work here, Tommy, because you and I both know that's not ideal, working with someone you're sleeping with.'

'In your opinion.' Tommy's chair scraped across the linoleum floor as he pushed back from the little staff table and stood. 'I wish I had enough money to get the hell out of this place.'

With a sudden surge of anger making his heart race, Jarrah held back for a second – lucky for Tommy, he had real thick skin. He had prison to thank for that. 'I promised your grandmother I'd take care of you, Tommy, and I thought I was doing a good job of that.'

'I'm not some stray dog that you picked up from the streets and need to take care of.' Grabbing his empty mug, he stomped over to the sink and rinsed it out. 'I want my own life, doing what I want, when I want to do it, with who I want to do it with.'

Jarrah's jaw set harder as he bit back words that would only fuel the fire.

Turning, Tommy rested his hands flat against the prep bench. 'I want to feel like I belong somewhere, and as much as I've tried to fit into the country lifestyle here, it's not for me.' Pausing, his jaw briefly clenched. 'If you'd like to know what I really want, it's to go back to Sydney, so I can get to know my family there.'

And there it was, the first step towards the truth. 'Your, or should I say, *our*, family down in Sydney are all crooks, Tommy, bad people who care about nothing but themselves.' Wanting to protect his vulnerable nephew, he instinctively took a step towards him.

Tommy held up his hand. 'Don't.'

As he halted, angst quickened Jarrah's pulse. 'For god's sake, didn't your parents' deaths teach you anything?'

Tommy's eyes narrowed and red rage stormed his regard of Jarrah. 'I've been told that my mother and father's deaths were caused by you.' There was a steely emphasis on every word.

The venom behind Tommy's unfair, untrue statement made Jarrah's hackles rise. 'Me? What in the hell, Tommy, I was in jail!' His stomach churned. 'Where did you hear such bullshit?' He knew exactly who would have fed his nephew such lies but wanted to hear it from Tommy's mouth.

Tommy couldn't meet his eyes. 'My grandfather told me.'

'You mean Carlo told you.' Now Jarrah's words were steely.

'Two of the same.'

His nephew's shrug of indifference was infuriating. 'Come on, Tommy, Carlo lies through his teeth every time he speaks.' He paused and took a breath, while finally understanding why Tommy had been so short-tempered with him and everyone else around here. 'I had nothing to do with their murders, not in the slightest.'

'He said that you pissed off a bloke in jail, and then the bastard took his revenge out on my parents when he got released.'

'No bloody way, that's not true at all.' Jarrah couldn't believe this was happening. 'The man that killed your mum and dad was seeking revenge because your grandfather had gotten Joey and his men to steal drugs and weapons from them.' He briefly squeezed his eyes shut against the heartbreak of losing his brother, and now possibly losing his beloved nephew. 'That son of a bitch, telling you such bloody lies; he needs to do us all a favour and go and rot in hell.'

'Shit, righto.' Tommy regarded Jarrah through cynical eyes. 'But why should I believe you over him?'

At a loss, Jarrah held up both hands. 'Because I've always been honest with you, Tommy, isn't that reason enough?'

Tight-lipped, Tommy's unyielding gaze shifted to the doorway.

'So when did you go and see Carlo?'

'When I was meant to be fishing.' Tommy's tightly folded arms dropped to his sides. 'I didn't tell you because I knew you'd be angry about it.'

Dropping his despondent gaze to his boots, Jarrah took a moment. It was only after two deep breaths that he could look at Tommy again. 'I'm more disappointed than angry, because I thought you knew better than to go anywhere near the Martinos.'

Hurt and regret flashed in Tommy's dark eyes, but only briefly, before his defensive scowl returned. 'I have a right to get to know my father's father. And make my own opinion on him.'

'If you say so, Tommy.'

'You're not my father, Jarrah.'

Tommy's icy tone stung. 'I've never tried to be your father, only your uncle, and hopefully a good role model.' He was trying to be patient, but his patience was wearing mighty thin.

Verbally backed into a corner, Tommy huffed and cracked his knuckles.

'Tommy, can you promise me you're not going to go back to see Carlo again?'

'No I can't, and I don't think it's any of your business if I do.' His darting eyes didn't land on Jarrah's.

'I'm going to pretend you didn't just say that.' He felt as if Tommy had just plunged the knife even deeper into his heart – he had to make this stop. 'And contrary to what you think, it is my business if you want to remain at Riverside Acres.' Tough love was all he had for Tommy right now.

Tommy glared at him, but the fleeting flash of hurt and regret told Jarrah that the Tommy he knew, the Tommy he'd raised, was still there, in amongst the mess that Carlo had created.

'I don't want to talk about this anymore.' Stomping past him, Tommy disappeared out the door.

Jarrah let him go. They both needed time to calm down. Enough had been said. For now. At the very least, he was relieved Tommy had come clean about visiting Carlo. Next he had to find a way to extract the truth about him delivering the envelope.

All in good time.

As he headed towards his office, his mobile rang out from his back pocket. Snatching it out, he eyed who the caller was, hit answer, and then pressed it to his ear. 'Hey, mate, long time no see.'

'Cor blimey, tell me about it, King.' Marty Williams' voice held the lilt of his legendary larrikin ways. 'I've been on the road for yonks, following the rodeo circuit all the way around Australia, and haven't had time to scratch my butt, let alone give you a call.'

'Ha, sounds like you're living the life of a bull rider, Marty.' Jarrah wasn't the least bit jealous. 'So what do I owe the privilege to?'

'I was wondering, on the off-chance, if you'd like to buck it out at the charity rodeo in Mossman next weekend. One of the guys pulled out last minute, leaving us short of a rider.'

Jarrah sank into his chair. 'You know I've hung up my spurs, right?' After laying quite a few of his demons to rest, he no longer had a death wish, and climbing onto the back of a raging bull came close to that.

'Yeah, I know, King, but this is for sick kids, mate, and the bulls, well, let's just say they're on the tamer side and not like the ones in the professional circuit.'

When it came to children and animals, Jarrah couldn't say no. 'Well then, if it's helping sick kids, then that's a different story.' There might be some cuts and bruises, and definitely a sore back, but hopefully nothing worse. It was worth a shot. 'You've twisted my arm, mate, so count me in.'

CHAPTER 13

The working week had flown, landing Millie at the annual Mossman charity rodeo on a balmy Saturday afternoon as if in the blink of an eye. Which was almost the time it would take for Jarrah's buck-it-out ride today: eight seconds, that's all it took to hit the leaderboard – or hit the dirt with his testosterone-fuelled ego barely intact. It was also all it took to send a bull rider to hospital, or worse. The thought terrified her, but she was doing her best to push it to the backburner. It had been many years since she'd attended a rodeo – the last one had been the PBR championships in Sydney almost five years earlier – so she wanted to thoroughly enjoy her outing, while remaining positive that Jarrah was going to be able to walk away from the toughest sport on dirt with his self-esteem and body intact. A feat considering he was more of a horseman than a bull rider.

With an expanse of powdery blue sky and not a cloud in sight, the weather had come to the party. Having relished the thrill of the saddle bronc, the first round of barrel racing, and the steer wrestling and roping, Millie had descended from her seat at the top of the grandstands and was now on the hunt for an early dinner. Wandering along sideshow alley, towards the rows of food trucks, she smiled at the line-up of kids dropping balls into the laughing clowns' rotating heads as their parents stood close by. A game of skill, perfect timing and concentration was required if they were to win a stuffed toy. As for her, clowns freaked her out, so as a kid she'd avoided going anywhere near the popular carnival game. Even now, she walked at a safe distance.

Above her, a cloud of fine dust seemed to hover, and all around the scent of popcorn, burgers, cattle and manure, and pork spit roast clung to the tropical air. The last one was making her stomach growl – she'd be buying a juicy pork roll, with lashings of gravy, a dollop of applesauce and extra crackling, after she'd browsed through one of her favourite shops. Passing the dodgem cars, she chuckled at the frivolity of the drivers and their white-knuckled passengers. There was laughter and squeals aplenty, scarcely heard above the volume of the music booming from the speakers. Stepping into the coolness of the R.M. Williams Western shop, set up in a huge tent, she browsed the reins, leather chaps, stirrups, saddles, boots and clothing. This place was a country lover's delight. But needing to keep her purse strings tight, she wouldn't be buying herself anything today.

Half an hour later, with her mammoth pork roll and a can of Coke in hand, she headed back towards the centre ring where country music blared from the suspended speakers, hung high above the arena. In prime position, a big screen gave the crowd an eagle-eyed view of each event. With the grandstand close to capacity, it seemed like every man and his dog had come from near and far to attend. Rowdy groups were gathered at the bar off to the side, families had settled into their seats with bags of fairy floss and tomato sauce–covered dagwood dogs in hand, and then there were the teenage girls, dressed to the hilt in their sparkly jeans, boots and button-up rhinestone-studded paisley shirts. It was clearly a big deal for the small FNQ community of Mossman, and she felt honoured Jarrah had invited her along as his plus one.

Heading towards the VIP section of the grandstands, she grabbed a seat in the third row from the top and settled in for the evening events. Tucking into her pork roll, swimming in thick rich gravy, she continually dabbed her lips and chin. She cracked open her can of Coke, took a sip, and then smothered a burp as she spotted Jarrah climbing onto the top railing, just behind the chutes. If she'd thought he looked manly in his usual country attire before, holy moly, in his leather chaps and matching black hat, lord help her. Her heart rebelled against her pure intentions and sped up as the same butterflies he always aroused spread their wings and fluttered. Unable to help overhearing the flashy group of buckle-bunnies sitting directly behind her, she grinned at their topic of conversation. It was none other than her chaperone to the event, the forever-charming, very fetching, Jarrah King.

'Oh my god, girls, just check out that King bloke, would you, he's so ruggedly scrumptious, and that scar on his face is so freaking hot,' a high-pitched voice affirmed.

'Tell me about it, Amy, that sexy beast of a man can ride me any time,' another declared.

'I wish I knew how he got it.' Amy's voice was distinctive.

A gasp was followed by 'I bet it was from a bull's horn.'

'Oh my gosh, yes! That makes him even hotter!' a new voice stated. 'If I got my hands on him, I'd do him like there's no tomorrow.'

A collective cackle was flowed by '… me too, in a heartbeat.'

'What about your boyfriend?' another said.

'He doesn't need to know about it. What happens at a rodeo stays at the rodeo, hey, girls.'

They burst into laughter, sounding like a pack of hyenas.

Millie rolled her eyes. Did they know how cheap and nasty they sounded? A sneaky glance over her shoulder confirmed they were likely in their mid-twenties and dolled up. With their low-cut tops, they were clearly keen to show their wares. As if a man like Jarrah would be interested in a much younger woman, especially one that evidently had no class at all. She knew him for the man he was now, but had he ever gone for the buckle-bunnies in the past? Her stomach roiled from a sudden shot of jealousy. A sense of protectiveness rushed over her. She bit her lip to stop from turning around and telling the pack of desperadoes to stay the hell away from her man. Because he wasn't her man, in the slightest, and she'd be making a complete fool of herself in doing so. It would be interesting to see how much attention he got at the afterparty, though, and how she'd handle it, if she stayed long enough to bear witness. Since she'd started working in the kitchen, staying up past ten-thirty was proving hard. But she had the next day off, so she should at least try to make midnight.

The hum of the crowd hushed as the announcer introduced the guy who was going to perform the national anthem. Tall and lanky, the singer wore a shirt that was starched to a crisp and his fawn felt hat was pulled low over his brow. As he reached the centre of the ring, the microphone crackled to life, and the crowd stood. Standing among her fellow Aussies, she sang the words, feeling so very proud, and so very blessed, to call Australia home.

'Righto, folks, it looks like we're ready to get the final battle of the barrel racing underway.' The compere's voice pitched with excitement as he began announcing the next competitor. 'Rose Jones is a local rider and has made a name for herself over the years, so make sure you give her a rousing entrance.'

Clapping along with the crowd, Millie was certain she'd heard of this Rose Jones before now. From what she could recall, Rose was from a farm called Jacaranda, and she'd been acing the barrel-racing circuit for over a decade. Maybe it had been when she was reading one of Jarrah's *R.M. Williams Outback* magazines that she'd come across her name. The crowd began to hush. There was a three-second pause, and then the horse exploded into action. Rose Jones and her companion leant into the corners like a Grand Prix motorbike rider would, making a tight figure eight around the barrels in mind-blowing time. The horse's stride was measured and powerful, and Rose's posture was faultless. Millie held her breath as hoofs hammered over the finishing line. A few more of the qualifiers followed, and wrapped up in the excitement of it all, before she knew it, the barrel racing was over and Rose Jones was named champion.

'Ladies and gents, girls and boys, now we've completed the barrel-racing event, next up our courageous riders are going to try and show the bulls who's boss.'

Millie sat up straighter as the first rider thundered out into the arena, hanging on for his dear life. He was thrown within two seconds. On his feet in less than that, he was sprinting for the safety of the rails with the bull hot on his heels. Getting his boot on the bottom rung, he vaulted over the top in the nick of time, barely missing being caught by the bull's deadly horns. A collective cheer rose and the bloke lifted his hat while offering a cheesy grin to his adoring fans. The bull snorted on the ground beneath him, snot flying from side to side as it looked left to right for its next target. Millie watched on in total admiration at the courage of the bullfighters, and their agility that kept the rider out of harm's way as they pushed the belligerent beast towards the gates leading to the holding yards.

Running her eyes over the tops of the railings, she met with Jarrah's silhouette just as he jumped down and disappeared behind the chutes. With the announcer's voice booming over the speakers, the guy was doing his best to work the spectators into a frenzy by telling them Jarrah had drawn the fiercest of the bulls. And he succeeded as the crowd erupted in cheers and boot stomping. The grandstand quivered from the rhythmic drumbeat of feet, but she couldn't join in the fun. Her quivering legs wouldn't be able to hold her.

Next up was a gangly bloke, who appeared to just hang on tight. He was bucked off in three seconds flat. Landing in a heap, he then stumbled to his feet and gave the crowd a wave with his hat. A goofy grin was planted on his face as he hightailed it over the fence with the bull aiming like a sniper for his back end. Another two rides ensued, with only one of the guys making it to the eight-second bell. Next up was Jarrah. Hands gripped tightly in her lap, Millie did her best to ignore the cheers and giggles of the girls behind her as she focused on his imminent ride. The big screen was honed in on him and she could see every little detail of his handsome face, including the scar that gave him more of an edge. Straddling the bull, he adjusted his grip on the strap.

Bunching its muscles, the bull bucked in the chute. It took four men to calm the situation as sweat tracked its way down her spine.

Please, God, keep him safe …

She was shocked by the awareness that she'd just asked a god she hadn't quite believed in for many years to take care of Jarrah. But there was no time to ponder her sudden belief as Jarrah nodded and the gate flew open. The bull shot out and into the arena like a cannon fired. Jarrah's left hand was high in the air as Devil's Advocate spun wildly, its trained ferocity unleashed. Man and beast danced to the beat of the spectators' hearts and the ticking of the timer. The seconds felt like hours as she held her breath. She almost wanted to close her eyes, but couldn't look away. At six seconds, the crowd were on their feet. As was she. The next two seconds felt like an eternity. But then the buzzer sounded.

Thank god!

Jarrah launched himself from Devil's Advocate's back and landed on his feet. The crowd went crazy. To her horror, the bull spun and came for him. But the bullfighters did what they did best, putting themselves between the man that had every snippet of her attention and the belligerent beast.

'I'm gonna get me some of that cowboy tonight, girls,' said a voice from behind her.

It would be over her dead body …

Not wanting to hear any more of their smut talk about a man that meant so much to her, Millie made her escape before she gave the bunch of girls a piece of her mind. She wanted to see Jarrah, to make sure he was as good as he looked when he left the arena, and to congratulate him on his perfect ride. Her footfalls quickened as she reached the bottom of the grandstand and headed in the direction of the back of the chutes.

'You looking for me, cowgirl?' A husky voice came from the shadows.

She spun, her smile wide when she spotted Jarrah among the other riders, some stretching, some sitting, and one down on his knees, praying. 'Oh, hey, Jarrah, yeah, I am.'

Going over to the railings, she leant against the cool steel. Jarrah met her on the opposite side, and his eyes danced over her before they locked onto hers. 'You enjoying the rodeo?'

'I sure am.' She liked how he kept glancing at her as he stepped away and packed his gear bag. 'That was a mighty fine ride too, King.'

'Why thankya, Mills.' He zipped up his bag and tossed it over his shoulder. 'I tell you what, though, I'm going to be bloody sore tomorrow. My body's not made for this kind of stuff anymore.' He ducked under the railings and stopped short of her. 'I need to inhale a burger with the lot, and then would you like to go grab a beer or two over at the bar?'

'Uh-huh, sounds like a plan.' Her hands in her jean pockets, she fell into step beside him. 'I didn't know you could ride like that.' She raised her voice to compete with the foot-tapping beat of the familiar Brad Paisley song blaring from the suspended speakers. 'I thought you were an amateur.'

'Ah, nope.' He offered a sideward glance and his cheeky expression matched his spirited tone. 'It's not my first rodeo.'

They joined a line of people at the burger truck. 'So you've ridden professional before?'

'A few times, yes.' His blue eyes sparkled with mesmerising spirit. 'In my past life, I was Queensland champion for two years running.'

'Really!' She gave him a playful shove. 'You never told me that.'

He chuckled. 'You never asked.'

She grinned at his reply. 'Seriously?'

They reached the counter and Jarrah stepped forwards to order. 'Did you want a burger too?'

'No, thanks, I've already eaten half a pig for dinner.' She patted her full belly. 'A roast pork roll,' she added in answer to his look of confusion.

He grinned. 'Ahh, gotcha.'

Standing aside as he placed his order, she admired the humble man he was, although she had a feeling that in that other lifetime he was referring to, he would have been quite the heartbreaker, and quite the rule breaker too. She had a rebellious side too, and she thought again how alike they were. She liked his layers, very much, and peeling each one back was a journey all on its own.

An hour and a half later, they'd enjoyed a couple of bevvies and she was relaxing into the rowdiness of the bar alongside Jarrah and his hilarious mate, Marty.

'I best get back to loading the bulls, King.' Marty tossed an arm over Jarrah's shoulder. 'Thanks for stepping up tonight. I'll catch you on the flip side, buddy.'

Jarrah gave his mate's back a hearty slap. 'No worries, and don't leave it so long between visits next time.'

'I'll do my best,' Marty affirmed with a grin almost as wide as the brim of his dusty old hat. 'It was nice to meet you, Millie.'

'You too, Marty.' She waved him off as he disappeared into the thick of the partygoers.

Jimmy Barnes' voice rang out of the massive speakers, to the party tune of 'Rising Sun'.

'Oh my gosh, I love this song,' she shrieked, jiggling on the spot.

'In that case,' Jarrah held out both his hands, beckoning for her to join him, 'can I have this dance?' He swayed in time, his boots tapping and his face a picture of absolute joy.

She almost said no, but then thought why the heck not – she hadn't seen this side of him. 'I reckon you can have this dance, yes.' She possibly hadn't ever seen this side of herself either.

Taking hold of her hands, Jarrah drew her to the dance floor, and moving in time to the catchy beat, spun her left then right, his hand never letting her go. She spotted the dolled-up girls who had been sitting behind her in the grandstands, dancing around them, moving their hips provocatively. The most boisterous of the bunch was especially vying for his attention with flirtatious glances, but Jarrah kept his gaze wholly and solely on her, making her feel like the only woman in the room. They sang the lyrics at the tops of their lungs, as did the rest of the throng. It gave rise to goosebumps all over her, just feeling part of this happy mob. It felt so good to let things be for a little while, to belong for now. She needed to do this more, let her hair down and allow her caged spirit to be free.

Boogying and bootscooting, jiving and rock-and-rolling, two upbeat songs passed them by in a flurry of singing and laughing. But then the tempo slowed, and before she had time to get out of his reach and off the dance floor, Jarrah had grabbed her, and she was now pressed up against him, his hands resting in the curve of her back and her lashes flickering against where his chest peeked out of his button-up shirt. And for once, just this once, she didn't want to fight their intense connection. For the entirety of 'Stand By Me', she wanted to do just that. She wanted to be with him, to hold him, to be embraced by him. Peace filtered through her as they swayed in time to the nostalgic Ben E. King tune. Sighing softly against his chest, she felt protected, cared for, loved. So much so that when the song came to an end and Jarrah's hands left the curve of her back, she almost cried. With his fingers entwined with hers, he led her from the dance floor and back towards the bar, where he let her go and ordered them both a beer.

She gratefully grabbed hers from him. 'Thank you.' They clinked bottle tops and she took a thirsty guzzle. 'I think you just went and broke hearts in here, choosing me for that dance.'

He simply shrugged, offered her his mischievous smile, and with a lingering glance, took a swig from his beer. She couldn't help but revel in his undivided attention, when other women were clearly trying, extremely hard, to win it. If only she didn't have to return to reality tomorrow. If only she could allow herself to fall for this majestic man. If only she could be the one to discover where the scar on his cheek came from. And learn why he was so guarded about his life and his past. If only she didn't have to remain tight-lipped about who she was, and why she'd arrived at Riverside Acres. Part of her felt as if she could trust him – no, *knew* that she could trust him. With her life, if it ever came to that. But there was way too much at stake if she opened up to him. She knew, deep down, that falling for him would be a massive risk. And for the sake of discovering the truth, she wasn't prepared to take a gamble on him, because knowing her luck she'd be the one to throw the dice and lose it all.

* * *

Tapping his boot in time to Luke Combs' song 'Beer Never Broke My Heart', Jarrah was fighting the battle of his life – the urge to draw Millie back into his arms, tip up the brim of his hat and plant his lips upon hers, so he could let her know just how much he liked her, was overwhelming. Every second he got to spend with her, he found another quality that he was powerless not to fall for. She was strong, smart and so incredibly sexy, and she was stirring something deep and primal inside him, something he liked the feeling of, one hell of a lot. And she didn't even know it. Or if she did, she wasn't one to flaunt her power, or knowledge of it. And he liked that – no, actually, he loved that about her. Resting on the edge of his barstool, bearing witness to the way she was looking at him beneath those long dark lashes – her smile as sweet as sugar, her cheeks flushed from the drinks they'd enjoyed, and her eyes filled with all-consuming spicy fire – his mind, heart and body were at odds with one another. If he'd thought himself fuelled with adrenaline when he'd been pacing behind the chutes a few hours earlier, or while he was spinning her around the dance floor, it had been nothing on what he was feeling now. Right this very second. Maybe he shouldn't have had that second shot of tequila.

Too late now, King …

He ached to make long, slow, deep love to her, all night long and then some. He wanted to learn what made her happy, discover the secrets he knew she was holding under lock and key, and make her feel the safest she'd ever been.

'So, Mills.' He gave her a little nudge. 'Are you glad you stayed now?'

'Mm-hmm.' The lips he was dying to kiss beamed his way and there was a mischievous twinkle in her eyes. 'I can't believe I'm still out, seeing it's almost two am.' She glanced around at the party that was still in full swing. 'But I don't care because this is the most fun I've had in forever.'

'I'm glad to hear it.' He felt someone bump his side, and a buxom blonde pressed between him and the woman he craved with every fibre of his being, before he could say anymore. 'Can I help you?' It annoyed him, how this stranger thought it was her right to invade his and Millie's space, and in turn, insult Millie.

Completely oblivious to the uninterested vibe he was now exuding, the early-twenties buckle-bunny leant into him, her hands going against his chest as she pressed her lips up against his ear. 'How about I help get those jeans off you, cowboy.'

'Ahh, no, thanks.' He shot from his barstool and it tumbled backwards. 'I'll pass.' He caught sight of her group of friends, watching from the sidelines. 'How about you go back to your friends and enjoy the rest of your night.'

But to his disbelief, she didn't back off. She just smiled a little smugly and brought a fingertip to trace the scar on his cheek. 'How did you get this?'

The memory of the broken glass catching his flesh as he climbed out the window to escape the fire, with Amelia Price wrapped in his arms, jarred him, but he covered it well. 'A bull got me.' *That'll do …* He took her wrist and carefully, respectfully, pushed her arm back to her side. 'Now please, go back to your friends before this gets any more uncomfortable.' He made sure his expression displayed his distaste for her unprovoked, and now very unwanted, attention.

'Really? Whatever, your loss.' None too pleased, the blonde tossed her ponytail over her shoulder, glared at him, then stamped off.

Relieved, he looked to the only woman in the room he had eyes for. 'I'm so sorry, Mills.'

'Don't worry about it.' She shook her head and laughed it off. 'It's bound to happen.' Her little shrug of nonchalance was just another quality to adore. 'Now, come on, stop sweating the small stuff and let's get out of here.' Grabbing his hand, she dragged him through the crowd, out the front door.

'Where are you taking me?' He chuckled at her determination to drag him away. 'You know the LandCruiser is thatta way.' He gestured in the opposite direction with a tip of his head.

But she didn't respond, just kept tugging him forwards. It was only when they'd reached the quiet solitude of the bushland surrounding them that she finally spoke. 'Who are you?' Her hands had let go of his and were now planted on her hips.

His heartbeat ground to a halt. 'Pardon?'

Shit! What does she know?

'I said.' She considered him with shrewd eyes as she folded her arms. 'Who. Are. You?'

He fought to keep his cool as he pulled a ridiculous, baffled face. 'I'm Jarrah King, who are you?'

'Come on.' Her head tipped to the side. 'Now's your chance to be completely honest with me.'

'I am being honest.' He huffed a breath, more to try and steady his voice. 'What's gotten into you?'

One breath, two breaths, three … they just stared at each other, wordless, motionless.

Shit!

'Sorry, don't mind me.' She sighed and looked to the starry night sky. 'I think I've just had too much to drink.'

'All good, I reckon we've both had our fair share, and then some.' Relief flooding him, Jarrah reached out and took her hand. 'Come on, you can crash in the back of my LandCruiser, and in the morning, when I've sobered up, I'll drive us home, yeah?'

She was blinking fast now, and her bottom lip was clamped between her teeth.

'Millie?'

Her forehead puckered. 'I don't know if that's a good idea.'

He wasn't going to leave her alone. 'You got a better one?'

Her shoulders lifted ever so slightly. 'Not really.'

'Right then, it's settled, you're sleeping with me.'

A little smile surfaced on her yummy lips. 'You might want to word that a little differently, King.'

His brows shot up when he realised what he'd just said. 'Oh crap, yeah, true.'

'Don't worry, I knew what you meant.' She hooked her arm into his. 'Okay, cowboy, take me to bed so I can sleep off this alcohol and wake up with a hangover.'

CHAPTER 14

The hum of the roadhouse carried into the commercial kitchen as Tommy shoved through the door, piles of dirty plates in his hands. After dumping them into the sink, he retraced his steps, leaving his air of tetchiness trailing behind him. Used to his moodiness, and now somewhat unaffected by it, Millie did her best to ignore it. She had bigger fish to fry than worrying about a moody teenager. With the temperature feeling off the charts, she plonked the tray of blueberry muffins down and fanned her flushed face with her hands. A quick check of the air conditioner confirmed it was on, as was the overhead fan. Deep down, she knew her body's furnace wasn't due to the humid weather. Every nerve in her was heightened, and her heart felt as if it had been skipping beats for the past forty-eight hours. Even now, the lingering heat fuelled by mind-blowing desire still flushed through her body.

With her job on the line if anyone found out what had happened, she knew she should feel guilty for giving in to her raging libido, but she didn't. Never in her wildest dreams had she imagined the heights Jarrah could take her to. Nor had she expected to feel so much, so intensely.

It all still felt so surreal.

Needing, wanting, craving to relive it, she closed her eyes and recalled his body pressed up against hers, skin on skin, mouth on mouth, with their hands exploring each other ravenously. She still couldn't believe what they'd gone and done, in the back of his LandCruiser, under the silvery glow of the half moon, and also under the influence of a heck of a lot of alcohol. But, along with the moving recollections, she also felt a stab of hurt as she recalled what she'd heard him say beneath his breath when she'd stepped out of his LandCruiser at first light that morning, a sight in her bedraggled clothing, feeling as if she was executing the walk of shame.

Why did you go and do that, King ...

Hurt beyond belief, she'd almost spun around, pointed her finger and outright blamed him for their reckless actions. Actions that could lead to devastating consequences if Tommy ever found out. But even though he'd made the first move, it wasn't Jarrah's fault she'd reciprocated. It took two to tango, and gee whizz did they tango together so beautifully, for hours, tucked up within his swag. Having tormented herself since overhearing him, she wished she'd turned around and at the very least demanded he explain why he regretted what they'd done. Because she sure as hell didn't. And they'd barely acknowledged each other since – the angst between them was killing her.

Frustrated, hurt, worried out of her mind about how they were going to act normal around each other now, she realised she was clenching her hands into fists. Opening her eyes and drawing in a few deep breaths, she forced herself to relax. The sound of the four-wheeler motorbike coming to a stop outside drew her attention to where Jarrah was alighting. Before she could take a beat, her heart leapt towards him, and the ache it left behind winded her. Watching Scruff sticking loyally to his master's side, she blinked back hot tears. No way was she going to shed another tear after crying herself to sleep the past two nights. She was done with the merry-go-round of self-pity and then beating herself up. She had to get a damn grip on the steering wheel of her life. Otherwise, the web she'd woven by succumbing to her emotions was going to get her caught up and eaten alive if she wasn't careful. She needed to get to the bottom of why she'd come here in the first place, as soon as she could, and then get the hell out of Riverside. But what questions was she meant to ask, and to who, without drawing attention to herself?

Turning away from the window, she got back to chopping onions for tomorrow's special of a fetta, spinach and onion quiche. She turned her mind towards more important matters, like who she thought was behind her letter: she veered from Tommy, to Jarrah, then back to Tommy. Or maybe it had been the both of them, or neither. Maybe it was Penny and Jenny, or Mack, or Graham, or Marty, or … oh my goodness, could it have been Jasmine? She gasped with the thought. Frustration had her chopping angrily. After two weeks here, she was none the wiser to anything, and she was beginning to tire of pretending she was someone that she was not. She was sick of not knowing who was behind it all. She was sick and tired of not knowing who she could trust. And who she couldn't. Slamming her knife down, she felt her entire body vibrate with impatience. She wanted to know the truth. Before the end of the week, come hell or high water, she was going to unearth the buried secrets that hid here at Riverside Acres.

Tommy stomped back into her space with another armful of dirty plates. This time he didn't just dump them, but instead began rinsing and stacking the plates into the dishwasher. Like a bull confined in a china shop, his bad mood was omnipresent. Everything he put down was slammed. Every one of his footsteps was stomped, and the constant huffs and puffs made it sound as if he was having a whole heated dialogue within himself. Even though she was doing her very best to ignore him, Millie couldn't help but feel as if she was treading on eggshells as she manoeuvred around him. Working in this kind of environment was wearing thin. But what choice did she have? With her heart heavy and her mind weary from spinning in circles, she was very close to exploding. And that wasn't going to be pretty, if she, for lack of her better judgement, did. As if sensing the building tension from outside, Scruff appeared and whined a little from the opposite side of the flyscreen door.

Pausing to greet the only living thing here she fully trusted right now, Millie glanced to where Scruff had his nose pressed up against the screen and her heavy heart instantly lightened. 'Hey, buddy,' she said softly. Strolling towards him, she pressed the screen open and, stooping down, gave his head a ruffle. 'Would you like some of the meat scraps that I've saved for you?'

Tommy pushed past her, sending her off balance as he stomped outside. 'Excuse you,' she called after him.

Ignoring her, Tommy stuffed a cigarette between his lips then, striking his lighter, lit it as he walked away from her.

'What the actual f—' Her anger at boiling point, she shot to her feet and followed him out. 'Tommy.' She lengthened her stride to keep up with him. 'What in the hell was that all about? Tommy, don't ignore me!'

Ironclad silence ensued as he just kept on walking.

'Well, eff you!' she roared before her self-control had a look-in.

Tommy stopped in his tracks and spun to face her. 'What did you just say to me?' His narrowed gaze was cutthroat.

'You heard me.' She swallowed down a huge lump of regret.

He took slow, steady, menacing steps towards her. 'You do know that I'm your boss, don't you?'

'Yes, but,' she blinked as she fought for an answer, 'how about you try acting like one?'

Time stretched. She could hear her pulse pounding in her ears as Tommy glared at her.

'If you want me to respect you as my boss, you can't treat me like you do, Tommy.' Even though the way he was looming over her made her extremely uncomfortable, she refused to step back. 'I deserve to be treated like every other employee here.'

'You know what, I've thought long and hard about you the past couple of days.' Tommy inched another step into her space. 'You're not actually on the books, because we have to pay you cash, Millie.' An odd smile played on his lips. 'Therefore, there's no trace of you ever being an employee here, so don't play the "I'm an employee with rights" card with me.' He smirked at her lack of response. 'I'm onto you, Millie no last name.' Spreading his two fingers he pointed to his eyes and then to her. 'My eyes are on you. Always.'

Well, not always, or he would know about … 'What do you mean by that?' Her rapid pulse made her feel as if she were tap-dancing through a minefield.

He shrugged smugly.

He was clearly enjoying toying with her, the son of a …

Scruff came to her side and sat protectively in front of her, his gaze glued to Tommy.

'Huh, looks like you got this one around your little finger too.' He shook his head and huffed. 'Eff me, what's this place coming to?'

Bristling, she held her tongue as she watched him storm away from her. Only when he was out of sight did she release the breath she was holding. If he was trying to get her to completely lose her temper, it was going to take a lot more than that to rattle her cage. But if this was a case of him letting her know that he was privy to why she was there, then he'd certainly hit his mark. Was she right in thinking he was the one who'd sent her the letter that had her driving three thousand kilometres to here? Because he was definitely her number one suspect right about now.

'Hey, Millie.' Jarrah's voice carried from the opposite side of the driveway.

'Hey, Jarrah.' Her reply sounded strangled as she fought to rein in her rising panic.

His smile as wide as the bright blue sky, he wandered towards her with an easy gait, as though nothing had happened, as though they hadn't avoided each other like the plague the past two days. As he neared her, the air was suddenly teeming with his captivating testosterone, and it triggered her fight or flight response. But she couldn't run. She had to stand here and try and pretend she felt nothing. Wanting, needing, to act normal, she desperately tried to slow her racing heartbeat so she could at least string together a comprehensible sentence.

Pull yourself together, Price. He's just a man. That you slept with. And now …

There was a slightly awkward pause before he broke her train of thought. 'How did you pull up Sunday arvo, after such a big night?'

Was he serious? Clearing her throat, she stumbled over a mountain of words as she tried to do the same as him, and ignore the elephant standing between them. 'Hmm.' She squinted into the glare of the sun. 'I was a bit seedy.' She chuckled in a bid to hide her nerves. 'And I have to admit that my hangover headache is still lingering.'

'Well, I got a cure for that.' He held up two beers that she hadn't noticed were in his hands, and passed her one. 'Hair of the dog, works a treat.'

'Can't, but thanks.' Her gaze snagged on the arms that had held her so possessively tight two nights ago. 'I'm still on the clock.'

'Now?' He glanced at his watch. 'It's five-thirty, Mills, you should have knocked off ages ago.'

The fact that he shortened her name annoyed her this time around. 'Yeah, maybe, but I was just getting some prep done.'

'You work way too hard here.' He held the beer out again. 'Knock off for the day and enjoy a well-deserved cold one.'

Her head spinning, she took it from him and gladly took a swig to hide her trembling lips. 'Ahh, yup, it tastes better than I thought it would.'

'See, I told you.' His smile, and dimples, deepened. 'Should we pull up stumps while we enjoy these bad boys?'

She tipped her head. 'Stumps?'

'Yeah, the stumps, over there.' He pointed to two short upright logs, beneath the shade of the big old gum tree. 'For seats.'

'Ha, you meant literally.' How did this man have such an uncanny way of unburdening her heart in an instant? A feat considering he was the main cause of her load.

'Or do you want to kick back on my verandah and watch the sun bow out for the day?' There was something unfathomable within his gaze.

She needed to find out what it was. 'The verandah might be a little more comfortable.'

'True that, come on then.' He waved her towards the homestead.

After a tongue-tied stroll, they sat side by side on the day bed, a decent gap between them as they gazed out at the view that she'd come to love with all her heart. Jarrah's horsey, leathery scent lured her the entire time they drank their beers and chatted about everything but the obvious. She'd never been so physically aware of a man as she was with him, and her attraction to him was driving her nuts. Oh how she wished she could just get over him. Like he apparently had gotten over her. And now they were back to being friends. Just. Friends. The contemplation angered and hurt her. She bit back the need to tell him. *Maybe being here is a mistake*. She needed to go. Now.

Quickly finishing her beer, she stood. 'Thanks for the bevvy, Jarrah, I better get back to it and let you do the same.'

'Our first one went down way too fast.' Jarrah shot to his feet. 'I'm just going to duck inside and grab us another.' He hesitated. 'That's if you want one?' His gaze pleaded with her.

Even though she was confused by his desperation for her to stay, when he'd very clearly been avoiding her the past couple of days, she nodded. 'Okay, just one more, and then I'll go lock up the kitchen and head home for a shower and some dinner.' Her curiosity as to whether or not he'd raise what they'd gone and done was overriding her level-headedness.

Leaning against the banister while she waited for him to return, both for support from her buckling knees and needing a distraction, she drew in a deep breath as she admired the tropical panorama that Jarrah worked tirelessly to keep looking so pristine. She was so immersed in the exquisiteness of it all, she jumped when she heard the back screen door slap shut.

Spinning around, she couldn't believe what she was looking at. 'What in the heck are you doing?' Her eyes narrowed with amused suspicion.

Offering her a confident smile, Jarrah finished strapping his wacky apron on. 'I'm going to cook us dinner.'

Her eyes widened, as did her smile. 'Oh my gosh, Jarrah, you loon.' She cracked up laughing as she pointed at the nude old-man bod skilfully printed on the apron in a way that made his head look like it was attached to some nudist hippy. 'That's freaking hilarious.'

He pulled a confused face. 'I don't know what you're on about.'

'Oh, stop it, you know exactly what I'm on about.'

He briefly looked down, and then brought his mischievous gaze back to hers. 'Oh, you mean this old thing?' He pointed to it. 'I thought it might give you a chuckle.'

'Well, your plan worked a treat.' She accepted another beer from him and went and settled herself back on the day bed while he cooked a couple of scotch fillets.

It didn't take him more than half an hour to have dinner prepped and on the outside table. Her steak was cooked to perfection, charred on the outside, yet juicy on the inside. And the potato bake, along with his version of an Italian salad, buffalo mozzarella and all – good lord, she was in heaven. She couldn't help but think he'd planned on having her here all along, in the hope she'd join him. But for what reason? Was he about to say things she didn't want to hear? No. She wouldn't let him. She needed to get in first and put a stop to this. It was now or never.

'Jarrah, about the other night, I ….'

Leaning forwards, he pressed a finger to her lips, and in that connected moment, she swore she saw flames dancing in his blue eyes. The attraction between them was undeniable, but that didn't mean she had to do something about it. On the contrary, she needed to put an end to it.

'Whether you like it or not …' Sitting back, she took a beat. 'We have to talk about it.'

Sighing, Jarrah nodded. 'I know we do.' He sat up straighter and met her gaze once again. 'I'm sorry for doing something so reckless and stupid.'

'Reckless I get, but stupid?' She couldn't hide how much his revelation hurt. 'Thanks for that, Jarrah.'

'No, you've got it all wrong.' He stood and came to her side of the table. 'Do you mind?'

She scooted along the bench seat and turned towards him. 'Keep going, because I'm all ears.'

Shifting uneasily, he wrung his hands and cleared his throat. 'You deserve way more than a bloke shagging you in the back of a LandCruiser.'

'Wow.' She flinched from the stab of hurt. 'That's how you see what we did? A shag?'

'No, not at all.' He huffed. 'Faaark me, I'm so crap at this.' Frustration crinkled the corners of his eyes as he momentarily squeezed them shut. 'Please, just give me a sec to find the right words.'

Seeing just how much he was struggling, she remained quiet but placed a hand on his bouncing knee, steadying him. How could she not care for the man who owned so much of her heart?

The windows to his soul met with hers and remained there. 'I like you, Mills, a lot, probably way too much given I've only known you for a couple of weeks. But in a really weird way, it honestly feels like I've known you for most of my life.' A wary smile surfaced. 'And I suppose, in a way, I was hoping you feel the same about me.'

Totally blindsided, with half of her heart rejoicing and the other half retreating, she took a little bit before she could answer. 'So you're saying you want whatever this is to go further than the other night?'

'Do you?' His gaze was hopeful.

'I'm not sure, I …' Words got stuck in her throat. Jarrah had no idea who she was or why she was here. They were living a lie. This, them, couldn't happen. But she desperately wanted it to. 'I wish …'

The lump of emotion grew bigger, halting any hope she had of answering him as the fifteen years of grief she'd tried so hard to push down, to hide from the world, began to bubble to the surface, as if trying to reveal who she really was to him, so they could jump the hurdle and be together. Forever.

Stop this nonsense, Millie, right now!

Blinking faster, she struggled to take a breath as gathering tears made Jarrah's concerned face blurry.

'Hey, Millie, I'm here.' His strong arms came around her. 'Just take a breath. That's it, slowly, hold it, then exhale.' His voice was soothing, yet strong. 'I've got you, you're safe, and everything's going to be okay.'

Leaning against him, she surrendered, and sobbed into his shoulder as he soothed her by stroking her back. His manly scent enveloped her, and for a few breaths, she felt weightless, safe, valued. Little did this wonderful, big-hearted man know that nothing was okay, that everything about being here felt dishonest. And deeply wrong. But for one second, followed by another, and another, she allowed herself to tumble into their false reality, where she believed that he could shield her from anything or anyone ever hurting her again. And as he held her close, she permitted him to peek over the wall she'd so methodically built, so he could see all the broken bits of her, and somehow, in his own unique way, make her feel whole again. Because she sincerely trusted he'd be able to do just that. If only she could allow herself to freely love him, and for him to freely love her. But that meant telling him exactly who she was and why she was here. And by doing that she had a gut feeling she'd find out exactly who he was, and why she was lured here, to be around him, to get to know him. What if he'd been involved in the deaths of her family? The extreme thought jarred her, terrified her. Inhaling one last breath of him, she quickly untangled from his arms and slid out of his reach.

'Millie, please, let me help you.'

She shook her head. She didn't want to believe that he was capable of such evil. The silence between them lengthened, stretched, and then reached a point of being uncomfortable.

'Are you going to be okay?' His tone was so gentle, so caring.

Taking a deep breath, she nodded. 'As okay as I can be, yes.'

His hand went to reach for her, but then dropped back to his side. 'Is there anything I can do to make this easier on you?'

'Thanks, Jarrah,' she said hurriedly. 'Honestly, I'll be fine. You've got enough on your plate, you don't need to worry about me.' She stood and eased out from behind the table. 'I'm going to go now, thanks for dinner.'

And before she broke down again and allowed him to comfort her once more, she hightailed it across the verandah, down the steps, and into the enclosing darkness without looking back.

CHAPTER 15

Tommy, Millie, Tommy, Millie ... why do the two people I care for the most in this world have to be so far out of my reach?

Tossing and turning for what felt like the hundredth time, Jarrah rolled onto his side and squinted at his alarm clock to see 3.23 am glaring back at him. A quick glance through his parted curtains confirmed this to be true, as a sea of brightly sparkling stars pinpricked the velvet black sky. The burdens weighing down upon his heart had meant he hadn't slept a wink, and he was done with trying everything from counting backwards to counting sheep, then cows, then chickens for heaven's sake, to the last resort of listening to a guided sleep meditation that did nothing but annoy him when the person kept telling him how to breathe. Thanks to his spiralling thoughts of both Tommy and Millie, his lack of sleep would undoubtedly be an unwelcome guest throughout his long day ahead.

With a heavy sigh he resigned himself to the fact that he wouldn't be sleeping anytime soon. Especially not when thoughts of Millie and how she couldn't get away from him quick enough were circling his mind. He didn't want to regret telling her he liked her, but it was hard when her silence made him feel as though his feelings weren't reciprocated. His only saving grace was his certainty that he couldn't have imagined the powerful connection he'd felt with her when they'd become one beneath the starry sky. And the way she'd broken down and sobbed against him the night before. It was as if she did like him more than a friend, but couldn't allow herself to admit it. It made him wonder if there was another reason, or reasons, she was shutting him out. Was she married? It would fit with her not wanting to give him her last name. Was it her husband she was running from, hiding from? Or were her secrets ones that would shock him to his very core?

Quit overthinking everything, King …

It had been a stupid idea, giving in to his craving to caress her every inch, but at the time, when she'd surrendered to his touch and given all of herself over to him with unbridled passion, he'd never felt so wanted, so uninhibited, so deeply moved. He could still hear her gasps, her sighs, could still feel her fingers trailing up his back, her nails digging into him as she reached the pinnacle of ecstasy, and how she shuddered when he'd brought her to the peak of euphoria. Then the way she'd looked at him afterwards, with her head resting on his chest and her smile soft and dreamy, she'd completely and utterly won him over. He could still taste her sweetness and feel the beat of her heart pressed up against his, and as each day passed, all of this only made him ache for her more. There was a prowling need inside of him that she'd stirred to life, a need he wasn't sure would ever be fulfilled without her being his lover, his companion, his – dare he think it – wife and mother of his children. He knew he wouldn't just exist with her by his side. He'd live a full life with her. The kind of life that would leave a lingering smile upon his lips whenever it was that he took his last breath. And then he'd wait for her in the afterlife. He'd have to go first, because he wouldn't be able to live on this earth without her. And yet he was facing that very miserable prospect with her leaving here, forever.

Ahhh, Millie, I want to know who you really are …

For now, he knew she was so much more intricate than he'd first imagined her to be. There were parts of her he already recognised and identified with on the deepest of levels, and yet there was so much more to learn, to know, to adore her for. Intimately, both physically and spiritually, she'd known just how to evoke the very parts of him that he'd buried down deep. Fragments of his former self that reminded him he *was* a man who longed for soul-deep love. The thought of never being able to experience such an intense, profound moment with her ever again made his heart echo with the same old emptiness that she had filled so exquisitely with her touch, her kiss, her whispers of desire.

With her memory as his only companion, he stretched out on his king-size bed and stared up at the ceiling, praying daylight would come soon so he could try and distract his thoughts with some hard labour. He knew there were way more things he should have said to her last night, *could have* said. But he'd found himself tongue-tied for fear of scaring her even more than his revelation of liking her did. How in the hell was he meant to put such complex emotions into words without sounding like a crazy man? He knew if Tommy got wind of his sentiments, and just how far he'd taken them the night of the rodeo, his nephew would be like a dog with a bone. And they had enough to sort out between them without adding this to the mix.

He needed to be very careful.

And he needed to get up and do some work, before he drove himself nuts.

Climbing out of his tousled bed, he did just that.

By midday, he'd worked himself to the bone, but Millie still occupied a large portion of his mind. Too weary to try and combat her possession of his thoughts any longer, he gave up the fight. It was a battle he was never going to win. And the same could be said for the situation with Tommy. It was going to be up to his nephew to make the right choices. There was nothing he was going to be able to do, or say, to stop Tommy entering into Carlo's dark underworld if that's what he wanted to do. Joey had been proof of that, and Tommy was so much like his father. Sadly, Jarrah's instincts told him that Tommy was going to have to learn the hard way. He just hoped and prayed it wasn't going to be with his life. Hopefully, fate would play its hand in ending the toxic relationship between grandfather and grandson before it grew into a poisonous, suffocating weed. God, how he hated his father with every fibre of his being – and he was certain that, unlike Millie, his father reciprocated his feelings.

Climbing behind the wheel of his LandCruiser, he then turned in a slow circle, making sure to be steady with the accelerator so he didn't send dust spiralling out behind him and towards the homestead, where it would settle on everything in sight. After almost a week of dry weather, he needed some rain to help compact the dirt driveway, and by the looks of the black clouds marching over the mountains, a storm was on the way. Wanting the fresh air, he wound down his window, and by the time he'd driven past the roadhouse and motel rooms, rain-scented wind gusted in. He smiled to himself. The encroaching tropical storm wasn't far off.

A gunshot rang out, echoing, reverberating.

What in the hell?

Another shot trailed the first and it came from the direction of the machinery shed. He floored the accelerator, hoping to god nobody was hurt, or worse. Skidding to a sliding stop, he killed the engine. Seconds later, Tommy strode past the bonnet, a saddle over one arm and a shotgun in his hand. His cocky gait didn't scream emergency.

Jarrah rested his forearm on the windowsill. 'Is everything okay here, Tommy?'

'Yup, right as rain.' Tommy just kept on walking. 'Nothing to see here,' he hollered over his shoulder.

'Righto, smartarse,' Jarrah grumbled. Sucking in a fortifying breath, he stepped out and followed Tommy into the shade of the shed. 'Is there a problem I need to know about?' He looked at the gun sceptically.

'Why do you ask?' Tommy dumped the saddle in his arms onto the sawhorse.

'For Christ's sake, half the town would have heard those two gunshots, Tommy.'

'Oh, that.' Tommy arched a sly brow as he unlocked and opened the door of the gun cabinet. 'It was nothing.' He placed the shotgun back and slammed the door shut, locking it again.

Jarrah bristled as he waited for Tommy to turn and face him. 'Nothing?'

'Yeah, nothing.' Hands making fists at his sides, Tommy looked like he was fighting the urge to throw a punch.

'You know the rules about guns here, Tommy.' Jarrah was fighting to keep his tone cool, calm and collected. 'We only get them out if the feral pigs become a danger to us, our livestock, or our customers.'

'Yeah, I know.' Tommy plucked his phone out from his back pocket and began scrolling.

In another time, another place, Jarrah might have grabbed Tommy by his collar and made him listen up. He shoved his hands into his pockets to stop from doing just that. 'So what did you shoot at then?'

Tommy kept on scrolling as he shrugged. 'A couple of empty cans.'

'So let me get this straight.' Adrenaline making it hard to stand still, Jarrah shifted from boot to boot. 'You know the rules, but you decided to break them.'

Tommy shrugged again. 'Looks that way.'

'Bloody hell, Tommy, could you put your phone down for a minute.' Jarrah heaved a sigh.

As he lifted his eyes, Tommy's stare was frosty as he shoved his phone into the back pocket of his jeans. 'Right you are, boss man.' There was a stubborn set to his jaw and a hint of loathing in his gaze.

'Tommy, come on, mate, you don't still believe that BS your grandfather told you about me being involved with your parents' deaths, do you?'

Silence was Jarrah's only reply as Tommy stormed out of the tack shed.

Bitter disappointment, coupled with overwhelming hurt, swept through Jarrah. But as much as he wanted to have it out once and for all with his temperamental nephew, he zipped his mouth shut. Words said in heat were usually regretted. There'd be no benefit in arguing with him. Step by stomping step, Tommy wasn't only burning his bridge here at Riverside Acres, he was essentially blowing it to smithereens. There was only so much of this attitude he could take, before sending Tommy on his merry way. The very thought sent his heart plummeting. Then there was the aching weight of Millie. He needed to go over to the roadhouse and try to smooth over any remaining uncomfortableness with her. They were friends. And she worked for him. He didn't want her leaving here any sooner than she planned to because it felt awkward between them. Again.

His strides long and deliberate, it didn't take him long to reach the back screen door. 'Howdy doody, Millie.' The screen slapped closed behind him as he stepped into the buzz of the kitchen.

She turned to him, flour smudges upon her cheeks. 'Oh hey, Jarrah.'

He was going to get straight to the point. 'I'm sorry about last night.'

'Don't worry about it.' She bit down on her bottom lip, and kept it clamped between her teeth as she unpacked the dishwasher.

Her silence destroyed any hope he'd had of them going back to some kind of normalcy. With all his heart he wanted to close the distance and give her a hug. But he was worried if he risked touching her, she would flicker like an image upon water, then disappear like a mirage, leaving him aching even more to know what could have been if he'd held his horses and allowed things to fall into place.

Say something, King, anything to fill this horrible silence …

'Are we all good, Millie?' It was fairly evident they weren't, but he didn't know what else to say.

Nodding then plonking the cutlery basket on the bench, she rested a hip against the side of the counter as she started to unpack everything, but still said nothing. Jarrah's voice of reason roared. This was so hard. She felt so far away from him and he hated this gaping divide. It was taking every bit of willpower he could muster not to grab her and declare everything all over again, more passionately this time, in the hope she'd rise up on her tippy toes, wrap her arms around his neck, and kiss him like she never wanted to let him go. He could try and smooth things over all he wanted, so they could return to being friends, but he couldn't deny that he was crazy about her. Actually, he was crazier than crazy. He was boots over head, inevitably, undoubtedly, falling harder for her as each day passed.

'What is it, Jarrah? I can see you need to tell me something else.' She threw a glance in his direction. 'So just say it, please.'

He fidgeted a little, wishing he could come right out and speak his truth, but fear of a second rejection halted him. 'I was just going to ask if your Jimny is running good now.'

She shook her head and her blonde ponytail swept over her shoulder. 'I see what you're doing and I'm not playing that game.' She went back to the dishwasher and dumped the empty cutlery holder inside before shutting the door and turning all her attention to him. 'I know I basically ran off last night, and I'm sorry about that. It's just, I wasn't ready for you to tell me something so *intense*, and I panicked.'

'Me liking you doesn't have to be so,' he grimaced at the way she'd pronounced it, '*intense*.'

'I'm not planning on sticking around here, Jarrah, so there's no use in us trying to make something out of this, wouldn't you agree?'

'Yes, and no.'

'Which one is it, Jarrah?' She huffed. 'Yes or no?'

'Honestly, it's both.'

Scruff had joined them, and was looking from one to the other, his kind brown eyes clouded with worry and his forehead puckered.

Millie hunkered down to his height. 'It's okay, buddy, we're all good here.' There was extraordinary compassion in Scruff's eyes as she gave his head a loving ruffle.

Witnessing just how much Scruff adored her, a pang of yearning struck Jarrah's heart, strong enough to send his hand to his chest to try and somehow soothe it. With all her attention on Scruff, he closed his eyes, taking a moment to will the sensation away. Deep breath in, deep breath out. Millie's soft sigh had him opening his eyes to meet hers.

'I'm guessing there's a lot we don't know about each other, Jarrah, and we're not going to peel back the layers in the short amount of time I'm here.' She placed a gentle hand on his arm. 'Therefore, I don't want to step over any more boundaries, because I don't want to hurt you, and I don't want you to hurt me.' Even though she was softly smiling, there were tears in her eyes.

The pain of witnessing her despair almost snapped him in two. 'I totally understand, Millie.' He cleared his throat and nodded. 'I'll leave you to get back to it, then.'

Before she could bear witness to his own raw emotions, he strode out and into the sunshine, desperate to catch the breath she'd just stolen from him. Tomorrow, he'd return to his motto of never looking back, because he wasn't going that way. Not ever. Not even for Tommy. And as for him and Millie, that dreamlike night was a thing of the past too. Their chance was gone. And there'd be no second chances. For any of them.

* * *

The following morning, Millie couldn't get enough of the salty sea breeze as it tossed rolling waves onto the shore and tousled her loose hair. Perfect imprints of her bare feet and Scruff's paws trailed behind her in the soft, wet sand as she made her way towards the jetty. Her plan was to sit on it for a little while, her legs dangling over the edge and her attention in the moment. Because after pining over Jarrah the last couple of days and lying awake half the night crying about what they could have had under different circumstances, she needed to centre herself, and the only way to do that was to get away from Riverside Acres, and Jarrah, for a couple of hours. And what better place than the beach to come and air out her heart on her day off?

Above, seagulls dipped and dived, calling to one another. She enjoyed the crunch of sand between her toes as she wandered the horseshoe-shaped coastline. Tilting her floppy straw hat to ward off the golden rays of sunlight, she gazed dreamily towards where the water met with the horizon. The breath of the ocean was helping to soothe her soul, along with putting things into perspective. One more week, that was what she was giving this venture, before she packed her bags, said goodbye to Jarrah and Scruff – no need for such sentiments for Tommy – and headed back to Sydney. Staying here any longer would only complicate things further. After almost three weeks there, she was none the wiser as to who had sent the letter, and why she'd been told to come there. Woefully, she was starting to believe it had been a waste of time, and whoever was behind the letter had known that, and the sick son of a bitch was enjoying controlling her life as if she were a puppet.

Scruff raced ahead of her, his nose poking into the holes that the little crabs had escaped into. She wished she could strip off, race to the water's edge and plunge beneath the waves, but who knew what was lurking there. The crocodile warning signs, as well as the newspaper clippings Jarrah had pinned behind the bar, had worked on her – unlike some other people who dared to brave the water. Even Scruff was being constantly reminded to get away from the edge of the water. She'd been hesitant to bring him, but Jarrah had insisted, saying Scruffball would keep her safe from any weirdos. She found his need to protect her endearing. Not that she was going to allow the feeling to spread. He'd gotten beneath her armour once and she couldn't let him do it again.

Reaching the jetty, she called Scruff back to her side. 'Come on, buddy, let's go and ponder the meaning of life for a little bit, hey.'

Scruff was eager to do whatever she wanted to, and his nails clipped the timber boards as they traipsed towards where a rainbow stretched from one side of the water to the other. And then, with nowhere left to go, she and her mate sat side by side, both staring into the distance. By the time she decided to turn her Jimny around and head back to Riverside Acres, it was almost two hours later.

Wandering over from the stables, Jarrah met her as she pulled up. With dark rings beneath his eyes, a slight slump to his shoulders and in need of a shave, he looked utterly worn out. She felt for him, probably way too much. And she wanted to nurture him, to somehow make him feel better. Just like he'd done for her. In so many ways. But she couldn't.

Scruff leapt through the window in his excitement to greet his master. 'Did you enjoy your trip to the beach, mate?' Chuckling, Jarrah ruffled his floppy ears.

'He sure did.' Tossing her tote bag over her shoulder, Millie hopped out and went to Jarrah's side. 'He even sat and contemplated life with me for a couple of hours.'

Footfalls approached, and she caught the stench of alcohol as Tommy stomped past her. Swaying a little as he approached Jarrah, he was evidently drunk. This wasn't going to go well. Not in the slightest. Hooking her fingers into Scruff's collar, she held him beside her and held her breath, praying she was wrong.

'So what are you pair up to, huh?' Folding his arms while trying to stand on unsteady legs, Tommy eyed them. 'Is there something I should know about?'

It was a loaded question. One that Jarrah very clearly wasn't in the mood to answer. And he didn't. 'Go home and sleep the booze off, Tommy.'

Scowling, Tommy snapped in response, 'Why don't you go and get stuffed, Jarrah.'

Jarrah scowled back. 'I'm done talking, Tommy.'

For a split second Tommy looked as if he was about to grab Jarrah's collar. 'Yeah, righto, whatever.' He staggered away, and back towards his room. 'I'm watching you two.'

Looking to Millie, Jarrah held his hands up in the air, a gesture that said *I'm at a loss.*

She felt for him, so much. 'You good?'

'No, but yeah.'

She couldn't leave him like this. 'Do you want to have a beer and mull it over with me?'

'I don't feel like mulling it over, but as for the beer, yeah, why not.' He took off his Akubra and ran a hand through his hair. 'Your place or mine?'

'I think yours, my neighbour's a little cantankerous.' Referring to Tommy, she grinned, trying to ease the heavy air he'd left behind.

'Agreed.' Jarrah returned her grin. 'Done deal.'

Grabbing them both a beer from the outside fridge, and then heading inside to turn on the stereo – Garth Brooks' honky-tonk voice soon rang out – Jarrah reappeared, clicking his fingers and singing the lyrics to 'Long Neck Bottle' as he plonked down beside her on the day bed. He bouncily bumped shoulders with her, catching her eyes and trying to encourage her into a sing-along. It was the closest she'd been to him in days, and an avalanche of emotions crashed down upon her. Swigging her beer, she did her best to shake off heart-wrenching sentiments as she laughed at his antics. They were friends. And that was that. She needed to grasp this fact. Even though she longed to grasp him.

Stop with your schoolgirl nonsense, Millie …

Halfway through the song, Jarrah leapt to his feet and bopped from side to side. 'Dance with me.'

'Pfft, no.' She planted her butt further into the day bed. 'I'll stay spectator, thank you.'

'Oh come on, Millie, don't be a spoilsport.' He circled around and then held out his hand. 'It's a fun song, and it'll make me feel better if you dance with me.' His eyes implored her. 'Pleeeease.'

'Oh, for goodness sake, I will, but only if it will stop you being so damn annoying.' Jumping up, she spiritedly held out her hand, and he took it. 'Woooh,' she squealed, as he country-style rocked and rolled her across the verandah.

Millie lost herself in their merriment as they enjoyed the music. Scruff joined in too, playfully nipping at their heels with his tail spinning in excited circles. Once again, it was just the three of them, living their best lives while living in the moment. Jarrah had this knack of bringing her right into the present and holding her there, nice and tight, so she couldn't focus on anything else but each passing second spent with him. Everything they'd been battling faded into the background, and she was right back where she'd been the night of the rodeo, before they'd torn each other's clothes off – helplessly, head-over-heels, falling for him. Then the song changed, as did the tempo, and 'The Dance' echoed. Jarrah kept hold of her and placed a hand in the curve of her back. Relieved to not be looking him in the eyes, for fear of losing all self-control, she rested against him. She knew every word of the moving song like the back of her hand. And how fitting it was. It was all about it being best not to know how things will end, because if you did, then you may deprive yourself of some of the most beautiful experiences – she might miss the pain, but then she might also miss the dance. And she didn't want to miss dancing with Jarrah, because he made her feel as though she was floating on air.

As if reading her thoughts, he smiled down at her, and the earth shifted beneath her gliding feet. Electricity arced between them, settling in her stomach like a million butterflies' wings as she felt herself slipping back into him, becoming one like they had that unforgettable night beneath the stars. But this time they were fully dressed, and they'd be remaining that way.

CHAPTER 16

Gripping her shopping trolley tight, Millie tried to ignore the eerie sense that someone was watching her. At the end of each aisle, she paused and glanced over her shoulder, her suspicions not justified. Even so, panic prickled her scalp and had the hair rising on the back of her neck. Drawing in a breath, she wiped her sweaty hands on her shorts and told herself to calm down. But two aisles later and the creepy sensation still wouldn't leave her alone. Pausing in front of the dairy fridge, she could see the reflected outline of what she considered to be a man a couple of metres behind her. She spun on her heel, ready to catch her stalker, but there was nobody there. Turning back to the fridge door, the silhouette had gone. A shiver ran down her spine.

She wasn't losing it.

She wasn't seeing things.

Convinced she was being followed, she left her trolley and took hurried steps so she could glimpse up every single aisle in quick succession. There were people, like her, out doing their shopping, but nobody stood out as suspicious. Shaking her head, she considered leaving, but she needed the groceries in her trolley to make Jarrah dinner tonight, like she'd promised. Her chilli con carne topped with spicy guacamole was her way of saying thanks for all the meals he'd cooked for her, so she wasn't going to let some unnerving hunch have her leaving here empty-handed. She was also going to let him know she'd be leaving as soon as he found a replacement for the cook's position. She'd already extended her stay a few weeks longer than planned, so a week preferably, two weeks tops, was the limit of her time left here. It was a conversation she'd been avoiding the past couple of days, but it had to be done.

Returning to her trolley, she sucked in a breath, squared her shoulders and took determined steps. Gathering what she needed, along with an impromptu few ingredients to make Eton mess with fresh berries, she lined up at the tills. A commotion behind her had her spinning to see a pile of cereal boxes that had just been knocked to the floor, and then she caught sight of Tommy out of the corner of her eye, slipping through the sliding front doors of the IGA. Apprehension filled her. Fear whispered in her ears. Everything she'd been feeling while wandering the aisles slipped into place. Tommy had been her stalker. She was certain of it. But why? What did he think he was going to uncover by sneaking around, following her? With her suspicions, shouldn't it be her that was spying on him?

After placing the bags of groceries into the back of her Jimny, she climbed behind the steering wheel and took a moment to gather her nerves and her thoughts. She'd been suspicious of Tommy the second she'd met him, and all throughout her three weeks at Riverside Acres he'd done nothing but made her feel extremely unwelcome. What did he know? How was he tied to the night her family died? What did he gain by dragging her all the way here, only to treat her like crap? Surely there was more substance to the letter, and the photograph, than that. She had to find a way to unearth the buried secrets here. And when she did, because by hook or by crook she was going to, there'd be consequences for whoever thought it would be gratifying to drag her over the hot coals of her past to be here. And all for what? A sick joke? Revenge? To harm her? Well, she'd be ready. So bring it on.

Standing out the front of her motel room a couple of hours later, she savoured the scent of her chilli con carne simmering away on the little two-burner stove inside. The sun had hit its peak, blasted heat, and now, thankfully, late-afternoon shadows stretched out as it sank away, providing shade from what had been a day of relentless sunshine. She glanced at her watch. Jarrah would be arriving soon, and she marvelled at how she wasn't wearing a bit of make-up, not even her usual brush of lip gloss, her hair was a tousled mess, and she was dressed in baggy shorts and a sloppy T-shirt, and she didn't care one bit. It felt good to feel so comfortable around a man, especially one as eye-catching as Jarrah. She just hoped her chilli lived up to his expectations – she'd built them up a fair bit over the last couple of weeks.

Tossing the stick for Scruff, she put her hands to her hips as she waited for him to retrieve it and bring it back for what felt like the hundredth time. She'd come out to her patio to sit back and enjoy the views, to enjoy some Zen-like downtime before she had to have a difficult conversation with Jarrah about leaving, but her doggy mate had other ideas. Not that she minded – his antics distracted her, made her laugh, and made her love him even more. It was going to be hard, saying goodbye to Scruff. He'd given her nothing but love from the second they'd met. Flopping beneath the shade of the old gum tree, Scruff finally dropped his stick and panted like billy-o. He'd clearly had enough for the afternoon. Crossing the driveway to be nearer to him, she leant on the rustic timber railing of the paddock opposite, and her gaze fixed to the two palomino horses that called it home, and then towards the thick tropical landscape beyond. She loved how the rainforest remained untouched by man's hand, and how it was filled with so much of everything that made her feel whole.

If only she could stay.

'Millie.' Her name carried on Jarrah's voice.

Turning to see him wandering towards her, she felt an easy smile break out on her face at his kind-hearted regard of her. 'Hey, Jarrah.'

He tugged the brim of his hat in greeting. 'What's appertaining?' His eyes crinkled from the glow of the setting sun as he stepped into her space and leant against the same railing as her.

'I'm just admiring Mother Nature's handiwork again,' she admitted, smiling dreamily.

'Mmm, nice.' He leant his chin on his folded hands. 'I don't mean to brag, but I reckon this place is her pièce de résistance.'

'I'd have to agree with you.' She quirked a brow as she straightened. 'And why not brag, you have the right to, being the sole owner of Riverside Acres.'

'Ha, yeah, I suppose I do.' Jarrah dropped his arms from the railing and turned to her. 'Something is smelling bloody good.' His deeply ingrained smile as he drank her in made her insides shiver. 'I'm guessing that's our dinner?'

Did this man want her no matter how rough and unready she looked? 'It sure is, let's hope it tastes as good as it smells, hey.'

'My bet is that it tastes even better.'

'Oh, no pressure.' Chuckling, she shifted her gaze and studied him for a few seconds. 'Jarrah, I have something I need to tell you.'

'Okay.' His relaxed posture stiffening, concern twisted his handsome features. 'I'm all ears.'

She was standing stock-still, but her heart was careening out of control.

Oh shit, oh shit, oh shit, oh shit …

'I think Tommy was following me around the grocery shop today.' Not exactly the 'I'm leaving as soon as you find a replacement' she had been planning on saying. 'And I have no idea why.'

His head tipped. 'Following you?'

'Yes, following me.' It felt strange, saying it out loud. 'I could feel someone behind me the entire time I was in there, but every time I spun around whoever it was had gone, and then, as I was finishing up my shopping, somebody knocked over a stand of cereal boxes in their hurry to get out of there, and I spotted Tommy, looking very suspicious, hightailing it out the front doors.'

'That's really odd.' His frown deepened as he drew in a pensive breath. 'Are you sure he wasn't just doing a bit of shopping?'

'Not one hundred percent sure, no, but my instincts aren't usually wrong.' Her mouth feeling as if it was suddenly full of cottonwool, she shrugged and took a second to swallow down her tension. 'Let's face it, Tommy has never liked me, but why would he want to follow me?'

As Jarrah considered this, she watched his expression closely, looking for a sign, a hint, anything to tell her he knew something she didn't. There was a passing moment when she thought she spotted perception, realisation even, but it was so fleeting she couldn't be sure.

'Do you think he's out to get me for something I'm not aware of?' She knew the question was a little loaded, but she'd started the ball rolling and she didn't want it to come to a dead end.

'There's no way in hell that's possible.' Jarrah shook his head. 'Tommy might be a moody bugger, but he's not someone that purposely sets out to hurt anyone.' He eyed her solemnly. 'And you're sure someone was following you?'

She nodded and said quietly, 'Fairly certain, yes.'

'Okay, I believe you, I'm just not one hundred percent convinced that Tommy was your stalker.' A flash of something surged through his gaze. 'But whoever it is, I've got you, Millie. Nobody will want to hurt you, especially in my line of sight.'

'Hopefully not.' She offered a grim smile. 'It really rattled me today, feeling like I was being shadowed by some weirdo with an agenda.'

'You're safe here, I promise you that.' He reached out and gave her arm a reassuring squeeze. 'I'm not sure what brought you here, to Riverside Acres, whether it was fate or by accident, or if you were running from someone, or something, or both, but I hope you know that as long as you are here, I will make sure you're looked after. Always.'

She cleared the gathering emotion from her throat, just enough to be able to speak. 'Thank you, I appreciate that.'

You're the most beautiful soul I've ever met, Jarrah King …

Here she was, trying to trip him up, and here he was, taking the utmost care of her. Drawing in a quick breath, she bit her bottom lip to stop from crying. There was something so strong, so solid, about him that made her believe she could truly trust him. And she wanted to, with all her heart, but the niggle that he knew something about her letter wouldn't stop.

'Millie.' His strong hand came to her cheek and he gently guided her eyes to his. 'I've got you.'

And by god he did. With their eyes locked onto one another's, she felt another fragment of him land within her heart, adding to what she already held there for him, and him alone. His transcendent aura helped to pacify her racing pulse, and for a few heart-stopping, breathless seconds, she thought he was going to lean in and kiss her. Again. Just like he had the night of the rodeo. When one thing had led to another. And they'd made the sweetest, wildest, most ravenous love she'd ever experienced. Oh, how she wanted to be led down that path with him again, to arrive in that land of euphoria he so skilfully brought her to.

Even if it was for just one last time.

But then his hand dropped from her cheek and he stepped back a little, as if stopping himself from following through on everything his gaze had just revealed to her. Even though she was thankful for his self-control, given that hers was missing in action, she felt the weight of disappointment settle in her stomach. Damn it. She *liked* him. A lot. Way too much. She had to get a grip and stop acting like some lustful woman, falling headfirst for some sexy-as-hell cowboy who was way too kind, way too thoughtful, way too mesmeric, just *way too much* to be real. There had to be a catch. There had to be a red flag. There had to be something she was missing. Men like Jarrah King did not exist. He was playing her. He was in on whatever scheme had brought her here to Riverside Acres, to him.

* * *

Don't do it, King, don't kiss her. Just don't!

It was all Jarrah had been able to think when Millie peered up at him with a flood of want and need in her enthralling gaze. All he'd known in that breath-stopping moment was that she needed to be kissed. She needed to be loved. And only by him. But he couldn't, wouldn't, complicate things again. When he forced himself to step away from her, and the reality of Tommy possibly following her really hit him, his thoughts had immediately changed course. Up until her arrival, he'd felt left alone, safe, and somehow free to move on with his life. But since she'd been there, things had felt unsteady. Maybe that had everything to do with Tommy's deceitfulness, and nothing to do with her. But if Tommy had been the one following her, there had to be a reason for it. And something told him the reason could have something to do with Carlo Martino. But what? Why her? Maybe he was just being paranoid. Maybe her arrival was just a coincidence. Either way, he couldn't risk her being caught up in whatever game Carlo and Tommy were playing.

That had been an hour ago, and now, sitting at her little dining table, his belly full of her delicious cooking and his heart full of her captivating presence, he shook his head at himself; it had been ridiculous to think she had anything at all to do with Tommy's deceit, or Carlo's schemes. Just watching the way her head tipped in laughter and her lips moved as she spoke to him, made his insides sizzle with heat. And even though he was keeping his cool, his heart pounded, as if trying to break free of his rib cage, and he couldn't stop the craving to lie with her, to make love to her. Lord help him, because right this very second all he wanted to do was kiss her all over, hold her close, wake up with her, then repeat.

Placing down her empty wine glass, she hiccupped, and then giggled. 'Would you like something sweet now that our dinner has gone down?'

You're sweet, Millie, can I have you, now that my dinner has gone down?

Jarrah's breath caught at his wayward thought, and he had to take a moment to gather himself before he dared open his mouth again. For if he spoke right this second, he'd tell her exactly what he wanted to do to her, all night long. 'Sounds good to me,' he finally said.

'Great, I'll grab our dessert out of the fridge.' She stood. 'Do you want to grab us a couple of plates, and a spoon each?'

'On it.' He hopped up from where he'd been saddling his dining chair.

'Oh, wowsers.' Millie gripped the edge of the table, all the colour draining from her face. 'I don't know what's come over me, but I feel really dizzy.' Her knees buckled and she collapsed to the side.

Jarrah dived to her rescue. 'Millie!' Within the safety of his arms, she grabbed hold of his shirt, as if she was scared that he was going to let go of her.

'It's okay, I've got you.' Thanks to his years of riding bucking bulls and working with horses, Jarrah prided himself on the fact that his reflexes were sharp. In this instance, he was pleased they'd come to good use, relieved to have caught her before her head had hit the floor. 'Here, let me get you over to the couch.' Keeping his arm wrapped around her, he carried her weight and then eased her down.

Laying her head back, she stretched out her legs. 'I don't know what just happened.' She rubbed her eyes. 'But it didn't feel good at all.'

'I think you fainted, so be careful if you try and sit up,' he cautioned. 'You don't want to make yourself dizzy again.'

'That's weird.' She carefully propped herself up with some pillows. 'I've never fainted before.'

'Maybe you're dehydrated.' He took steps towards the sink. 'I'll grab you some water.'

'Okay, thanks.' Her reply was a little hoarse.

He returned with a glass filled to the brim. 'Here, drink up.' As he passed it to her, it splashed onto her leg.

'Cheers for that.' She chuckled. 'But I want to drink it, not drown in it.' She took the glass with both hands, as if to steady it, before taking little sips.

He adored how amid her vulnerability, she still had her spirited streak, and was about to tell her that when a loud, insistent knock at the door had him rushing to see who it was.

'Tommy.' His nephew's brow-raised expression met him. 'What's up?'

'I could ask you the same thing.' Rolling his shoulders, Tommy peered past Jarrah and towards Millie. 'I thought it was against the rules to be having sex with the staff?'

Apart from wanting to focus back on Millie, so he could make sure she was okay, Jarrah wasn't in the mood for this. 'I can still smell whisky on your breath, Tommy, so how about you go back to your unit and sleep it off.'

'Yeah, whatever, mister "do what I say and not what I do".' Tommy waved an arm through the air. 'I'll leave you and your bed-notch to it then hey.'

Jarrah's anger shot to boiling point in a millisecond. 'What did you just say?'

'You heard me.' Tommy pointed in Millie's direction. 'She's nothing but a cheap skank and you're a dickhead falling for the likes of her.'

Red rage swallowed Jarrah whole. 'How dare you speak about her like that.'

'I'll speak however I want, about whoever I want.'

'Not on my property you won't.'

'Stuff you.' Tommy shoved Jarrah in the chest.

Jarrah shoved him back, and stepped outside. 'I'm warning you, Tommy, don't start something you're not going to like the end of.'

Coming for him, Tommy threw a punch. And in the blink of an eye, Jarrah had defended himself and Tommy was on the ground.

Struggling to his feet, Tommy glared at him as he wiped the blood from his lip. 'That's the first and last time you're ever going to do that.' He stormed away, and a slamming door sounded.

CHAPTER 17

Fresh out of the shower, Jarrah grabbed a clean T-shirt and pair of jeans from the basket of clothes he was yet to fold. Having spent the night tossing and turning, he'd come to the conclusion that Tommy needed to make his choice: remain living here at Riverside Acres and pull his moodiness into gear, as well as apologise to Millie for his foul mouth, or move to Sydney and stay there. As hard as it would be if his nephew chose the latter, he had to stick to his guns. He wasn't going to allow him to flit between two very different worlds. He wanted no part of Carlo's criminal activity, nor did he want Tommy dragging it back with him, which he inevitably would, if he hadn't already. He regretted with all his heart losing his temper when Tommy lashed out at him, and throwing a punch in return. But then again, Tommy had to learn to pick his battles, and who to pick them with. He'd had enough of his nephew playing the martyr. This had to stop. And to achieve that, he had to stop seeing

Tommy as the child he'd raised. Tommy was a man now, with his own thoughts, and was wholly and solely responsible for his own actions. He still loved him. How could he not? Tommy was a big part of his world.

He'd also come to the conclusion that not falling head over boots for Millie was proving way easier said than done. And it wasn't only her physical appearance that stirred him – it was something unfathomable that pulled him towards her like fast-flowing water towards a raging waterfall. In the six weeks she'd been there, she'd seeped beneath his skin, so unobtrusively, so innocently. He didn't completely understand her yet, but he vowed to. He just hoped she stuck around long enough for him to do so. Deep down in his gut he felt that she was on the run, from a past, or from someone dangerous. There was definitely something she was hiding behind those beautiful eyes of hers, and he wanted to discover what it was so he could offer her protection, support, compassion, whatever she needed from him to get through it.

Running his fingers through his damp hair, he made his way downstairs. Wanting to pop in and check on Millie before he headed into town, he decided not to make himself his second coffee for the day. He'd just grab one at the roadhouse. Kill two birds with one stone. Delicious smells greeted him as he made his way across the drive, down the rise, and towards the back door of the kitchen – freshly ground coffee, sizzling bacon, roasting tomatoes, and the freshly baked damper that had been selling quicker than she could make it.

'Good morning.' Millie's smile was wide.

'Morning.' He searched her smiling face. 'You seem on top of the world today.'

'Best place to be.' She grinned. 'Cooking makes me happy.'

'Eating your cooking makes me, and everyone else, happy.' Sensations zinged through him, making him want to grab her and take her into his arms. 'No more feeling dizzy?'

'Yes and no.' She grabbed the tea towel from her shoulder and wiped her hands. 'I felt a little off when I woke up to my alarm, but I'm okay now.'

'Good to hear, but I still reckon you should go into town and see the doc, just to have a check-up.' He shrugged at her look of indifference. 'I can ring and make you an appointment with mine, if you like?' She pouted in thought and then nodded. 'Yeah, righto, what's it going to hurt.'

'Good.' He plucked his phone from his pocket. 'I'll give them a call right now.'

She eyed him, chuckling. 'Keen then.'

'I'm just looking after you.'

'I can see that.' Her smile softened and reached into her eyes. 'Thank you.'

Jarrah returned her smile as the phone began to ring in his ear. She didn't need to thank him. Together or not, friends or lovers, he'd go to the ends of the earth for this woman, and then some.

* * *

The following morning, with her ritual morning coffee made, Millie padded out of her motel room and onto her patio. Slumping down in her fold-out chair, she wrapped her hands around the mug and took tentative sips while watching the glorious day unfold. Pinks, oranges and pastel blues splashed across the sky right before the sun rose in all its glory. For a brief moment, she clenched her eyes shut against the glare and enjoyed the feel of the sun's rays reaching for her and warming her from the outside in. Ahhh, Riverside Acres. With its tropical rainforest, lush mountains and crystal-clear running creeks, she was going to miss so much about this place.

But most of all, she was going to miss Jarrah.

Her throat ached with emotion, and she allowed herself a few minutes to recover before rising to her feet and padding back inside. Jarrah had gotten her an appointment at the doctor's at ten-thirty, and he'd also given her the day off, with strict orders to stay away from the roadhouse so she could rest. Mary would be filling in for her today. She still had a few hours to kill before heading into town, and she planned to go for an easy stroll. The fresh air would do her the world of good. She headed inside, dumped her cup into the sink and padded into the bathroom. Stripping off, she was just about to hop in the shower when an intense wave of nausea had her racing for the toilet. But by the time she'd reached it and dropped to her knees, the urge to heave her coffee back up had passed. Standing carefully, then slumping down on the lid of the loo just in case it returned, she leant forwards and took slow breaths. Maybe the pressure of being there was finally taking a toll on her?

You're okay … it's all going to be okay …

But she wasn't okay. Soon enough she'd be heading back to Sydney, likely none the wiser to who had summoned her there, or why, and with her heart held in the hands of Jarrah. It was no wonder she was suffering from bouts of stress. She sat there for a little longer until she felt completely confident that she'd be able to stand. The warm water of her shower helped her to feel a little better. Once showered and dressed, she made her way outside and turned left, past the machinery shed and then the stables. Horses shifted and nickered in their stalls and she wondered if Jarrah was tending to them. Or maybe it was Tommy. The latter made her anxious. Wanting to avoid Jarrah's nephew at all costs, she wasn't about to risk finding out which one of them it was. She quickened her steps, but her getaway was botched when, thankfully, it was Jarrah who stepped from the stables, a shovel in his hand.

'Oh, hey, Millie.'

'Hey.' She met his gaze and the dark rings beneath his baby blues stirred emotions. 'Have you and Tommy sorted things out after what happened last night?'

His expression was pained. 'Not really, but we'll hopefully get there.'

She studied his forlorn face. 'I wish there was something I could do.'

'Yeah, me too.' He sniffed hard, as if fighting off emotions. 'But there isn't, I'm afraid. Tommy's a man, and he must take responsibility for his life and his actions, like I do.' He shook his head. 'I never should've hit him, but it was hard in the moment, when I was trying to defend myself.'

'You can't beat yourself up over it, Jarrah. What's done is done, and I can vouch that he was the one who started it.' The fact that Jarrah had been defending her honour made her feel both lucky and sad – she didn't want to be the cause of their angst.

'I know, but I still regret hitting him.' With his riveting blue gaze pinned to hers, his broad shoulders lifted into a half-shrug. 'I'm really sorry about how he spoke about you too, Millie.'

She was about to tell him he didn't need to apologise for his nephew's actions when the thunder of hoofs halted their conversation. Tommy came around the corner atop a jet-black horse, and the fluttering in her stomach morphed into waves of apprehension.

'Well, I'll be off, let you get back to it.' The backs of her eyes were scalded with tears that she refused to shed as she quickly made her exit. 'I'll touch base when I get back from the doctor,' she called over her shoulder.

'Please do that,' Jarrah called back.

She kept walking as she responded. 'Will do.'

A few hours later, after a day of brilliant sunshine, grey clouds were now making their way across the blue, swallowing up the sky, giving relief from the balmy heat. Sitting on her patio, Millie briefly closed her eyes and tried to enjoy the feeling of the breeze cooling her face. When she'd gotten back from town, she hadn't been able to find Jarrah, so she'd headed back to her motel room and made herself a coffee. He'd find her soon enough, she was sure. Tracking her gaze up the gentle rise, to where a small herd of his cattle ambled, then off to the left, where agisted horses grazed in their paddocks, she sighed. There was something so very peaceful about watching livestock. There was no obvious reason for the ominous feeling that had been sitting in the pit of her stomach since getting her blood tests, but try as she might, she couldn't shake it. The doctor had been a little more concerned than she'd expected him to be. There'd been a mention of diabetes, and a few questions about her family history, but she wasn't going to know the results for a couple of days, and not wanting to unnecessarily worry herself, she was doing her best to turn her attention elsewhere.

The crunch of tyres grabbed her attention and she turned to see Jarrah and Scruffball hop out of his LandCruiser and head towards her. 'Hey, you pair.' She gave him a friendly wave just as Scruff skidded to her side, his tongue dangling out the side of his chops.

'Hey, I thought I'd call past and check how your visit to the doc's went?'

'Yeah, good, I think,' she replied as she petted Scruff's head. 'He sent me for some blood tests, I should know the results in a couple of days.'

'Oh righto, well, it's good that he's being thorough.' He pointed to the chair. 'Mind if I join you?'

'Of course not, would you like a cuppa?'

'No, but thanks.' His chuckle was husky. 'I reckon I've had four, or maybe even five, coffees, already today, and that's way above my quota.' He rolled his eyes. 'I already can't sleep, so I probably don't need to add caffeine overuse to the list of reasons why I've become an insomniac.'

Wishing she was pressed up against him, she tried to shove the thought away. 'I'm sorry to hear that; not being able to sleep sucks.' She couldn't believe just how much she wanted what they couldn't have.

'Uh-huh, it sure does, big time.' His nod was exaggerated. 'Sounds like you know all about it?'

'Yes, I sure do.' Maybe now was the time to tell him why she hadn't been sleeping?

His Adam's apple bobbed in his throat as he cleared it a few times. He looked so broken, so torn, so much so that she wanted to reach out and offer him some comfort. But she didn't, and instead shoved her free hand beneath her rump, as if that would stop her urges. Apprehension flooded her but she blinked the sensation away as she straightened and lifted her chin, then quietly cleared the emotion from her tightening throat. She needed to be honest with him and tell him she'd be leaving soon, and while she did it, she hoped to goodness she wasn't going to cry.

'Jarrah.'

He seemed a million miles away when he turned to her. 'Hmm?'

She hesitated, weighing up if now was a good time – he looked so sad. 'Are you okay?'

'I feel a bit meh, but I'll be right.'

She didn't want to come between him and Tommy, but she wanted to at least be there for him, as he had been for her. 'You can vent to me, you know, it might help.'

'Why vent, it's not going to change things.' His smile was grim. 'And I don't really want to put it all on you.'

'You're not putting it all on me by simply talking to me about it.'

He thought about this but then tossed a hand through the air. 'It's my problem, not yours.'

'Fair enough.' As his gaze went back to the countryside, she regarded him thoughtfully. She knew all too well what it felt like to take the weight of the world upon her shoulders, and she sympathised with him doing the same. 'Have you always been like this, or did something make you feel like you had to close off, to be able to deal with things?'

The look he shot in her direction was fired from somewhere raw and enflamed and damaged, and she instantly regretted being so candid. 'I'm sorry, I shouldn't have said that.' She shook her head and looked away from him. 'Me and my damn foot in mouth.'

'Don't worry about it, I get that horrid foot in mouth disease sometimes too.' He veered his now playful gaze from hers, and back to the sunset-hued sky.

But as beautiful as it was, the sunset sky didn't hold her captivated. Instead, she looked at him, and for the longest of moments, said nothing.

'Why are you staring at me?' He turned to her, and his regard was thoughtful. 'Am I really that fascinating?'

She could see ghosts in his eyes, and caught a glimpse into the tortures in his soul. 'You're a mystery, Jarrah King.'

'So are you, Millie.'

'Two peas in a pod,' they both said in union.

This lightened the mood instantly, and their laughter and easy conversation carried them into the twilight.

CHAPTER 18

The new day had dawned promisingly bright, giving Millie a false kind of hope. But despite her eagerness to soldier on, and through, whatever her results revealed, her fear was beginning to overcome her sense of calm reasoning. Now, with her heart in her throat and her adrenaline pumping, she stared at the doctor sitting opposite her, praying the conclusion she'd jumped to on her way there was very, *very* wrong. *Please don't let it be the C word.* Damn Doctor Google for scaring her out of her wits.

Pull yourself together, Millie, she commanded silently. 'So, why couldn't you tell me about my results over the phone?'

'I'm very happy to tell you that your blood work came back normal,' the doctor said with a smile.

'Oh, thank god.' Her hand went to her chest.

He met her gaze and held it. 'If all my patients were as healthy as you, I'd be out of a job.' He inhaled sharply, his smile fading. 'There is something you need to know, though.'

She was suddenly sick to her stomach. 'What is it?' She noted the twinkle in his eyes and relaxed a smidge.

'You're pregnant, Millie.'

Tears burnt behind her eyes, but she managed to hold them back. 'I am?'

'Yes, you are.'

There's a life, growing inside me?

As she blinked faster, her hands and gaze came to her belly. 'Do you know how far along I am?'

'My guess is about four weeks.'

She looked at him through tear-blurred eyes.

Jarrah's the father …

The thought echoed over and over again as the doctor spoke words to her that she was no longer hearing. She nodded, as if she were listening. Before she knew it, he'd risen from his chair and was guiding her towards the door. Then she'd paid on autopilot and her legs had carried her away from the receptionist. She wasn't sure how she'd gotten from the doctor's office to her car. But now here she was, sitting behind the steering wheel of her Jimny, staring out her windscreen as if she were staring into space. Suddenly stifled, she wound down her window, allowing in what little wind there was.

Resting back, she watched all the people moseying by as she attempted to drag in steady breaths – all the while her heart felt like it was about to beat right out of her chest. After miscarrying, and being told she might find it hard to fall pregnant in the near future, this news was an absolute blessing. Not an ideal situation, but a blessing all the same. What if Jarrah didn't agree? What if he expected her to get an abortion? What if he wanted nothing to do with his child? There was no way she wasn't going through with this pregnancy. She'd already lost a child. She wasn't about to lose another. Panic fuelled her pulse. She wanted this life growing inside of her to be born into this world, so she could love him or her with all her heart and soul. Thank goodness all of this was covered under the confidentiality clause with her doctor, as he knew her real name, given she had to provide her Medicare card at her first appointment.

She closed her eyes, rested her head back, took her rose-coloured glasses off and candidly thought about Jarrah King. In a matter of weeks, he'd somehow found a way to climb over her walls and swim through the cold waters of her heart. There had to be a motive. He was too good, too nice, to be true. She scrutinised him, thought about the time she'd spent with him, and contemplated their uncanny connection. Until now, she'd been busy trying not to act upon whatever this was building between them. But now there was another life involved. A life she'd protect with her own. It was a whole other ball game. She'd been trying not to notice the red flags, the signs, and there'd been a couple. His lack of a past, her sense that she'd met him before, the heated undercurrent between him and Tommy, the way he acted like he knew her when she knew damn well they'd never met before. How could they have? She'd been trying to push aside the gnawing sensation that he had something to do with the letter. But now she was allowing herself the liberty of seeing things clearly, it was possible. She'd been brought to Jarrah's property for a reason. He had to have had something to do with the fire. And as for Tommy, he might be too young to have played a hand, but he was involved in the scheme to get her there, she was sure of it. Had she fallen for, and fallen pregnant to, a man who'd played a part in the murder of her family?

No way, surely not. Fate couldn't be that cruel, could it?

Maybe she was barking up the wrong tree, in a forest far, far away from the actual truth. Maybe Jarrah was innocent in all of this. Maybe it was all Tommy. Maybe she was just grasping at straws, trying to come up with a reason to hate Jarrah, so she didn't have to tell him she was pregnant, so she didn't have to risk being told he wasn't happy about it.

Argh!

She smacked the steering wheel with both hands. She really needed to find a way to calm her jangling nerves, and that certainly wasn't going to be with her usual go-to of alcohol. So what, or who, was going to help her? Turning the key, she revved her Jimny to life, backed out, and headed in the opposite direction to Riverside Acres. She had no idea where she was going, but for now, she knew she didn't want to go back to where all her problems were waiting for her. Reaching a junction, she veered left, and a quaint little church beside a cemetery caught her eye. In days gone by, when she was a little girl, she used to go to mass every Sunday with her parents and little brother, but since losing them, she'd lost her faith. What kind of god would be so brutal? She hadn't felt able to set a foot inside God's house since the day of her family's funeral. But now she felt utterly compelled to stop and somehow find the courage to go inside, so she could forgive God for taking three of her most precious loved ones from her, and also find a way to forgive herself for surviving. And maybe, in between all of that, by some miracle, she would find the comfort and answers she was seeking.

Pulling up beneath the shade of a huddle of towering trees, she killed the engine. It took her a couple of breaths to be able to take her seatbelt off and shove her door open. Her heart felt as if it were rattling in her chest as she stepped out and shoved her keys into her pocket. Pausing, she took her time and breathed deeply, slowly. The scent of freshly cut grass and blooming jasmine flowers filled her senses. She could do this. If not for herself, then for her baby. Her child deserved a mother that was put together. The headstones of the neighbouring cemetery were her only audience as she negotiated the pebbled pathway and after drawing in another deep breath, climbed the four steps of the church while trying to ignore the sensation of waves crashing in her stomach.

Standing at the front door, she peered inside. The leadlight windows dappled striking colours over the pews and the scent of burnt sage lingered. Dipping her fingers into the holy water by the entrance, she did what her mother had taught her to do, and made the sign of the cross. Then, with one cautious step after another, she slipped into the quiet sanctuary and settled into the back bench seat. For now, going any further inside felt like a sin. As her eyes darted from the altar to the high open-beamed ceilings, to the statue of Jesus hung from the cross, it was hard not to go back there, to that heartbreaking day, when she'd squeezed Ebony's hand so very tightly as she'd stared at three coffins lined up, side by side, one so much smaller than the other two. With the recollection, she felt her heart split down the middle, and like a dam breaking its banks, she broke down and sobbed harder than she had in a very long time.

She wasn't sure how long she'd been crying for, when a gentle hand came to rest upon her back. 'Hi, my dear, is everything okay?'

Lifting her teary gaze, she tried to smile at the priest, but her lips trembled. 'Not really. I hope it's okay to be in here?'

'Of course.' His smile was filled with genuine warmth. 'Do you need an ear?'

She pointed to hers and tried to smile. 'I've already got two.'

'Humour is one of the ways to cope with sadness.' The priest chuckled. 'Talking about it is another.' There was immeasurable wisdom within his gaze. 'Can I sit?'

'Yes, of course.' She nudged a little up the pew.

'You can choose to talk.' He placed both his hands onto his knees. 'Or we can just sit quietly, my dear, it's up to you.'

'I'm pregnant,' she blurted out before she could stop herself. 'And I don't know if I should tell the father or not.'

'I see.' His brows furrowed, more in thought than judgement. 'That's a blessing, yes, to be with child?'

'Yes, it most certainly is.' Little did he know just how much.

'I'm glad to hear it.' He looked to her, and not just at her, but also within her. 'That's what you need to focus on, then, how fortunate you are to be carrying a child, and simply trust that everything else will fall into place as it's meant to.'

She took a moment to really hear what he was saying. 'So, I need to focus on the good, and not make any rash decisions about the bad.'

'Something like that, yes.' He folded his hands in his lap and looked to the statue of Jesus on the cross. 'And as he taught all of us, sometimes, even in the most challenging of circumstances, the bad actually turns out to be very good.'

'I like that.' She lightly placed a hand over his. 'Thank you.'

'My pleasure, dear.' He nodded and offered a kind smile. 'Any time.'

She stood and smiled gratefully. 'I'm so glad I came in here.'

'Me too.' He straightened beside her. 'I hope I gave you some peace.'

'Yes, you have. Thanks again.' She took quiet steps outside, noting how her heart felt a little lighter as she descended the steps.

An hour later, and she was back in her spot, on the patio of her motel room, when the crunch of boots on the gravel drive approached. She instinctively knew they were Jarrah's footfalls and, as nervous as she was, she managed to plant a smile on her face as she turned to greet him.

'Hey, Millie, how were your results?'

'Yeah, good, he reckons I'm as fit as a fiddle.'

I'm carrying your baby, our baby.

'Oh, good.' He flopped down in the chair beside her. 'I was starting to get really worried, seeing as you took so long in town.'

'Oh, I decided to take myself out for some lunch while I was there.' She hated lying, but she wasn't ready to tell him she was sitting in a church, telling a priest what she should be telling him.

'Nice, where did you go?'

Liar liar pants on fire!

Her mind raced. 'That place at the end of town, you know the one.'

'Hmmm.' He frowned. 'You mean the Sugar Shack?'

She'd never even noticed the place. 'Yeah, that's the one.'

His frown deepened. 'Was it nice?'

Tight-lipped, she nodded. 'Mm-hmm.'

'Yeah, righto.' Jarrah's perplexed expression was gathering momentum. 'I thought you didn't have much of a sweet tooth, especially when it comes to main meals.'

'Oh, I don't usually.' She was crap at this lying malarky.

He regarded her, as if he was seeing straight through her story. 'Fair enough.'

She fidgeted in her seat. 'Would you like a cuppa?'

'I'm good, cheers, Millie.' He quirked a brow. 'But have you got anything stronger?'

'I'm all out of beers and wine, I'm afraid.' She wouldn't be touching a drop of it now she was pregnant.

'No worries.' He leapt to his feet. 'I'll go grab us a couple of beers from home, if you like.'

'Oh thanks, Jarrah, but count me out.' She avoided his gaze as she crossed her legs beneath her. 'I've decided to detox for a bit, so no alcohol for me.'

'Oh wow, okay, good for you.' He rubbed a hand over his dark stubble. 'In that case, I'm going to head home for a beer, or two, so I'll catch you later.'

'Yup, catch ya,' she said as she watched the father of her unborn baby saunter away.

CHAPTER 19

After a massive day working in the humid tropical heat, Jarrah felt as if he'd been dragged over hot coals, and then some. A brutal headache was brewing, his eyes burned, and he had to forcibly swallow the ache that had risen from his heart and into his throat. As he trudged from the machinery shed and across the drive, all around him the air felt dense, weighted, as did his spirits. Something had to give. He and Tommy had to find some common ground and make a truce. After mulling everything over and over, all day long, his mind was exhausted and his body was bone tired. It didn't happen often, but he had to silently admit that he was well and truly rattled. Millie was acting a little odd, and had been for a few days now. And as for his nephew, knowing Tommy had gone behind his back to see Carlo, and likely would again, was almost too much to bear. Let alone not knowing why he'd agreed to deliver an envelope to a woman who had been Amelia Price's best friend. Maybe Carlo had grown a conscience and was paying grievance money to Amelia. Now wouldn't that be the surprise of his life, to find out his father did actually have a heart.

Pfft, yeah right.

Taking off his hat, he raked a hand through his sweaty hair. It was almost sixty-thirty on a Friday afternoon, and the sun was on its downward descent behind the mountain ranges. As dusk swept over his land, he took one last look at the splendour of the sunset before stepping into the roadhouse and wandering towards his office. He still had half an hour of paperwork to do before he could call it a day, and he couldn't wait to get it done so he could head home and enjoy some much-needed downtime.

He was midway through adding up the GST owing to the tax office when his office door flew open and rebounded off the wall. 'I need to show you something.' Tommy strode in, a yellow envelope in his hand. 'Right now.'

'Okay.' This was the first time Tommy had spoken to him since their fight, and Jarrah's curiosity was piqued. 'What is it?'

'I knew she was full of crap the second I met her.' Tommy smacked the envelope down on the desk. 'And now I have solid proof.' He stabbed it with his finger.

Jarrah reached out and warily dragged it towards him. 'Should I be worried?'

'Turn it over, open it up, read it, then decide.'

Jarrah slowly turned it over as Tommy paced. When he read the name in bold, black letters his heart leapt into his throat. It was as if he'd just jumped from a plane, without a parachute. His past was here, right now, in his office, staring him in the face. And here he'd been thinking he could outrun it. With trembling hands, he plucked out the folded notepaper, along with a black-and-white photo of a very young Amelia Price and her father. He had to read the letter twice to let it sink in, to believe it. To come to grips with the fact that the girl he'd saved from the fire was here, just a few hundred metres away, a grown woman now, and he'd fallen for her, made love to her, imagined having a life with her. He couldn't be mad at her for lying about who she was; his father had made sure to cover all his bases. But man, he was blown away by what had been staring him in the face ever since she'd arrived here, and he'd been too blinded by his attraction to her to see it. Millie. Amelia. One and the same. How could he not have put two and two together?

He waited until his vision stopped swirling, and Tommy's scowling face came into focus, before he dared to speak. 'Where did you find this?'

'Under the driver's seat of her car.'

'And what were you doing, snooping through her car?' Jarrah used everything he had to keep his voice steady, his tone even.

'I dunno, a hunch, what does it matter?' Tommy shrugged. 'I don't trust her, and now I know why.' He sank down in the chair on the opposite side of the desk. 'And there's something else I need to tell you too.'

Feeling as if his entire world had just been pulled out from beneath his boots, Jarrah was having trouble drawing a breath. 'Go ahead, I'm listening.' His fingers drummed the desk.

'I'm the one who delivered it to her apartment block.'

And there it was, the frankness he'd been praying for. 'Your grandfather got you to deliver it?'

'Yeah, he did, and he paid me a thousand dollars for it.' Tommy's downhearted gaze was filled with regret and sorrow. 'I didn't know it was anything to do with you, or Riverside Acres, or your past being dragged up.' He shook his head sadly. 'I'm so sorry, Uncle, I can see what you mean by him being a master manipulator now. He told me it was to do with some rent a woman owed him.'

Jarrah whooshed a breath. 'I tried to warn you, Tommy, but I think you had to experience it firsthand to know I wasn't exaggerating.'

'Yes, my bad.'

'Yes, it is.' He caught Tommy's eyes and tried to hold his attention. 'I can forgive you this time, but just remember that if you do it again, it's not a mistake, it's a choice.'

'I one hundred percent get that.' Tommy nodded. 'So what are you going to do about Millie?'

'I need to have a think before I act rashly, and I need you to give me the time and space I need to deal with this properly, okay?'

Tommy's next nod was swift. 'Yup, done deal.'

'Promise me, Tommy.' Jarrah's tone was cautionary. 'Because I don't want this ending up messier than it already is.'

Tommy looked Jarrah dead in the eyes. 'You have my word, Uncle J.'

And Jarrah believed him. 'Good, now can you leave it with me?'

'Yup, sure can.' Tommy straightened and took steps towards the doorway. 'I'm around if you need me, okay.'

'Thanks, Tommy, that means a lot.'

Jarrah wished he could feel complete relief in knowing Tommy was now being sincere with him. But hell, no. There was only a smidgen of relief swirling beneath the mountain of heartache he now had to deal with. He wasn't sure if he was going to beat around the bush or come right out and say it. Either way, he and Millie needed to talk. And he knew this wasn't going to go well. Not in the slightest. If anything, this would be the reason she ran for the hills and never looked back.

Losing no time between walking from his office to the front door of her motel room, he sighed, then knocked. 'Millie, you here?'

The door opened and her smile met him, then faded. 'Jarrah, hey.' He must have appeared anxious, hesitant even, because her hand came to his arm. 'Is everything okay?'

'No, not really, we need to talk.' He could feel the flames that had been dancing between them since the very first time they'd met, but right now, given what he knew, the heat of it was suffocating. 'Can I come in, or do you want to sit out here?'

She bit down on her lip. 'Out here, it's less stuffy.'

'Righto.' He settled in his usual chair, as did she.

Placing her elbows on the little table, she rested her chin in her hands. 'So, what's up?'

Words that were going to shatter both their worlds got stuck in his voice box. He cleared his throat. Shifted uneasily. The silence stretched, lingered, as he did his best to calm his galloping heart. 'I don't think either of us have been honest about who we are, Millie, wouldn't you agree?' There, that was as good a start as any.

'Huh?' Confusion, or fear, or possibly both, crinkled the corners of her eyes. 'I don't know what you're talking about.'

He swivelled in his chair to face her. 'Millie, please, this is our one chance to be completely honest with each other.'

Bearing witness to her rigid posture, and the way she was now gnawing on her fingernail, he gathered she must have some idea as to what he was on about. 'Millie, please talk to me.' He willed himself not to spill everything that was weighing down upon his heart in his next breath, because he wanted to give her time to be honest too.

She finally brought her gaze to his. 'Honest about what, exactly, Jarrah?' There was no softness in her tone now, just defensiveness.

'Millie, I know.' In all his years, he'd never felt his heart beat so fast and so hard.

Her gaze turned suspicious. 'You know what?'

'I know.' That's all he felt he needed to say.

'You know, hey … interesting.' She turned her cheek and took a moment. When she looked back at him, her lashes were heavy with tears and her lips were parted as if a question she didn't want the answer to lingered there.

He clasped his hands atop the table. 'Go on, ask me anything you want to, and I promise I'll be totally upfront.'

She drew in a deep, sharp breath. 'Ask you what?' She shook her head.

Wow, she was really sticking to her guns. 'I can see it, Mills, with the way you're looking at me.' He offered a resigned sigh. 'You want to know who I really am, don't you?'

She paused, and her expression bunched as if she were looking inward, somehow searching for the right answer. And then her eyes widened and she gasped while studying him. He forced the long-ago echoes of her cries for help from his mind, along with the blood-curdling screams of her family. He ached to tell her he was the one who'd saved her. He ached to tell her his side. More than ever, he ached to console her, to somehow put her mind at ease. But the truth of who her father really was would likely shatter her even more, so that meant it would inevitably be more lies, and he couldn't do that to her. She deserved to know the truth of what happened and why. But he just couldn't bring himself to break her heart even more. Damn his father and what he'd done from the confines of prison. Damn him to hell!

Don't do it, King. Do not pull her into your arms and tell her everything. Protect her.

'Millie, please talk to me.' He went to touch her hand, but she jerked it away.

'Don't touch me.' Her gaze was fierce, storming with raw emotions as she shot to her feet and her chair tumbled backwards. 'I think it's about time you told me who you really are.'

Guilt twisted in his chest. He'd seen her like this before. Way younger than now. Terrified yet fighting for her life. Emotions collided inside his heart: shock, anger with himself, love for her, fear, blame, shame. And that was right about when his perfectly manufactured world seemed to crack and crumble beneath his feet.

* * *

Without outwardly admitting anything, Jarrah had dropped a bombshell. Millie's head was spinning with possibilities, and her racing heart was making it hard to draw a breath. Appearing at her side, Scruff nudged her hand. She instinctively comforted him by ruffling his ears as she tried to make herself believe that there was nothing untoward going on. That this wasn't about her pregnancy, their baby. That the letter wasn't at play here. That Jarrah had been nothing but open and honest with her. That she was overreacting. She needed to get a grip, take a breath, and let everything fall into place, as the priest had told her to do. So she leant against the wall for support and waited for Jarrah to speak, to ask, or to confess. So many secrets, they each had. God only knew what he was about to tell her.

'Jarrah, come on, for god's sake, spill.'

'All right.' He held up his hands. 'Just give me a minute, would you, because I only want to say this once, and in the right way.'

There was a part of her that couldn't shake the sense that she was going to regret her need to hear what he had to say, but her desperation for the truth, and to be truthful, was stronger. There was so much at stake here. She knew that. Having spent the last twenty-four hours knowing a part of him was growing inside her, her mind had painted a picture of what she wanted him to be, what she wanted them to be. Why had she been such a fool to allow the walls she'd built around her heart to crumble enough for him to reach inside of her?

Jarrah was out of his chair now, pacing with his head in his hands, as if he was trying to collect his scattered thoughts. As she watched and waited, she felt as if a storm was building inside her, with hot and cold fronts moving in from all sides. It was unsettling, worrying, heartbreaking, suffocating. Whatever bridge they'd built during their time together was now officially burnt, leaving her on one side and him on the other. They'd been so connected and now they were on opposite sides, with so much left unsaid between them. She swore, if the truth didn't come out, in one way or another, she was going to drown. And then, as if it were an epiphany, something dawned on her and she *really* saw him. Tipping her head, she watched the way his jaw clenched and unclenched. She glowered at the scar on his left cheek – one that would be left behind after a bad burn. And then she saw it, the yellow envelope with her name scrawled upon it, stuffed into the back pocket of his jeans.

Storming in front of him, she stood ramrod straight, with her heart racing a million miles a minute. 'You were the one that went to prison for killing my family, aren't you?' Her eyes pleaded with him for the truth.

Jarrah's lips clamped into a thin line and emotions rampaged in his eyes. It was within his silence that the truth reached out and hit her with striking velocity, and her heart ached at the evidence. 'You're a lying son of a bitch.'

'Millie, please, let me explain.' He reached out to touch her, possibly to reassure her, but she stepped back. 'I had nothing to do with their deaths, you have to believe me.'

'Don't, Jarrah.' She was surprised at how normal she sounded given the fact that her heart was shattering into a million tiny little fragments. 'If you were there that night, and you went to prison, it's clear to me that you had everything to do with their deaths.' Her tears broke loose and tumbled down her cheeks as red-hot rage burst into a flood of raw emotion. 'With every fibre of my being, I hate you,' she roared, every word full of venom, full of fury, full of heart-wrenching pain. 'And I never, ever, want to see you again.'

CHAPTER 20

Millie was only half listening to the drone of the newsreader's voice as she wriggled restlessly in the seat that was now stuck to her. On autopilot, other than stopping for fuel and a bottle of water she'd driven straight through Queensland. But now, nearing the New South Wales border, her head was pounding, and her heart seemed to be joining in. The clutch stuck for the umpteenth time, and she swore out loud as she pumped it while jamming the gear from fifth into third as she approached the T-intersection. Pulling to a stop, she looked left to right. A kangaroo bounded past on the side of the road, startling her. She had to take a moment to catch her breath. With her headlights igniting the road sign, she read the kilometres she had left – eight hundred and fifty-seven. Oh. My. God. With every muscle aching, she felt as if she'd been wound into a knot. She was carrying precious cargo, so she needed to stop. Now.

Less than two minutes later she was pulling up at a roadside motel. Turning off the ignition, she peered through her dusty windscreen at the glowing sign stating there were vacancies. Thank goodness, because if she drove another kilometre, she was sure she'd fall asleep at the wheel. Glancing at her reflection in the rear-view mirror, she cringed. With mascara smeared beneath her red-rimmed eyes, and her hair looking like she'd stuck her finger in an electrical socket, she looked like death warmed up. Grabbing a wet wipe, she dabbed at her cheeks. Then, undoing her knotty bun, she tried to tug her hair into some kind of respectable order. Satisfied she'd achieved looking somewhat normal – even though her life was far from normal – she turned and grabbed her handbag from the back seat, then, pushing her door open with her foot, she climbed out. A bell jingled as she stepped into the cool air-conditioned office that looked as if it was stuck in the eighties. A massive tabby cat lifted its head from the corner of the desk, instantly reminding her of Felix the second. Oh, if she could cuddle him to her right now.

'Can I help you?' came a voice right before an elderly woman appeared from behind a curtain.

'I'd like a room for the night, please.' Millie did her best to focus on the lady with huge glasses instead of the flowered wallpaper lining almost every inch of the room.

The woman shifted her glasses up her nose as she ran her gaze from the top of Millie's head to the toe of her sandals. 'Is it just for you?' She peered past her as if trying to see if there was another person in the car.

'Yes, just me.'

The lines in her forehead etched a little deeper. 'Okay, well, if it's just for one person, that will be eighty-five dollars, to be paid upfront please.'

'Yes, of course, I want to hit the road nice and early so that will be better anyway.' She rustled in her handbag and tugged out her purse. Grabbing a hundred-dollar bill, she passed it over. 'Here you go.'

'Thank you, I'll just grab you some change.' As she passed fifteen dollars back, she smiled now, gentle, kind even. 'Are you okay, love? You look a little pale.'

Her throat went tight. 'Yes, I'm just tired from the long drive.'

'Okay.' The woman held out a set of keys. 'Here you go, room number eleven, just down the end of the block. You can park right out front.'

'Thank you.'

'We're also still serving dinner.' The woman glanced at her watch. 'For another half an hour or so.'

'Okay, thank you.' Feeling as if she were about to burst into tears, Millie began taking backward steps towards the door. 'I might grab something once I've settled in for the night.'

'Yes, you do that.' The woman nodded towards Millie's belly. 'I'd say your little one might be hungry.'

Millie's jaw dropped open. 'How do you know I'm pregnant?'

'By the way your hands are resting protectively there.' The woman sucked in a quick breath. 'I can also organise for a sandwich and some fruit for you to take on the road with you tomorrow morning, if you like?'

Her tears were building. 'That's so kind of you, thank you.'

Escaping the office just in time for a fresh flood of tears, she quickly made her way over to her Jimny, drove the short distance to the hotel room, parked, and then went inside. As soon as she shut and locked the door behind her she plucked a tissue from the box on the bedside table and dabbed her cheeks. Sinking down on the side of the bed, she looked around her room. She'd cried so much she was surprised she had any tears left. And her eyelids felt like sandpaper every time she blinked. She needed a sweet cup of tea. Rising then flicking the kettle on, she popped two sugars into the mug along with a teabag. While she waited for her brew, she dared to turn her phone back on. It pinged and dinged with messages; some texts, some voice. Pressing voicemail then holding the phone to her ear, she held her breath.

'Millie, please, don't leave like this.' Jarrah's recorded voice sounded hollow, raw, desperate. 'I'm begging you, please come back so I can explain how I had nothing to do with your family's deaths, or this letter you got.'

Her heart squeezed super tight as she waited for the next message.

'Millie, please …' Jarrah's voice broke off in a sob. 'Nothing's what you think it is. I took the rap for something I didn't do.'

Could he be innocent? Surely not, if he'd gone to prison. She almost hung up before the last message but couldn't bring herself to.

'It's me, Jarrah. I really wish you hadn't left like this, but I get it. I'm so sorry, Millie. One day I hope I get the chance to fix this. And just so you know, it was my damn father who sent you that letter.'

His father? Why would a parent do that to his very own son? She really wanted to believe him. But how could she when they'd been living a lie for the past six weeks? His pain stung her heart but she wasn't going to call him back. Dropping the phone, she wrapped her arms around herself, at the same time wishing it was his arms she was encased within. What a crazy thing it was, to want comfort from the man who'd stolen so much from her. The very same man who was now the father of her baby. The baby she needed to take care of. A nice hot shower, followed by some dinner, and hopefully a bit of sleep before hitting the road again nice and early, would be one small step in the right direction.

Showered and tucked up in bed, with her dinner having been delivered a couple of minutes earlier, Millie tried to put her life into some kind of perspective. With the initial shock of her pregnancy subsiding, she felt the flicker of euphoria at the life growing inside of her as she stared out at the raindrops pelting against her hotel window. Torn between returning to Riverside Acres to hear what Jarrah had to say, or going back to her life in Sydney, she felt as if she was halfway between two very different worlds, two very different paths, and at the same time stuck in the middle of nowhere. Her hands went to her belly, and she blinked back another onslaught of tears. Jarrah's admission, through his lack of a response, burnt right through her heart and into her soul. The utter pain of his betrayal shocked her to her very core. But it didn't change the fact that this baby deserved a father, or to at least know of him. How was she going to navigate that?

'What should I do, little one?' she whispered, smiling softly through her distress. 'That's right, just let everything fall into place, exactly as it's meant to.' The priest's advice had stuck with her, but time would tell if his words were true.

Munching down on the hamburger she'd ordered, she thoroughly enjoyed the first mouthful, and the next. And the side of chips was nice and crunchy too. But then, halfway through her meal, a wave of dizziness washed over her and her stomach roiled in protest at the greasy meat. Clambering from the bed, she had to momentarily rest against the wall. The room closed in on her, and she felt suffocatingly warm. She dashed towards the bathroom and made it to the toilet just in time to drop to her knees and heave until there was nothing left. Wiping her mouth with some toilet paper, she remained on the floor for fear of falling over if she stood up. Pulling her knees to her chest, she leant her head forwards and allowed the racking sobs to overcome her. She felt so alone, so broken, so hurt. She wasn't too sure how long she stayed like that, or what brought her back to her feet. But she found herself taking steps towards the front door. She made sure it was locked from the inside, and then turned out the lights.

Resting back on the hotel bed, she snuggled beneath the doona. Beyond the room, the glow of streetlights reached through the frosted windows and between the curtains. If she left them ajar, at least the sun would wake her nice and early first thing. As she settled deeper into her pillow, tears welled up and rolled freely down her cheeks. Tonight, she was going to cry herself to sleep. Tomorrow, she would get in her car, snap her seatbelt into place, and then decide which way she would turn out of the hotel's driveway. Her heart was saying one way and her head was saying the other. Maybe some sleep would put the tug of war to rest. But one thing was for certain. She could never, ever forget what Jarrah and his gang of thugs had stolen from her that godawful night, let alone find a way to forgive him.

* * *

A week after the love of his life had left, Jarrah had rolled from his shambolic bed well before dawn, sleepless, shirtless and barefoot. Then he'd wandered around, his head everywhere else but where it needed to be – here and focused on Riverside Acres. But for the life of him, he couldn't stop replaying the images of Millie driving away, all the while his boots rooted to the ground and his heart heavier than he'd ever felt it. He'd almost raced after her, when her taillights had disappeared into the distance, so he could tell her everything. But what good was it going to do? She hated him. She never wanted to see him again. She'd made all of this crystal clear. And he couldn't blame her. He'd still been standing there ten minutes later when a tap on his shoulder from Tommy had snapped him out of his rigidity.

Feeling like a man lost in a fog, he tossed his half-eaten piece of toast into the garden below and squeezed the bridge of his nose. Closing his eyes, he rested his head back against the day bed and heaved a sigh worthy of blowing half the world over. It was yet another day he'd have to get through with this heaviness in his heart, and the unbearable weight of Millie's suffering upon his shoulders. Not that he was sorry for himself; there was no room for self-pity in this situation. All he cared about was Millie, and how she was coping, what she was doing, where she was. She hadn't answered any of his calls or replied to any of his text messages. He didn't want to give up trying to contact her, but there was a point when he had to accept she didn't want to speak to him.

With sunrise done and dusted, the day had well and truly begun, so it was time to get on with it. He tugged on his R.M. Williams then came to his feet, his boot heels punching out a steady staccato rhythm as he walked across the back verandah. In the coolness of the kitchen, he placed his empty cup into the dishwasher and then stared out at the sun sitting high behind the mountain ranges. He'd done everything in his power to leave the shadows of that night behind. But he now knew he'd been a fool to believe that his past would never catch up with him, because it had outrun him good and proper. And it had caught up with him in the form of the most mesmerising woman he'd ever met.

His mind went back to the week before, when Millie had realised who he was. The hurt and disappointment in her eyes had haunted him ever since. Knowing just how much he'd unwittingly broken her heart broke him. He'd allowed himself to fall for her, to love her, without knowing exactly who she was. But in his defence, it had been out of his control. She was impossible to resist. She'd captivated him from the second he'd laid eyes on her. He'd been a goner, putty in her hands, from the get-go. All along, even if he'd denied it to himself, he'd known she was the one, the woman he wanted by his side. He fantasised about her being his wife, the mother of his children. But that was all before he realised she was the girl he'd carried from the fire as the rest of her family had burned to death.

As he strode from the homestead and into his day, the events of the past month rolled over in his mind once again, and piece by piece, it was all starting to come together. He felt as if his heart had been hollowed out by her departure. And he couldn't bear the thought of living the rest of his days feeling like this. Missing her like this. He couldn't give up on her, on there ever being a *them*. He had to at least try to get her to listen. And then he had to find the fortitude to tell her the whole heartbreaking truth, with not one detail missing. For if he didn't, it would be the deepest regret he'd ever have to carry to his grave.

Finally firm on his decision, a wild, desperate, buoyant rush came over him. Nothing short of a bullet to his heart was going to stop him getting to Millie. Or Amelia Price. It all depended on who he wanted to see her as. Either way they were two of the same, just with very different life paths. In one, he'd saved her life, and this time round, she'd innocently save him from himself.

CHAPTER 21

Sitting at the dining table, staring at her stone-cold toast and coffee, Millie wished Ebony was back from her holiday; she missed her so much. She also wished things had turned out differently. A whole week and two days had passed since she'd run from Riverside Acres with the shattered pieces of her heart in one hand and her fingernails digging into the flesh of the other. Contrary to popular belief, time wasn't healing her. Nor was the distance she'd gone and put between Sydney and North Queensland. Between herself and Jarrah. She'd stupidly thought that when she returned to Sydney, it would be easy to forget he existed, and that she would somehow be able to slip back into the mundane day after day of her life and stumble forwards. Oh, how wrong she'd been. But then, how could she have expected otherwise when part of him was blooming to life inside of her?

Furious regret coursed through her. As did red-hot rage. And then there was the tenderness she still harboured for him, swirling amongst it all, painfully reminding her what could have been. Reminding her of what they'd gone and lost. Her mind flashed back to the moment in time his lips had met hers and her fingertips instinctively trailed her mouth as she recalled how powerful his kiss had been. The memory pinched her heart, and forced her to take a breath while blinking the sting of pain from her eyes. In another life, what she'd give right now to be wrapped up in his arms, with her head on his chest, as they tried to decipher the galaxy of stars glimmering above them. In another life, they'd be planning for their baby's arrival, with joy in their hearts. But so much had happened since the night they'd given in to their desires. She no longer trusted him. And trust was everything. So she just had to find a way to wade through the heartache, but it was so damn hard when she could imagine what it would feel like if he kissed her, like she was his, every single day for the rest of her life.

She had to stop thinking this way, or she was going to drive herself insane.

A knock at the door brought her to her feet. It wasn't easy to get into the building, unless whoever it was had snuck in, or they lived there. 'Who is it?'

There was a short pause, then, 'It's me, Jarrah.'

Jarrah? Here? At her door. Her heart skidded to a stop and she fought off a sense of hope because happily-ever-afters only existed in fairy tales. 'What do you want?'

'I just want to talk, to explain what happened that night.'

Willing herself not to give in to him, she clenched her hands as tightly as her heartstrings as she took cautious steps towards the door. 'I don't want to talk to you, Jarrah, so just go the hell away!'

Yes, you do, Amelia, so let him in …

'Please, Millie, I've come all this way, and I'm begging you.'

Tears stung. Covering her mouth, she only just stopped a sob from escaping. She could imagine him, on the other side of the door, his hardworking hands pressed up against it, his cobalt gaze filled with dark shadows.

For a split second, she almost, *almost*, let him in. 'I said, go away!'

There was another long, hushed pause. 'Okay, I'm sorry, I'll go.'

There was silence and then his footfalls began to fade away, creating a cavernous-seeming distance between them. But she held her ground and didn't budge an inch. All she had to do was stay strong for the next minute, two at tops, and then he'd be gone. For good.

He deserves to know about his child.

Crossing the room, she hid behind the curtain and watched him take steps across the street. Memories of their past tried to break through. She firmly reminded herself that that was then and this was now. Everything was different. They could never get back to that place. That place where they could have been each other's entire world. Hardening her softening heart with a sharp intake of breath, she blinked back tears. Not long now and she'd be free of him forever.

But would she ever truly be free of him when she looked into the eyes of her baby?

Their baby.

A rush of desperation had her flipping the narrative. She couldn't let him leave without telling him the truth, because at least then her conscience would be clear.

'Jarrah, wait.' Her voice carried out the window and towards him.

He halted and, spinning around, his gaze snapped up to hers. 'Millie?'

'Please come back up.' Her heart took a flying leap towards him. 'And I'll let you in.'

With both her hands going to her belly, she watched him all but run back across the road. He was at her door within thirty seconds. This time, she let him in. He took hesitant steps, his shoulders bunched and eyes downcast. For the length of ten heartbeats, she stood, shell-shocked, staring at him with her hands clenched in her pockets. That familiar, comforting scent of him, of horse and leather and earth, wrapped around her like a warm blanket – she had to remind herself to breathe. In. Out. Slowly. Repeat.

'Come and take a seat.' She waved him towards the dining table.

Nodding, he stepped past her, and it was only then that she noticed a ziplock bag clutched in his hand. 'What's that?'

He held it up. 'Evidence.'

'Evidence of what, exactly?'

He looked her directly in the eyes and drew in the deepest of breaths. 'My innocence.' His eyes filled with concern. 'And who your father truly was.'

'What do you mean?' She gritted her teeth. 'My father was a good man, a decent man, who worked hard and took care of his family.'

'In your eyes, of course he was.' Jarrah's expression was foreboding. 'We need to sit, and I'll tell you everything you need to know.'

Trepidation filled her as she waited for him to take a seat, then she pulled out the chair opposite him and did the same.

'I want you to have a look at these first, and then you can ask me anything you want.' He handed the bag over to her.

She cautiously took it from him and opened it with trembling fingers. There were four photos and a newspaper clipping. She started with the clipping.

Son of rumoured mobster boss and wife are shot dead. Joey Martino, and his wife, Anna, were found with gunshots to the back of the head in the early hours of Sunday morning. Their son has been handed over to social services. Police are calling for witnesses to come forward.

Not needing to read the rest of the article, she looked up at Jarrah. 'What has this got to do with my dad?'

'I'll explain after you have a look at the photos.'

Picking them up, she stared at the first one. It was her father, shaking hands with the older man from the newspaper clipping. The next one was of her father again, his arm wrapped around the same man's shoulders. And the last one, it was of her and her father, with the same man again. Hazy memories spun in her head, the fragments of each not fitting.

'I don't understand.'

Jarrah pointed to the first photo. 'Carlo Martino is my father, Millie.' She nodded – she'd worked out that this must be the case. 'And the photos are confirmation that your father worked for my father.'

No, this can't be happening. 'What in the hell are you saying, Jarrah?'

Drawing in a deep breath, Jarrah appeared to brace himself. 'That your father was a crooked cop.'

'I don't believe you.' For a fleeting moment she thought she was going to be violently ill.

Jarrah's expression was despondent. 'I'm so very sorry, Millie, but it's the cold hard truth.'

'How are these photos proof that my father was up to no good?' She shoved all four back towards Jarrah.

'My father is a known mobster, and I think you know that your father would've never shaken such a corrupt man's hand if he wasn't doing business with him.'

Realisation punched her already beaten heart. She didn't want to believe him, but Jarrah had a good point. Her gentle, loving, kind-hearted father was a crook? She just couldn't bear it. 'Why didn't you give this evidence to the police when you had the chance to?'

Jarrah shrugged and shook his head. 'What good was it going to do, other than ruin what little you had left of your life?' Looking past her, he took a moment, followed by another. 'My father is the reason your family are gone, so the least I could do was respect your father's memory by keeping his secrets safe.'

'So let me get this right, you were actually protecting me?' she said, with quiet conviction.

Leaning forwards, he took her hand in his. 'In a way I was, yes.'

'Why would you do that?'

'Because you'd been through enough, lost enough, and I didn't want your life to be any more complicated than it had already become.' He looked at where he was wringing his hands. 'I hate my father, and all he stands for, and I hate the fact he dragged my little brother into it all, which is why I've taken Tommy under my wing and tried my best to put him on the straight and narrow.'

'I see.' She let this sink in, nice and deep, before asking what she was dying to know the answer to. 'If you had nothing to do with their deaths, why did you go to prison, Jarrah?'

'The night it all happened, I was trying to stop my brother and his bunch of thugs lighting it, but I couldn't. Then when the cops caught me, because I was the only one left at the crime scene, I took the rap because Joey had a fiancé and little Tommy to take care of. Whereas I had nobody to worry about, apart from myself. And when I got out of prison, I changed my name and tried to leave all of it behind me.' He paused, as if collecting himself. 'When I failed to stop them starting the fire, and witnessed how quickly it was spreading, I did all I could and went in to try and save you all.'

'Oh my god,' she gasped. 'You're the one that carried me out?'

'Yes.' One word, and yet it had the power to change everything.

Millie's eyes burnt and her stomach roiled. Chewing her bottom lip to stop herself from sobbing, she looked down at her folded hands. 'Thank you, for saving me.' Her gratitude was but a whisper. 'And trying to save my family too.'

'I don't need you to thank me, Millie.' Coming to his feet, Jarrah moved to her side and knelt beside her. 'I just need you to believe what I'm telling you.'

Allowing him to take her hands, she relished his tender touch. 'I do believe you.'

'Oh, thank god.' He whooshed a breath. 'I'm so deeply sorry to tell you all of this, but after weighing up what to do, I couldn't bear the thought of never having you in my life, let alone you hating me.'

Noting the dark shadows beneath his eyes, her heart tumbled. She felt for him. One heck of a lot. And if she were being completely honest with herself, she was also deeply in love with him. 'I could never hate you, Jarrah.' And even though she'd willed herself to do just that, she meant it.

'You don't know how much that means to me, Mills.' He rubbed a thumb over the back of her hand. 'So, where do we go from here?'

'Before we go anywhere from here, I have something extremely important to tell you too.' It was her turn to speak her truth.

'Okay.' He let go of her hands but remined kneeling at her side. 'Should I be worried?'

'That depends.' She paused and sighed a pent-up breath away. 'I'm pregnant, Jarrah.'

His mouth opened but no words came out. He cleared his throat, sucked in a breath, and shook his head, blinking faster. 'You mean?' A myriad of emotions flickered in his eyes.

'Yes, it's yours, ours, we're pregnant.' She was filling in the silence, but needed to stop to allow him to speak, to say what was on his heart, in his soul, at her news.

'Wow, I'm going to be a dad.' Leaping to his feet, he dragged her into his arms. 'You've just made me the happiest man alive.'

'Do you really mean that?'

'Yes, I do.' He unravelled his arms a little, so he could lean back and look into her eyes. 'I hope this means you might want to give us a go?'

How could she not? He made her feel cherished, cared for, loved. And in that moment, her heart swung open, inviting his in. And all the hurt and distrust and anger faded away, leaving nothing but pure, deep, enduring love. 'That's a big hell yes from me.' Rising up on her tippy toes, she laced her arms around his neck, leant in, and met his lips.

Jarrah pressed her even closer to him, and she invited him to deepen the kiss. A low growl escaped him, driving her wild. She didn't want to talk about their past any longer – they'd have plenty of time for that in their future. For now she just wanted to feel, and surrender, and love him like he deserved to be loved. And she wanted him to love her, like she deserved to be loved. There'd be no coming back from the place he was about to take her to, and she worshipped the thought, because in reality she'd never wanted to return from the utopia he'd already introduced her to. This time around, she wanted to remain there with him. Forevermore. Of that, she was certain.

'Are you sure?' His gaze caught hers and held it.

No words were needed. She tore at his shirt, desperate to feel his skin upon hers, to feel his hands on her breasts and his lips trailing over the frantic pulse in her throat. Soon enough, their clothes were in piles at their feet.

Helping her onto the bed, Jarrah rested down beside her. Locking his gaze to hers, he ran the back of his hand gently down her cheek. 'I love you, Millie, and I'm going to love you forever.'

With her heart overflowing, she was hungry to be at one with him. 'I love you too, Jarrah, so much it actually makes it hard to take a breath.' Never had she ever wanted anyone, or anything, so much.

His gaze regarded hers. 'I know exactly what you mean.'

'Then make love to me, Jarrah, please.'

Jarrah didn't need any more of an invitation and she savoured every touch, every sigh, every whispered word, as he trailed kisses down her neck, across her collarbone, over her nipples, then lower, lower, until he reached her sweet place. Arching her back, she pressed into him, moaning at the mind-blowing pleasure.

His tongue was slow, soft, teasing at first, but then he built the crescendo, licking, sucking and kissing until she was teetering on the euphoric brink of ecstasy. And just as she was about to somersault into rapture, he stopped and, retracing his kisses, met with her lips. In a moment of feverish passion, she rolled him onto his back and climbed on top of him. It was her turn to set the tempo. Slowly, she invited him inside her, and once he was there, it felt as if her entire body fizzled with bliss. He grabbed hold of her hips, and moving in unison, they rode the waves of pleasure together, climbing higher and higher until there was nowhere left to go. Indulgence rippled throughout her at the very same time he cried out with gratification. Gasping, sated and now even more in love with him, she collapsed against him while trying to catch her breath. Nuzzling her neck, he rolled her to the side and cuddled into her from behind. No words were needed right now. They'd just silently told each other everything they'd needed to know. Wrapped within his arms she felt so at peace, so safe, so filled with happiness.

Hours later, a beautiful warmth pressing into Millie's back woke her. Blinking heavy eyelids open, she smiled when she spotted Jarrah's tattooed arms, wrapped tightly around her, holding her as close to him as he could, with his hands resting protectively on her belly. His slow rhythmic breath brushed against her neck, giving rise to goosebumps – even in sleep, he could send sparks throughout her. As if sensing her gaze upon him, he stirred, and his eyes flickered open, and the smile he bestowed upon her was toe-curling.

'Hey, beautiful.' His voice was ruggedly husky, and sexy as hell.

'Hey, handsome.' Rolling to her other side, she tenderly placed her hand over his scarred cheek. 'Thank you, for saving me that night.'

He placed a hand over hers. 'I just wish I could have saved all of you.'

'I know you do.' She blinked faster as she bit her lip. 'So, back to your question from a few hours ago, where do we go from here?'

'How about you and our little one come back to Riverside Acres with me, and we all call it home?'

'I really like the sound of that.' She smiled brightly. 'Very much.'

'Good, because I plan on making you my wife in the not-too-distant future, too.'

'Oh, you do, do you?' Her comeback was filled with sass.

'Yes,' was his confirming reply.

Again, one powerful word that meant everything to her. And it was the very word she'd be saying to him when he got down on one knee to ask her to be his forever. And she knew this without a doubt, because until this very moment, she felt like she'd been counting every single breath just to stay alive. But now she'd finally found what she'd been missing, and that was Jarrah King, and for the very first time in her life she felt whole and happy, as if she'd finally arrived home to her person, her love, her life.

EPILOGUE

Five months later

After a glorious sleep, Millie felt as if she'd been walking on air since her feet had touched the floor at first light. And by the looks of the powdery blue sky stretching out as far as her eyes could see, it was going to be glorious weather too. Hearing Ebony and Tommy's happy voices floating in from where they were busy setting up the table for their dinner beneath the stars, she turned from the sweeping view of Riverside Acres out the French doors of her and Jarrah's bedroom, to her antique wedding dress hanging from the cupboard door. Beside it, she caught her reflection in the full-length mirror, and smiled softly. The content woman staring back at her, with the wide grin and the happy sparkle in her eyes, was really her.

Today was the day she'd be walking down the aisle to the man who'd saved her, who'd fought for her, and who'd shown her how good love could be. Stretching up on her tippy toes, she ran her fingers down the soft lace pattern of the bodice and then straightened the pearls that graced the empire waistline. After what had felt like a whirlwind few months, she still couldn't believe their big day was finally here. Her hands flitted to her belly, where their growing baby girl was awake and kicking, and she smiled. Only eleven weeks and they'd be meeting her for the very first time. There was so much to be happy for, to be grateful for. Her life with Jarrah was even more than she'd imagined it to be.

Her gaze dropped to her left hand, as she admired the most precious diamond ring in the world. She sighed dreamily as she recalled the moment Jarrah had dropped to his knee and asked her to be his wife, only two weeks after she moved to Riverside Acres. It was the most beautifully perfect moment, with just the two of them standing beneath a starry night sky, when he'd told her with such potency in his gaze that he wanted to love her, and be loved by her, forever.

Wandering towards the dressing table, she briefly thought back to Carlo, and how he'd so callously sent the letter to her, to mess with Jarrah, and in turn to regain what he felt was his claim on Tommy. Little had he known that he'd essentially make her life, as well as Jarrah's and Tommy's, full to the brim with joy and happiness. It was deeply satisfying to know they'd overcome Carlo's wickedness, just by being themselves and allowing unconditional love to win out in the end. She and Jarrah were so proud of Tommy, starting up his fishing charter business and staying on the straight and narrow. And he was doing well too, with every one of his five-day tours already booked solid for the next couple of months.

As she picked up her pearl earrings and admired them in the golden sunlight pouring into the room, her eyes stung with tears of joy and anticipation when she thought about the lives that they were all building, together, and how far Tommy had come in such a short amount of time. It just went to show what Jarrah's endless love and support for his nephew could achieve. It was just another reason for her to love him so deeply. Her Jarrah King really was one in a bazillion.

Racing footsteps came down the hallway, then her best friend exploded into the room. Ebony's face was a picture of absolute delight and excitement. 'Woohoo! This is it, Millie! Only a few hours until you're officially Mrs King, can you believe it?'

'I know, right, life can really turn around in the blink of an eye, that's for sure, my darling bestie!' Millie sat on the edge of her bed and smiled from the heart. 'I'm so happy you're here with me today.'

'Of course I am, I wouldn't want to be anywhere else.' Ebony plonked herself down beside her, and taking Millie's hand in hers, her eyes drifted to the wedding dress they'd shopped for weeks for, and found, together. 'You're going to look so beautiful, Millie, Jarrah is going to tear up when he sees you, I bet.' She sniffled and beamed brightly. 'I'm so happy for both of you, because you, my dear Millie, deserve this more than anyone I know.'

'Oh, Ebs, I love how much you love me.' Millie threw her arms around her best friend, and the two of them held onto each other tightly. 'I'm going to miss you so freaking much, living so far away from you.'

'Yeah, about that.' Ebony pulled back a little and smiled tenderly. 'Me and Felix are going to be moving up this way in a couple of months.'

Millie's breath caught. 'Oh my god, Ebs, what are you talking about?'

'I got the counselling job, Millie, at the Riverside hospital.' Ebony bounced up and down. 'I only just found out, five minutes ago, when they called me to give me the good news!'

Overjoyed their baby girl would have her only aunty close by, Millie leapt to her feet and danced on the spot. 'Holy moly! This is going to make today all the more amazing!'

'I'm glad it's made you even happier.' Ebony shot to her feet and met her, and they hugged again, both of them twirling in a happy circle as they did.

Millie's heart was so full, she thought it might burst. 'I love you so much, Ebs, thank you, for wanting to move up here with me.'

'I love you too, Millie. You're my sister, and always will be, so I wouldn't want to be anywhere else.' She cupped Millie's cheeks and smiled. 'Now let's get you ready to marry that amazing man of yours.'

Millie clapped her hands together. 'Yes, let's!'

Two and a half hours later, while taking a deep breath, Millie looked to Tommy and Ebony sitting on the only two chairs at the ceremony – they were the only guests she and Jarrah had wanted there, to share their special day. The song she'd chosen began, and she slowly took steps in time to 'It's Your Love' by Tim McGraw. Standing beneath the flower arch, Jarrah met her gaze and in that breathless moment, she was spellbound all over again. Looking as handsome as ever in his black tux, matching Akubra and snakeskin boots, his eyes glistened with joy and love. What a lucky woman she was, to be loved by him. This was the man she loved, the father of her child, and the sole owner of her heart.

Reaching him, he took her hand, and she smiled, looking up into his eyes. The celebrant began the ceremony, and when she said 'for better or for worse, for richer or poorer, until death do us part', she meant it with all of her heart. There'd be good days and bad days, there'd be joy and sorrow, but they'd always be together as one. She knew that in her heart of hearts. Theirs was a love she'd always longed for. A love she knew she was lucky to have found. A love that would last a lifetime.

As they exchanged their vows, Millie felt her heart swell even more with love for the man standing before her, beside her, with her. Their chosen words were simple, but their meaning was profound. Jarrah promised to love and cherish her, to support her in all of her endeavours, and to be there for her, and their baby girl, through thick and thin. Tears streamed down her face as she made her own promises to him – to love him unconditionally, to stand by his side always, and to create a life filled with joy and happiness, every single day of their lives.

With the exchange of rings, they sealed their love, and as the celebrant pronounced them husband and wife, they shared a passionate kiss. Applause erupted from Tommy and Ebony, and they stepped back, hand in hand, as Mrs and Mr King. This was the beginning of a new chapter in their lives, one filled with love, joy and possibility. And with each other's unconditional support, they'd conquer any obstacle that came their way.

Together.

Forever and always.

ACKNOWLEDGEMENTS

A rowdy wholehearted ovation to my remarkable team at Harlequin HQ – my marvellous publisher Rachael Donovan, I'm a very lucky author to have you at the helm of my career, you truly are amazing and I don't believe I'd be where I am today, without you by my side! To my meticulous, diligent, inspiring editors, Laurie Ormond and Kate James, you're both shining stars in what can sometimes be a dark cave of editing … dare I say you're both my favourite editors, EVER! I'm extremely honoured to be a part of the wonderfully supportive Harlequin family – you're all integral to my books. Thank you for making *Secrets of Riverside* the very best it could be.

Massive, heartfelt thanks, to YOU, the reader! I wouldn't be doing what I so avidly love, without each and every one of you grabbing my books off the shelf, and eagerly tumbling into my stories. I hope I've accomplished my writer's mission – lifted you up and taken you away from the pressures of life, given you precious time to swoon, cry, laugh, applaud, holler, believe in love again … whatever it is you felt compelled to do as you shared Millie and Jarrah's love story. Taking time out for ourselves is crucial in this day and age and we all deserve to indulge in a little, or in my opinion, A LOT, of recharging time. So if I've kept you up at night, or turning the pages until the early hours of the morning, if I've given you an excuse to let your housework go, or a good reason to get takeaway, ignore the laundry or stay in your PJs all day long, my job is done!

Until my next book has you relaxing somewhere peaceful, while my hero and heroine take you on a beautiful journey filled with ups and downs and everything in between, keep smiling and dreaming.

Mandy xoxo